# NATE

CELIA AARON

# NATE

Cover art by Perfect Pear

Cover model Amadeo Leandro

Cover image by Stefano Raphael

Content Editing by J. Brooks

Copy Editing by Spell Bound

# CONTENTS

---

# CHAPTER ONE

"IF YOU LOSE ANOTHER finger, who's going to get your girlfriend off?" I waved the thick blade in front of Vigo's eyes, which promptly began bugging out. "You've already lost the bird finger. I'm going to take this one." I slammed Vigo's hand down on the desk and pinned his index finger as David held him still.

"Just tell him." Peter hovered at my elbow, his pistol pointed at Vigo's sweaty forehead.

"I swear it wasn't me." Vigo shook his head as much as David's grip would allow.

I stabbed the knife into the desk, only half an inch from Vigo's finger. He screamed, and the scent of hot piss filled the musty back office.

Peter groaned. "Jesus, Vigo. Have some self-respect."

"It wasn't me." Tears leaked down Vigo's pasty face and dribbled along his stubbly cheeks. He was a low level nobody—the guy in gangster movies who always wound up with an anonymous death long before the credits rolled.

I stood and used the tip of the blade to scratch my chin. Did I think he was telling the truth? Maybe. Did it matter? No. What mattered was that on his watch, an entire shipment of the choicest weed Mexico had to offer went missing and wound up in the hands of the fucking Russians. Two of my men died, and the piece of shit Vigo was the only survivor. Sketchy as fuck. But even if he wasn't working with the Russians, I'd still have to make an example of him.

In the five years since I became the head of our organization, I'd worked nonstop to tighten the ship, streamline our services, and propagate a legitimate front for all the dirty-dealing that went on behind the scenes. The Russians, and now Vigo, were a threat to all my progress.

I ran a fingertip down the faint scar along my jaw—a bullet graze from the latest attempt on my life. They'd been trying to move in on our turf and take what was ours. From the minute the old boss, Vince, choked on his own blood, the Russians had been poking and prodding. Testing and taking. But that would all come to an end within the month when I allied with the Irish for control of the entire city. Then I'd handle the Russians—go fucking rathole by rathole if I had to—and eliminate every mobster who so much as looked at me wrong.

For the time being, though, I had to hold it all together. The easiest glue I'd ever found was fear. It sealed the holes right up and kept my men in line.

"Hold him." I pointed my blade at David.

"No!" Vigo squealed.

"I take no pleasure in this." I twirled my blade in my palm. "But be thankful it's not your life I'm taking." I leaned down and met Vigo's beady eyes. "If I so much as get a tickle in my ass crack that leads me to believe you're with the Russians, I'll send David to finish you."

David laughed low in his throat. If fear was my glue, it was his art form. His nickname, the Butcher, was well earned. Handy with a gun, but beautifully lethal with a knife, he could carve a man up like a Honeybaked Ham and smile while he did it.

"Send your girl on over to my place." Peter wiggled his free hand in front of Vigo. "I'll give her the three-finger special since you'll be out of commission."

Vigo's tears began anew as I pinned his index finger to the desk. I would make it quick, then send him on his way to the hospital.

"Don't fuck up again." I kept my gaze tied with his as I swung the knife in a vicious downward arc.

His finger came off clean right at the joint, a spurt of blood shooting out and spraying the front of my light blue button-down. He screamed as I pulled a handkerchief from my pocket and wrapped the nub. It matched his missing bird finger, though given the scarring, my cut had been far more precise.

David released Vigo, who clutched his maimed hand to his chest.

Peter snagged the finger. "Can't have you trying for a medical miracle, now can we?"

Vigo blubbered as I wiped my knife on his shirt sleeve then pocketed it.

"Get him an ambulance." I pointed to Peter. "Industrial accident."

He nodded and pulled his cell from his pocket. The three of us left the Trenholm Shipping office as Vigo sniffled and wailed behind us. Three of our guys stood next to the trucks, their eyes wide as we passed.

"The fuck you think this is? Break time?" David banged his fist on the side of one of the trailers. "Get to fucking work."

They started moving, loading pallets of bottled soft drinks onto the trucks. The visible bottles contained Coke. The not-so-visible bottles also had coke, the non-fizzy kind. Peter bumped into the foreman, then continued walking ahead of me to the car.

I sank into the back of the Benz as Peter took the wheel. David slid in next to him. It was unorthodox to have two seconds-in-command, but the Raven brothers formed a tight pair, always had ever since their days growing up in foster homes and eventually on the streets. I'd crossed paths a few times with them when we were kids, gotten into scraps and taken enough Raven beat downs to respect them. We'd all worked together for the last boss, Vince. And when I picked up the pieces of his shattered reign and took over, they'd sworn allegiance to me on the first day.

"What'd you do with the finger?" David kept his head on a swivel, peering through the bulletproof glass of the windshield as if a threat would appear out of the cloudy May sky and swoop down with machine guns blasting.

Peter snorted. "I planted it in the foreman's pocket."

David shook his head.

"He'll squeal like a bitch as he pulls out that fat little nugget when he's going for a cig later." Peter was the only Raven brother with a sense of humor. When he wasn't busy being a number-crunching nerd, he reminded me of myself before I'd taken over the syndicate. I'd been funny back then, too. Everything was a fucking laugh. Not anymore. Now, everything was exhausting. Balancing an empire on the head of a fucking pin while dumbasses took potshots at you didn't inspire humor.

I leaned back against the leather and took a deep breath. "Take me to the house."

"What about the table at Paredo's?"

"Cancel. Give Jimmy my apologies." I gestured to my blood-splattered shirt. "I don't think he wants me showing up at his restaurant looking like I just walked off Elm Street."

"He wouldn't give a shit." Peter shrugged, but turned onto the freeway leading out of town. I'd set up shop in a large estate in Gladwyne. The rich-as-fuck neighbors minded their own business from their mansions while my men and I fortified a house that looked like it belonged in the English countryside. With two wings, a large pool, and a twelve-car, two-story garage, the house was far beyond anything I'd ever dreamed of owning. Being the boss came with perks. The house had belonged to the Genoa family for a century, but when the last Genoa boss fell, it had fallen empty. Now it was mine.

We passed through the secured gate with a nod to a sentry in a crisp suit. The driveway meandered through trees and landscaping until the house appeared, ringed with spring flowers, pretending to be a warm family home instead of a hive of bad men with murky agendas. The sun was low on the horizon, almost gone, by the time Peter pulled up out front. I rose and climbed the few steps to the entrance.

George opened the door and greeted me, the butt of his black pistol peeking from beneath his suit coat. He had a semi-automatic stored just inside the front door. We were on high alert after the Russians stepped up their meddling, and especially after their last assassination attempt only two months prior. I'd barely avoided a shotgun blast to the chest that time, and it took hours for my personal doc to remove every pellet of buckshot from my left arm.

"Mr. Franco." Opal, my housekeeper, greeted me with a smile. She was excellent at pretending nothing was amiss despite the armed men who frequented the house. She'd been the housekeeper here, then at the last boss's house, and then back here again once I'd taken it over. "I thought you were dining out." Her eyes dropped to the crimson across my shirt. "Oh, I see. I'll whip you something up."

"It's fine." I waved her away and pulled off my suit coat.

"No, I'll send it up." She smiled.

There was no point arguing with her. I'd learned that much in the past five years. I trudged past her up the stairs, fatigue sinking into my bones.

"One more thing, Mr. Franco?" She called behind me.

"Can it wait till tomorrow?" I wanted to be alone, to sit and rest and try to figure my way out of the ever-growing mess of my empire.

She hesitated. "Sure. Yes, I'll bring it up at breakfast."

"Thank you." I continued toward my bedroom, stripping my shirt and undershirt off as I went.

Tossing them on the floor of my bedroom, I closed the door behind me and leaned against the cool, heavy wood. The deep navy hues of the wall and duvet gave me a sense of safety, the familiarity of the room easing my frayed nerves and blocking out the echo of Vigo's agonized scream that played on repeat in my mind.

The house was still, though I knew my men prowled around on silent feet, seeking out any threats. Under my control, they'd seen an increase in pay and a move toward less seedy work. No more prostitutes, and an effort to get away from the hard drugs. We'd ditched the heroin trade the prior year and were working toward ending our reliance on cocaine deals. My men were happy, and I made sure they stayed that way. It was the only thing that would keep me alive. Fear could only go so far.

The quiet filled my ears and attempted to overcome a whirlwind of thoughts and worries. I closed my eyes and simply leaned against the door, being still for a single moment. The first time in a long time.

Then I heard a splash.

I opened my eyes in the gloom and walked toward the wide windows looking out onto the back yard. The sun was gone, twilight fading into night, but the pool was lit, and under the surface, someone swam.

I walked onto the narrow balcony and leaned down, peering at the water. The lights illuminated long blonde hair and a delectable body wrapped in a tiny yellow bikini. Had one of my guys' women come over for a swim? She hit the wall beneath me, then shot out again under the surface, heading toward the stairs at the far end of the rectangular pool.

Leaning farther over, I watched as she rose from the water and climbed the steps, her back to me. Her tanned skin gleamed in the low light, and her body made my mouth water. Long legs, round ass, narrowing waist, and what I could only assume would be a pair of perfect tits. My cock stirred for the first time in a long time.

Whoever brought her here made a mistake. I wanted her for myself, and there wasn't a man on this earth that could stop me. It had been far too long since I'd felt the soft skin of a woman. The one who'd just landed in my lap was without equal. And if she had a smart mouth to go with that package? I was a goner.

I straightened and was about to go down to her when she twirled on her feet and stared up at me with the bluest eyes.

Sabrina waved and smiled, her as-suspected perfect tits bouncing with the movement.

"Fuck." I swore under my breath and tried to mentally will my dick to deflate. It didn't work.

She moved closer around the side of the pool, her body glistening with water. And then she said the thing that should have killed my erection, but didn't. "It's so good to see you, Uncle Nate!"

# CHAPTER TWO

N ATE COUGHED INTO HIS palm, the muscles of his bare torso flexing as he stared down at me. He looked even better than I remembered. Dark hair, bright eyes, and a toned body.

My heart swelled, and my glee barely remained caged inside me. My ploy had worked perfectly. I stood beneath his balcony, and he kept glancing away, trying to look at anything but me. It didn't work—his gaze always returned to my face and lower. The growing darkness cast him in shadow, but I could feel his eyes roving over me.

"You, um, you're back from school then?" He gripped the balcony railing.

"Yep. I'll be heading to Temple in the fall, remember?"

He likely didn't remember at all. I'd sent him an email about it in the winter when I'd gotten accepted, and he had responded with a perfunctory "congrats."

We hadn't seen each other for five years. He'd kept me at my boarding school and sent me on vacations rather than seeing me during the summers or over holidays. I'd stayed away from Philly, and I'd abided by his wishes. But not anymore. I was eighteen and ready to come home. I was also ready for Nate Franco, though I knew he wouldn't be ready for me.

"Right. Temple." He rubbed a palm down his jaw, the other hand gripping the railing so tightly the knuckles were turning white.

"In town. So, I can stay here ... if that's all right with you?" I clasped my hands behind my back, knowing full well it pushed my chest out farther. My breasts weren't large, but they filled out the bikini top. "I know you don't have to be my guardian anymore since I'm of age, but I was hoping I could stay around even if we aren't really related or anything."

"Stay around?" His voice had a rough, gravelly quality. I'd forgotten that tiny detail, but it all came back in a rush of memory. *"You're safe now. I swear."* The first words he'd ever said to me ricocheted through my mind, the rich timbre of his voice just the same. The moment I'd fallen for him sealed into my memory, even if I hadn't understood it at the time. I'd been too young, too traumatized.

"Yeah. Here at the house." I smiled. "With you."

"That's ..." He cleared his throat, but didn't seem inclined to continue.

"Are you hungry?" I unclasped my hands and toyed with the string bikini tie around my neck.

His head tilted, following my movement. After a heavy pause, he gritted out, "Yes."

"Come down to eat?" I tugged on the string just a little.

He slapped his hand down on the rail. "I—no." He coughed again and shook his head, as if trying to clear away a haze of thoughts. "I have work to do."

Had I overplayed it? "Oh." I pouted and dropped my hands to my sides. "I was hoping we could talk about college."

"Maybe tomorrow. At breakfast." He backed away, though I could feel his gaze. "Like I said, I've got lots of work, so I'll see you then. At breakfast."

"Okay." I shrugged and walked around to the stairs, swaying my hips as I went. Dropping onto the top stair, I reached up, stretching my body taut, then dove into the pool and swam end to end. When I emerged again, his balcony doors were closed, and I couldn't see him, but the prickling sensation along the nape of my neck told me he was still watching. I made a show of arranging my towel on a pool chair and lying down, letting the warm night breeze dry my skin.

Reaching up, I slowly pulled the string at my neck, untying it and peeling the strings down to the thin material of the triangles over my breasts. I stared at his window, and I wanted to pull the top all the way off, to show him what was his. But I didn't. I let the strings lie on my stomach and I wriggled down onto the lounge chair, the fabric still covering my hard nipples.

Closing my eyes, I imagined him coming down to the

pool. He'd stand above me, then pluck the bikini top away so he could see how hard my nipples were for him. His green eyes would survey me, take it all in, and then he'd drag his fingertips down my wet body until he found the slickness between my legs.

I threw my arms over my head and pressed my thighs together at the heat my imaginings stirred inside me. I should have known better. Fantasizing about Nate had become my favorite pastime at boarding school. I'd spend my alone time thinking about him, planning how our first time together would be, imagining his body on top of mine. The other girls at school were losing their virginity and racking up boyfriends while I had an imaginary, smoking-hot relationship with my guardian. Seeing no evidence of my interest in boys, they judged me to be a prude. But they were wrong. My issue was simple: I didn't want a boy. I wanted a man. One man in particular.

My mind wandered further, to what Nate would do to me once we were both naked. I'd spread my legs for him, showing him something that I'd never offered to anyone else. What would he say? I longed to reach down and pleasure myself, but if one little twirl of my bikini top had spooked him, a full-on masturbation sesh below his balcony might be the wrong approach.

I sighed and wrapped my towel around me, then sat up. Walking around the pool, I gave one more glance to his window and decided I would continue my imaginings alone in my room.

## CHAPTER THREE

### NATE

I sat back at my desk and listened as David gave a rundown of all our operations for the day. We expected another large shipment of weed later that night. This time, we'd send a contingent of men to guard it along with Peter. David would continue his search for the rat. There had to be one. It simply wasn't possible for the Russians to know our moves with such detail unless someone was squealing to them.

"If you find him, bring him to me."

Peter nodded, but David's eyes glinted, his signature violence trying to claw its way free.

I pointed my finger at him. "David, you'll get your chance at him, but I need to see him first. Got me?"

"I got it." David cracked his knuckles. That alone would make grown men with bigger balls than me piss themselves. The Butcher was aching to put a hurting on someone. "As long as I get to finish him."

"You will." I rubbed my temples as the clock in the hall chimed nine.

"We'll get to work." Peter rose, and he and David left for the day. I'd join them on the marijuana shipment later. Nothing could go wrong with this one. If we lost it, we'd be out of the dealing game for a week. A lot could happen in a week. New dealers would poach on our turf, and we could end up fighting the Russians as well as the other syndicates openly, just like the old days. I couldn't have that.

It was time for breakfast, but I hesitated at the door to the hall. Sabrina would be there, and after last night—the night I spent in a cold shower half the time—I needed to play this the right way. She could go to Temple, but she needed to find a place on campus or in the city near the school. Staying here would be too dangerous. I hadn't let her come to the house for quite some time, mainly because of the threat from the Russians. Getting her out of here was the smartest play. And not just based on safety. I needed to erase her from my mind, keep her at a distance. The thoughts I'd had about her before I knew who she was—I shook my head. And then the rest of the thoughts I'd had about her even though I knew good and damn well who she was. My cock tried to kick awake in my pants, and I balled my hands into fists.

"Focus, perv. She's your ward. Not your plaything," I mumbled to myself, though I didn't put much conviction into it. *Uncle Nate*. Her words echoed in my mind. That had been a nice touch, one that screamed "DO NOT

FUCKING THINK ABOUT IT," but I'd thought about it quite a bit since the moment I saw her in the pool.

Sabrina had grown from a timid, beautiful girl into a woman that could turn heads and shred hearts. Smart enough to get a full scholarship to Temple and with a body that made me want to—I stopped myself from continuing the thought. I was responsible for keeping her safe after her foster parents had been murdered in some ugly business to do with the old boss. That was five years ago, and Sabrina was all but forgotten in underworld dealings. Raised in the finest boarding schools money could buy, she was a stranger to this life, and I intended to keep it that way. I took a deep breath and let it out before adjusting my semi like a fucking teenager.

Sunlight filtered through the bulletproof windows along the wide hallway at the back of the house. The wood floors gleamed with fresh polish as I turned left into the main hallway, the walls still decorated with art procured by the Genoa family ages ago. I had no idea what they were worth, or if they were any good. Seen one, seen 'em all—that about covered art, as far as I was concerned.

The scent of bacon and eggs wafted through the house, tempered by the perfectly bitter tang of fresh coffee. Voices bounced off the mahogany paneling, one high and sweet and the other belonging to Peter.

My back stiffened as I strode into the breakfast room. Sabrina, her blonde hair falling in loose waves down her bare shoulders, sat at the table. She wore a sun dress with tiny spaghetti straps, the fabric so thin it was nearly see-through. Her eyes turned to me, the bright cornflower blue dazzling when she smiled.

"Nate." She stood, giving me a clear view of just how short her light pink dress was. Mid-thigh was a stretch. I wanted to drape her in my suit coat. Peter grinned.

"Don't you have work to do?" I bristled and strode around to the chair at the head of the table.

"Yes, boss." He gave Sabrina a small nod. "Good to meet you."

"Same here." She took her seat and placed her napkin in her lap.

When Peter was out of the room, I managed to relax a hair. But then she turned that smile on me again. So bright and full of life. Did she have any idea how radiant she was?

"Since I'll be staying here, I was wondering if I could redecorate my old room?"

I compared how she looked now to the small, scared girl I rescued from a shoot-out five years prior. The eyes were the same—enthralling, and the hair still had a golden hue, but the rest of her was different. Her face wasn't as round and had turned into more of a heart shape. Smooth skin, even white teeth, and plump lips. Disconcerting, to say the least. I had a distinct image of her in my mind whenever I happened to think about her away at school. It was always the same terrified little girl, her big blue eyes begging for me to save her. That child was gone, and a stranger had appeared in her place. A *hot* one.

Opal entered from the kitchen with my coffee and a

plate of bacon, eggs, and two fluffy pancakes. She beamed at Sabrina. "So nice to have another woman in the house for once."

I sipped my coffee and gave her a stern look. She took the hint and bustled out again as Sabrina took a bite of her waffle.

"God, this is so good." She swallowed. "We didn't get food like this at school." She cut another bite, then glanced up at me. "Are you going to eat?"

I realized I'd been staring and hadn't said a damn thing. Setting my coffee down, I leaned back and focused on keeping my gaze on her angelic face. "I don't think it's a good idea for you to stay here at the house."

Her face fell, and it was like taking a bullet. "But I just got here."

"I know." I draped my napkin across my lap. "And I'm sorry. But—" How could I phrase this? "The *business* has been having some trouble lately, and I want to keep things running smoothly. You'd do better on campus or maybe in an apartment? I can have that arranged for you."

She placed her fork on her plate. "Business?" Crossing her arms under her breasts, which drew my eyes to the hard points of her nipples—*Jesus*—she said, "I know what sort of *business* you're in, and I'm not scared."

I shook my head. "You don't know what you're talking about."

"You're the head of the Genoa crime family. Or maybe you call it something different now since the Genoas aren't around anymore. My father was a Russian drug importer. You saved me after the old boss kidnapped me and killed my adopted parents."

I swallowed thickly and tried to find the right thing to say. I failed.

"Did you think I forgot about all of that?" She shook her head. "I know what sort of life you're in. I don't care."

"You think you know. But you don't. Things are dangerous right now. Hovering on the edge of a knife. There's a target on my back. And anyone close to me, the same target is on them."

"I'm staying." She set her lips in a hard line. A little firecracker. I wanted to watch the fuse burn until the explosions began.

Frustration welled in my voice despite my efforts to keep my tone even. "I'm glad you think you have a handle on all the intricate workings of the Philly under-world. You don't. You had a great time in boarding school, and I'm glad." I took a deep breath. I *was* glad. I'd wanted her to have as normal of a life as possible after her rough start. "And I'm proud that you earned a scholar-ship to Temple. I want you to go and pursue your studies."

"I can do that and live here at the same time."

"Why?"

"Why what?" Color rose into her face, gilding her cheeks with pink. Unforgettable. Art made sense for a split-second—I would have paid for someone to paint her just as she was at that moment.

I leaned forward and rested my elbows on the table. "I mean why do you want to stay here? What does it matter? Don't you want to be free to do what you want somewhere in the city?"

"Free to do what I want? Seriously?" She rolled her eyes, acting her age for a split second. "You think I don't know that you've had the same guy watching me for five years?"

I smirked. "You made Hargut?"

"I made him the first week at school. At first, I thought he was a creeper. Then, when I realized he'd been given free rein of the school grounds, I knew he was personal security."

Guilty as charged. I'd made an arrangement with her school to hire one of my guys, Hargut, on as staff to keep an eye on her. "I had to keep you safe."

"If you want me to be safe, isn't the safest place here with you?" She plucked her fork from her plate and ate another bite of waffle.

She had a point. The house was heavily fortified. It would take a tank or a rocket launcher to get through the front door. Even so, I didn't need her underfoot. Or in the pool. Or anywhere near me, especially when it made my dick misbehave like it was doing right then under the table.

"I'll have someone look for an apartment for you."

"No." She drained her orange juice and stood. "I'm staying."

The sun hit her dress, revealing a straight shot between her thighs. She wasn't wearing panties. I gripped the arms of my chair and forced myself to stay seated. What would I do anyway? I had half a mind to yank her across my lap and spank her ass until it was red, then eat her pussy until she came all over my face. *Get your shit together*.

"You don't decide if you stay or go. I do." I stood and tossed down my napkin. Thank god my suit coat covered my lap. "You're going. I'll make some calls and see what's available near Temple. Until then, you can stay here."

She stepped toward me, her blue eyes glaring up into mine. "You can't just kick me out."

I glowered. "I can do a lot of things."

The pulse at her throat jumped, and she glanced to my lips. "You're different than I remember."

"How so?" I cut the distance between us until I caught her floral scent. One more move and she'd be in my arms.

"You used to be the funny one." A slight smile played at the corners of her lips.

"You want me to make you laugh while I kick you out?" I stuffed my hands into my pockets to keep from touching her. Had a man ever been so tempted? This was bullshit.

"No." She frowned. "You just seem so much more... troubled, I guess." She reached up and ran her fingertips down the scar on my jaw. "Banged up." Her hand traveled higher, smoothing down my cheek with a too-familiar touch.

I leaned into her warmth for a split second before stepping back. Fuck, I needed to think with the head on my shoulders, not the fat fucker hanging between my legs. "Then I guess we've both changed."

"Yes." She darted her tongue along her bottom lip. "But some things are still the same."

God, this girl. I had to get away from her before I did something we'd both regret. "Don't get too comfortable. You'll be leaving soon." I turned and walked toward the doorway to the hall.

"Can I at least redecorate my room?" Her sweet voice dripped down my spine like warm honey. "Hello Kitty isn't exactly my taste anymore."

I waved a dismissive hand at her. "Sure. Knock yourself out. Opal can get whatever you want." At the door, I hesitated. "Are you going out today?"

"Didn't you just say you want me out?"

I glanced at her over my shoulder. She had one hip jutted out, her arms crossed beneath her breasts. A spanking. Definitely a spanking for that one. "I do want you out, but just not in that dress."

She glanced down, then met my eyes with a sly expression. "Why? What's wrong with it?"

When I realized she was playing me, my cock engaged in open warfare with my zipper. Brattiness was my weakness, and she had it in spades. "You know what's wrong with it."

"I love it." She held out the hem, precariously close to revealing what was underneath. "I can't imagine why you don't like it." She fluttered her eyelashes, taunting me.

I didn't have time for her games, but fuck did I want to play. Forcing a clipped tone into my voice, I said, "Hargut will accompany you when you go out. If you want him to see your perky tits, that's on you." I strode into the hall instead of throwing her over my shoulder like I wanted. God, the things I'd do to her tight little body and her smart mouth. Gagging her with my cock shot to the top of my list, right behind the spanking. And damn, I would turn her ass redder than Santa's cheeks on Christmas Day.

Anger boiled inside me at the thought of Hargut seeing her in that dress, but I pushed it down. I needed to be running on all cylinders, and her little peep show had thrown me right out of whack.

One thing was for certain. The sooner she moved out, the better.

# CHAPTER FOUR

I HAD ZERO INTENTIONS of moving out. But my plan wasn't going quite as easily as I'd imagined. The Nate I remembered would have jumped at the chance to get with a girl like me. But he wasn't biting. Instead, he was backing away and trying to send me packing. Of course, this only made me want him more. Over the years we'd been apart, he'd turned into a gentleman—at least where I was concerned. Problem was, I didn't want a gentleman. I wanted Nate. Down and dirty. Just the way I remembered.

Staring down at myself, I took in what I had to offer. Medium breasts, but perky, as he'd pointed out. A decent waist and, I could admit, a larger butt, that led down to long legs. Boys at school had told me I was pretty—of course, that was when they were trying to get into my pants.

I worked out, took self-defense and kickboxing electives. Not a vamp by any stretch, but I wasn't a plain Jane. And I could have sworn Nate had been affected by me. His pupils dilated, his breathing faster. I didn't have the nerve to look down and try to spot a stiffy, but I suspected he was attracted to me.

So what was I doing wrong?

"Did you drop something?" Opal walked into the breakfast room and gave me a questioning look.

"No." I smoothed down my dress. "I was just, um..." I had no real explanation for why I was staring down at myself, so I changed the subject. "Nate said I could redecorate my room."

Opal gathered the plates. I reached for the empty glasses, but she waved me away. "This is my job. Been that way since before you were born."

"Okay." I moved out of her way as she efficiently cleared the table. "But do you think we could shop later?"

"I've got some chores to do, but I'm sure Mr. Franco wouldn't mind you shopping without me." She paused and met my gaze. "But make sure you take Hargut with you. You know who I mean, right?"

"Yeah." I'd seen him every day for five years straight. I could recognize him even if he dressed in drag.

"He can pay for the things you want." She finished gathering the dishes. "I'll see you when you get back, and we can work on changing the room."

"Thanks."

She smiled, her motherly eyes warming me a bit. "Anytime."

I turned and walked into the marble foyer, a sparkling chandelier overhead casting a gentle light along the wide staircase. Nate had already left, gone out to do whatever it was mob bosses did. I supposed I should have been more concerned about his profession, but I was the daughter of a Bratva drug importer and his mistress. I'd watched him die when I was just a child, and, at the time, I'd been slated to die right along with him. But through some twist of fate, the hitman had taken pity on me, stolen me away, and had me adopted into a nice family.

But it didn't take long for the life to catch up with me. I was taken, my adoptive family murdered, and then I was thrown directly into Nate's path. He'd saved me. The moment I'd seen him in that blood-soaked house when I was barely thirteen, I knew he would be my world. Now at eighteen, nothing had changed for me. Even though Nate seemed more world-weary, had collected a few more scars, he was still the man who made me feel safe despite the nightmares dancing around me.

I took the steps to my room and quickly changed into a pair of jeans, a t-shirt, and a hoodie. No need to show the goods off to anyone but Nate. Pounding back downstairs, I found Hargut standing at the front door talking to the armed guard.

"Hi. Did Opal tell you about the shopping?"

"Yep." Hargut smiled and held out a beefy hand. "I guess it's long past time for us to meet."

I took his bear paw and shook, finally getting a close look at my longtime shadow. Mid-fifties, portly, and with thin, graying hair, he had a quintessential dad bod. But he had a warm smile and kind eyes.

"And this is George." He gestured to the guard.

"Nice to meet you." His gaze slid down my body before he met my eyes. Mid-forties, salt-and pepper hair, and with a strong build, he seemed like a good choice for security, even if I didn't care for the way he looked at me. "So you two are going shopping?"

"Right." I forced a smile. "I want to redecorate my room."

George grinned. "Going to stay a while, then?"

"That's the plan."

"Good." He gave me another once-over as silence fell between us.

My skin began to crawl under his scrutiny.

Hargut cleared his throat, pulling my attention away from George. "I watched you grow up from a little girl to this." He opened the door for me. "Kept an eye on you as if you were my own. Straight A's, good scholarship, all those extracurriculars. I never missed one of your soccer games."

The pride in his voice surprised me. I turned and met his eye. "I didn't realize you were so involved." Happy to escape George's intense gawking, I walked out into the morning sun.

Leading me to a black SUV, Hargut continued, "I have a daughter that's about fifteen years older than you. When she was little, I didn't get a chance to do all the things with her that I should have. The job, you know?"

He walked around to the driver's side, and we both climbed in. "I know it sounds silly, but with you, it was sort of like I had a second chance at it. To do what I should have done and support you, even if you didn't know I was there. When the assignment came up, I jumped at the chance. Nate trusted me enough to let me be your protector, and that was that."

"Wow, that's so...sweet." I looked at him with a newfound appreciation. I barely remembered my real father. My adoptive father was kind but distant. And, other than that, I hadn't had much experience with fatherly types. "I didn't know you actually paid attention to all that stuff."

"I did. Watching you grow showed me what I'd missed with my own little girl." He put the car in gear and eased down the long driveway to the road. "My daughter would say too little, too late. She's a doctor in New York City now. Barely even calls or comes by to visit—even when I was assigned to you at that school right outside the city." He sighed, and then forced a smile. "But that's the past. I hear you're looking to redecorate your room? Want to bring it up to date?"

"That's the idea." I nodded. "And...well, thanks. For watching out for me."

"You were pretty easy to take care of. No meddling with boys or drugs or any of that. A real straight arrow." He smiled, that same glimmer of pride in his eyes.

My own began to mist, so I slid my shades on.

He waved at the guards hovering around the front

gate. "What are you feeling? Want to try King of Prussia?"

"Sure. I'm down for some mall ratting." I settled in for the ride. "What did you do for the syndicate before you became my guardian?"

He shot me a sideways glance. "Nothing good." The butt of the pistol pressing against his suit coat backed up his words.

"How long have you known Nate?" Getting whatever information I could on him seemed like a good idea.

"Oh, let's see. I knew his old man—may he rest in peace. So I probably met Nate about the time he was ten years old or thereabouts. I may have known him earlier, but he didn't do anything memorable until he was ten."

I perked up in my seat as Hargut guided the car onto the freeway. "What did he do?"

He laughed, the sound bubbling up from his round belly. "He was full of piss and vinegar at ten, already raising hell in the neighborhood, running game with his friends, and hanging with Conrad Mercer and his old man."

I shivered. "The hitman."

"Right. Con's retired now—or dead, depending on who you ask—so don't you worry about him. I know your history there, but I can guarantee you that the last thing Con ever wanted was to hurt you. He saved your life, right?"

A flashback of the barrel of his gun pointed at me when I was just a child skittered through my mind.

"He didn't kill me." I wasn't sure if that was quite the same as saving my life.

Hargut nodded, as if he, too, noted the difference. "Well, all that's over with. Going to make something of yourself instead of hanging around with the likes of Nate and me."

"I'm going to talk Nate into letting me stay at the house." I flipped on the air conditioning and started fiddling with the radio knob.

"That's not, ah, that's not what the plan is."

I shrugged and stopped on a popular music station, Justin Timberlake's newest song rippling through the speakers. "Maybe it's not your plan, but it's mine."

"Wouldn't you rather stay somewhere closer to school?" he offered gently.

"I already had this conversation with Nate." I sighed and stared at the cars next to us. Apparently, we hadn't gotten the memo that it was white SUV day, since there were three white Range Rovers blocking my view.

"Nate has your best interests at heart. He always has. That's why he sent you away from all this. You needed structure. Going to school and figuring out the sort of woman you wanted to be. That's what Nate wanted for you."

"Nate doesn't even know me." Frustration coated my words. "He hasn't made an effort to get to know me. He just sent me off to school, told you to tag along, and kept living his life while I wasn't in it."

He glanced at me. "I didn't realize Nate was so important to you."

"He saved me." I shrugged. How could I explain that Nate hadn't just pulled me out of a dangerous situation, but that in the weeks following, he'd made me feel safe in a way I never had, not even when I lived with my adoptive family? If I tried to tell Hargut, he'd probably brush it off as some sort of juvenile crush, and maybe I wouldn't blame him. After all, I was eighteen and Nate was thirty-three. But the deepest part of me—the part that had an absentee mother, a father who was murdered before her eyes, and a life that only looked on the outside like it was normal—couldn't shake the bond that linked me to Nate. He was the one I imagined holding me every night at boarding school as I struggled with my nightmares. And when I got older, I had plenty more imaginings that morphed from G to NC-17 at the speed of puberty. I'd never pictured being with anyone else. Nate and I were braided together, our threads intertwining from the first moment we met. I couldn't explain it, but the link was real, and sometimes, when I'd remember the violence of my past on dark, lonely nights, that link was the only thing that kept me grounded.

The air had grown heavy between us as I'd sank back into blood-soaked memories, the car too quiet under the sound of the wind and the tires.

Hargut cleared his throat and drummed his fingers on the gear shift. "So, what sort of décor are you looking for?"

Grateful for the reprieve from my thoughts, I said, "Something blue maybe. Some light gray walls with a china blue bedspread is sort of what I'm envisioning."

"Classy." He nodded and turned onto the King of Prussia exit. "We can always get some different furniture, too, if you don't like what—"

Gunfire shattered Hargut's window, and he slumped over the steering wheel as the white Range Rovers hemmed us in. My scream was drowned out by the sound of metal on metal as the cars scraped alongside, guiding us to the shoulder and easing to a stop.

"Hargut!" I reached across the center console and shook him, but he lolled to the side, unmoving.

The SUV against my door backed up, and two men got out and approached. I felt inside Hargut's coat and wrapped my hand around the butt of his gun as my window shattered and the door was wrenched open.

I pulled the gun from the holster and swung it around.

"You going to shoot me, little girl?" A thick Russian accent greeted me as the man at the end of my barrel smirked, his blond hair light in the sun but his dark eyes stone cold.

I pulled the trigger. Nothing happened.

He grinned and yanked the gun from my hand before grabbing a handful of my hair and hauling me out of the car. Fire raced down my scalp as he yanked. Speaking in Russian to his men, he walked me to the nearest Range Rover and shoved me in the back, then climbed in behind me as a cacophony of honking horns and shouting cut through the air.

"*Idti!*" He slapped his hand on the driver's headrest,

and we shot down the ramp. I glanced back, but Hargut hadn't moved.

*Go.* He said go. I thought I'd lost all my Russian after I was adopted, but some words still made sense.

The man slung his arm around my shoulders and pulled me tight to his side as we turned back onto the freeway and headed downtown.

"Get off me." I tried to shove him away, but he wrapped his hand around my throat and slammed me against the seat.

"Stop fighting, *kukla*." His dark eyes pierced mine. "You are mine now. My perfect little doll." He glanced to my lips. "Don't you remember me?"

I tried to shake my head, but he closed his palm tighter around my throat even as I clawed his wrist.

"Your father and I were close. I was his apprentice. Fourteen years old."

A spark of memory tried to surface. A blond boy who helped my father with the powder while I played with my dolls. A boy who never spoke to me. Dmitri, my father called him.

He laughed, but the cold sound was like sharp nails raking down my mind. "I say apprentice, but your father found more uses for me than simply learning the drug trade." His eyes bored into me as his voice dropped to a hiss. "Did you know your father preferred boys? Did you know how he liked to hold them down? Hold *me* down?"

I tried to shake my head but got nowhere.

"Your father said that a piece of trash like me should never go near a beautiful girl like you. His little doll."

The explosive anger rolling off him made the fear inside me ferment to all-out terror. "If only he could see us now." He kept the grip on my neck as he used his other hand to stroke my cheek. "Finally together."

"Let me go." The words barely carried.

"Never." He smiled and moved closer, his warm breath against my lips. "You're mine now. That idiot Nate never should have let you out of the house. Especially now that you've grown up so beautifully. Your father didn't have any finesse. Not like I do. I'm going to ruin his precious little doll. I've already ruined his other toy." He ran his hand down my neck, my chest, and cupped my breast. "But I'm going to do you slowly. You deserve a thorough job."

I tried to wrench his wrist away, but he only gripped me harder until I cried out.

"My little *kukla*. I can't wait to get you home so I can enjoy every last bit of you."

He held out a hand and snapped his fingers. I was too afraid to look anywhere but in his eyes. Fight or flight wrestled inside me, but his grip told me I wasn't going anywhere. And his size—at least two-hundred pounds of muscle and rage—reinforced that fact. I needed a weapon.

"What are you going to do?" The weak words poured from my lips.

He smirked, a cruel twist of his lips. "Whatever I want." Yanking me forward, he wrapped a black hood over my head. An antiseptic scent filled my nose, and I tried not to breathe. My lungs began to burn as the men spoke in rapid Russian. They were agitated, their voices rising. All I could make out was that someone was following us.

"Fucking Hargut." Dmitri shoved me to the side.

My lungs felt as if they would burst, and I had to take a breath. Screeching tires and shouts were the last things I heard before everything disappeared into the inky black fabric before my eyes.

# CHAPTER FIVE

## NATE

"WHERE IS SHE?" MY roar seemed to stun George at the front door, but he pointed up the stairs.

I took them two at a time until I came to her room. Opal sat next to the bed where Sabrina was sitting up but holding her head in her hands.

"She just woke up," Opal offered as she twisted her fingers together in her lap.

"Are you all right?" I rushed to Sabrina and sat next to her.

Lifting her head, her wide eyes met mine, then trailed down the blood staining my shirtsleeves. "Whose is that?"

"Not mine." I inspected her face—no visible injuries, thank god.

"Whose?"

"Don't worry about that now." I glanced to her throat where reddish finger marks marred her skin. Fury boiled and raged inside me. When I found the motherfucker who'd put his hands on her, I'd do him slow.

She touched my bloodied sleeve. "Hargut? Is he okay?"

I hoped she wouldn't ask, and I considered lying to her. But in the end, I simply shook my head. Her face crumpled, and a sob ripped from her throat. I pulled her into my arms and held her as she cried.

Hargut had managed to catch up to the men who'd taken her and rammed their car off the freeway. By the time my guys got there, he was already bleeding out, but he'd ripped Sabrina from her kidnappers, leaving two bodies and an injured Russian in the median as shocked bystanders stared from their cars. My men had grabbed him and the surviving douchebag, racing back to the house before the cops showed up.

Lying on my front steps, Hargut tried to apologize for letting her get taken, even while I held my hands on the fatal wounds in his chest. I watched him take his last breath as Peter dragged the surviving Russian around the side of the house. I would end him here in the basement after David questioned him. He wouldn't say shit. The Russians never did. But I would enjoy working out my anger on the cockbag.

"You sure you aren't hurt?" I pulled Sabrina away and inspected her face.

"I'm sore, but I don't remember the accident. I don't know what happened. But Hargut was there. Hargut—" She choked on a sob, her beautiful blue eyes awash in tears as I pulled the blanket back and ran my hands down her torso, then her legs, checking for injuries.

She hissed as I pressed along her hip. "There."

I popped the button on her jeans and unzipped them, then peeled them down to her thigh. A large purple bruise was spreading in a thick line down her side.

"I don't think it's broken." I did my best to ignore the delicate pink lace of her panties. "Opal, get her some ice and painkillers."

Opal rose and shuffled out.

I smoothed my hand over her soft skin, feeling around the bruise. "Anywhere else?"

"No." She sniffled. "That one hurts the worst."

Her tears affected me more than they should have. It took me back to an even darker time, one where she'd been traumatized so badly that she thought I was her savior. I wasn't. I was just an asshole who happened to be in the right place at the right time to pretend to be the hero. It seemed like my luck was holding in that respect, because she was looking at me as if I were the only man on the planet that could keep her safe.

"Come here." I welcomed her into my arms again.

She clung to me, her body shaking. "He watched out for me."

"I know. He did his job." I stroked my hand down her hair. "Shhh."

"H-He has a daughter. Someone needs to tell her."

"I'll handle all that." I turned her so she sat in my lap, and I leaned back against the headboard.

She nuzzled against my neck, her wet lashes tickling

my skin. And just like it had been five years before, I was wrapped around her finger. I would do anything to stop her tears, to make her feel safe even though she already knew—far better than most people twice her age—how horrible this world could be.

"I've got you. Nothing will happen to you here."

She nodded against me. "I know."

I held her for long minutes as her tears died down. My mind was on overdrive the entire time, and I itched to kill whoever thought it was a good idea to try to steal her from me, though I had a pretty clear idea of who it was. Hargut had managed to describe the kidnappers— fucking Russians. But how did they know? Sabrina hadn't been fifteen minutes from the house when they struck. There was only one conclusion. The rat was hard at work fucking up my life. Whoever it was, I intended to torture the fuck out of him. Let the Butcher take his time with all the Medieval shit he enjoyed, then I'd bring my A-game for the finale. Do some depraved bloodwork that would make the hardest man in the room want to blow his lunch all over the floor. That's what happened to rats.

Opal brought ice and gave Sabrina some Oxys.

"Can you talk about it?" I asked once she'd had the pills in her system for a bit.

"His name is Dmitri." A shudder ran through her body.

The head of the Bratva in Philly. Fucking fabulous. He was spearheading the efforts to blow my deal with the Irish. The fucker seemed to have a personal vendetta for me. After his move on Sabrina, the feeling was mutual.

I ran my hand up and down her back. "Did he say anything?"

"I knew him. He worked for my father. He said I was his doll. He said he ruined my father's other toy. What did he mean? He wants to hurt me. He said he was going t-to—" Her voice hitched, and I shushed her and rubbed her back more as red-hot fury rushed through my veins.

"He won't touch you." I would kill him with my bare hands. "That's enough now. You need to get some rest."

"Stay." She nuzzled against me. "Please?"

I had a man to kill in the basement, but I supposed it could wait. Giving David some extra quality time with the Russian prick was no skin off my back.

I glanced around at the cartoon cat that stared down at me from the wallpaper and the curtains. "I'm not sure if hanging around in the Hello Kitty palace is really my style."

She laughed against me, the sound soothing my frayed nerves. "Don't lie. I know you love it."

A smile twitched along my lips. "You got me."

"Believe it." She sighed and snuggled closer, her breaths becoming slow and steady.

I should have told her that I wasn't the sort of man you could stake a claim on, but I kept silent as she drifted off into a drug-induced sleep. Spending time with her like this made me feel more human than I had in a long time. Maybe she was right about me changing. I'd hardened in the years we'd been apart, but she managed to bypass the tough outer layers and lodge in my heart. The need to protect her overcame all else.

When David had called and told me there was trouble and Sabrina was involved, I couldn't get to her fast enough. All those years at school, she'd been safe. But now I'd fucked up by letting her stay at the house. She'd have a target on her back until the shit with the Russians was cleared up. And by "cleared up" I meant, "all the pieces of shit who dared touch her were bleeding out under my goddamn feet." She was mine to protect from the first moment I saw her, and I wasn't going to let her down.

The only problem with this plan? She wasn't a kid anymore. No matter how many times I tried to think of her as the scrawny girl from five years ago, the boner perilously close to her ass said differently. She wasn't a child; she was a grown woman who would test my severely limited ability to control myself.

My first parole officer had always told me I failed to do the "proper cost/benefit analysis" before committing crimes. I figured what he meant to say was, "you're an impulsive bastard with outrageous good looks." Either way, I didn't have much in the way of self-control when it came to things I wanted. And, at that moment, what I wanted most was sleeping peacefully against my chest. But she was the one thing in my life I hadn't cocked up. She needed to stay that way. Literally and figuratively.

Only one solution presented itself. I had to end the Russians sooner rather than later. I promised to protect Sabrina, and I would stick to it, even if it meant protecting her from myself. But the sooner she was out of my house, the better. That was something me and my neon blue balls could agree on, for once.

————

A muffled scream met my ears as I descended the wooden stairs. The cool basement greeted me, the walls made of the same pale stone that rose two stories overhead. With over a century of use, the dirt floors were tightly packed, hard as cement. Long fluorescent lighting cast a dim, sickly glow on the scene as the metallic tang of blood infiltrated my nostrils.

The thud of knuckles on skin woke my senses and took me from the warm bed filled with Sabrina's soft floral scent to the stark torture scenario laid out before me.

"He say anything?" I strode up behind David, whose undershirt was splotched with sweat and blood. He lived for this, for enforcing the blood-coated rules of our syndicate whenever it was necessary.

"Just some screams and a few Russian curses." David spat and backed up, crossing his arms over his chest as he leveled a hellish glare at the quivering captive. A year younger than me, David made up for the age difference with heft. I worked out. I kept my body in top condition, but I was a novice compared to the Butcher. Built like a fucking tank, there was a reason no one saw the light of day again after he went to work on them.

I slowly, methodically rolled up my shirt sleeves as the Russian's breath whistled in through his broken nose.

His eyes barely shown through the puffy flesh around them, and the rest of him looked like it had been through a fucking grinder. I didn't flinch. This was the fate he'd chosen when he stole Sabrina, when he decided to take what was mine.

Lowering to my haunches in front of him, I stared up into his dull eyes. "I already know you're Dmitri's man."

His nostrils flared the slightest bit.

"What's his name?" I asked David.

"Oleg."

"Nice to meet you, Oleg. I'm Nate. Dmitri's the one who hit my last weed shipment, no?"

He glanced to the side then met my gaze again.

I shrugged. "It was him. You admitting it will only confirm what I know. I can only assume he's got designs on tonight's shipment as well."

No response.

"I bet you know who the rat is, don't you? Who's been telling your boss all my little secrets?" I rose and walked around him, taking in the wedding ring on his left hand. "Got a wifey at home?"

He turned his head at that.

"Hey, David, when's the last time you got some strange?"

"Been a while. You?"

I smirked at him over the Russian's head. "Your mom hasn't been in town for a few days, so I'm overdue."

He glared at me but kept silent and let me work.

"I bet you've got a pretty wife." I walked to Oleg's front. "She's going to be so lonely." I sighed and leaned against the metal table full of bloody tools. "The Butcher here, he's really into redheads. She a redhead?"

His eyes widened.

"Bingo." I shot a look at David. "He's got a ginger at home. Where's his ID?"

He reached across the table and grabbed a beaten-up leather wallet.

I flipped through it to his ID. "Lives on Westing Lane. I bet it's a nice little seventies ranch house, isn't it? I used to fuck a girl in that neighborhood. Her parents' room was right across the hall. We had to be quiet. That was okay, since she was really into choking. You feel me, right?" I laughed, and the dumb shit actually seemed to give a little nod in agreement. I leaned down and stared into his eyes. "I'm good at choking. Your wife will appreciate the skill, I'm sure."

He shook his head, the tremble in his body increasing.

"But." I cocked my head to the side. "You could tell me who the rat is, and she won't be touched."

"I don't know." His voice rasped through his throat.

"Progress." I elbowed David and leaned against the table next to him. "But I don't believe you."

"I don't know. Only Dmitri knows." He coughed, blood spilling from the corner of his lips.

"That's unfortunate." I tsked and flexed my fists.

"I'm telling the truth."

I glanced to David, who gave a faint nod, which meant the dumb shit was telling the truth.

"Why Sabrina?"

He went back to the silent treatment.

I turned to David, kicking up a conversation as if we didn't have a bloodied prisoner sitting five feet away. "You know what chicks are really into these days? That BDSM shit. With the whips and the flogging and the pain."

"I've flogged my fair share." David smirked. "Probably more than my fair share."

"What's your favorite part?"

"When they cry." No hesitation.

"Cold." I laughed, playing it up. Mine was an act, but David? I wasn't so sure. Fuck, I needed a cigarette. "And redheads really do it for you?"

He grunted. "They fight back the most, more blood that way. And their tears"—he grinned—"you get enough of those, mix it with her blood, and you've got all the lube you need to—"

"He says he owns Sabrina," Oleg spat out. "That you took her, and so you have to pay. She's his."

"Well look who got chatty all of a sudden." I turned back to Oleg. "Why does he think he has any right to Sabrina?"

"He worked for her father, Petrov." He coughed, more blood dribbling from his puffy lips. "Petrov was a *merzkiy detoyeb*."

I gave Peter a what-the-fuck look.

"Sabrina's dad was a..." His brows drew together as he worked on the translation. "Pederast. Liked boys. Abused Dmitri, I figure."

So this was about revenge. Punish the daughter for the sins of the father.

I turned my gaze back to the prisoner. "So that's why he's been all over my ass like a horny gorilla?"

"*Da.*"

Now I *really* needed a cigarette. Sabrina was firmly at the rotten core of the feud between my crew and the Russians. The moment she'd left the safety of her boarding school, Dmitri pounced. And I was the idiot who said, "*Go shopping, get out of my house, have a great time, parade around in public. Here, let me draw a big, red bullseye on your back before you go.*"

"Is Dmitri planning on hitting my shipment this afternoon?"

Oleg snorted back and hocked a bloody wad of snot onto the floor at my feet. "*Yebat' sebya.*"

"He said—"

"Go fuck yourself. Yeah, I know the cuss words, at least." I peered down at Oleg, weighing whether threatening his wife would get me any further with him. He stared back, stripped bare and with the heavy weight of impending death dulling his eyes. He was done.

I dropped all pretense and grabbed the Glock from my back waistband and aimed at his face. "You have my word that your wife won't be touched."

"*Spasibo.*" He dropped his gaze to the floor.

"You're welcome." I pulled the trigger.

# CHAPTER SIX

SABRINA

M Y HIP THROBBED IN steady waves of discomfort as I sat up and peered around my room. Hello Kitty smiled back as the sun, low on the horizon, filtered through the curtains. The room was quiet, and I was alone, but I still caught the scent of Nate. He'd held me until I'd fallen into a pleasant sleep that eventually turned into one nightmare after another—each of them ending with me at the end of a barrel. I'd woken with a start, my sweaty shirt clinging to me.

Distant voices carried up the stairs, all male, as if there were a gathering below. I threw my legs off the edge of the bed and stood. The room spun for a moment before settling down. I eased to the bathroom and checked myself in the mirror. A light pattern of bruising rose along my throat. I shivered at the memory of Dmitri's hand pressing against me. Another streak of bluish brown down my collar bone. Sliding my pants down, I checked the ugly bruise on my hip. It looked like

I must have been thrown against the door's armrest when Hargut rammed the car. Just the thought of him brought tears to my eyes. I swallowed them back. He'd been brave. I would be, too.

I cleaned up and pulled my hair into a messy pony-tail. Walking with a slight limp, I crept down the hall to the bannister. Dozens of men were lined up in the marble foyer, their voices hushed but carrying in the wide space.

Going downstairs didn't seem like an option, but I didn't want to go back to my room, so I took a seat on the top step and waited. Out of sight, but with a great view of everything going on, I tried to figure out what was happening. More men arrived over the next few minutes until the foyer was packed.

They quieted as Nate entered from the hallway to the right. My breath hitched in my throat. He wore a perfectly fitted suit with a white shirt beneath, open at the collar. His dark hair was parted on the side, the strands neat and smooth as he stood and surveyed his men. At six feet three or so, he was imposing—taller than most of the men in the room. And the look on his face was stern, far more serious than I'd ever seen him. Two men followed close behind him. One was Peter, who I'd met earlier. I didn't recognize the other one, but I would remember him—large and terrifying, his face was a mask of dark intentions.

All eyes were on Nate. Standing there like a gorgeous, lethal man who exuded effortless power, he seemed to be calculating as he met the eyes of each man before passing to the next.

"As you all know, we have a rat." His voice boomed out over the crowd. They shifted uncomfortably and parted as Nate walked among them. "I want to assure you that I'm going to find out who it is." He stopped in front of a younger man. "And when I do, there will be no mercy. I will let the Butcher pull out all the stops. Every nightmare you've ever had, it'll play out right here, under our feet."

The young man in front of him withered under Nate's words.

Nate moved on, staring down each person in his path. "Because more than anything else, I demand *loyalty*. The rat threatens everything we've built here. And he will pay with blood, all of it. Does anyone have any questions?" He turned and moved to stand at the head of the room.

Silence reigned.

"Does anyone have anything they want to tell me?" His voice dropped low, which made it even scarier. The intensity of his gaze spoke to some primal part of me, telling me to run. Like a blinking predator alert going off at some ancient level of my consciousness. I didn't move.

No one spoke. No one seemed to breathe as Nate bore down on them like a tempest.

"Tonight, we're receiving a shipment at Essington. I'm expecting company straight from Moscow." He crossed his arms over his chest. "We're going to kill every last one of them. It's time they learned what we do to anyone who takes what's ours."

A flurry of nods and agreement went up from the crowd.

"Don't hesitate. Shoot first, ask questions later. We'll protect this shipment, then the next, and the next." He smirked. "What's more, we're going to start taking."

Even more agreement with a chorus of yeahs rumbled around in the air.

"Peter will speak more about that when the time comes, but I need to be sure that every man here is ready to fight for what's his. To protect what we've made with our own hands. Are you ready to bleed for it?"

The men roared so loud that I clapped my hands over my ears. Nate's eyes cut to me, but he looked away quickly and continued, "Good. Because you will. But when it's all over, we'll rule this fucking city."

Another cheer that seemed to shake the chandelier.

"Get to work." Nate turned and retreated down the long hallway. Peter and the huge man followed as the room burst into movement and the men dispersed. In a matter of seconds, the entire foyer was clear except for George standing at the front door.

I padded down the stairs and turned toward the hall where Nate had disappeared.

"He's busy." Though I'd ignored George, he didn't pay me the same courtesy.

"He'll see me." I continued down the hall and hoped my words were true.

I turned into the study where Opal said he did most of his business. Comfortable couches and a wide desk presided over a sunny room whose walls were lined with books. Nate sat at his desk and stared at an unopened pack of Marlboros in his palm.

"It's not as bad as all that." Peter sat on one of the sofas as the other man—the one who looked like a beefy version of Death—stared at me.

"It might be." Nate peered at the cigarettes, then glanced at me as I eased into the room.

"You still smoke?" I asked. The faint sweet scent of tobacco floated through my memory. He'd used to roll his own cigarettes, though he'd try to hide his smoking from me.

"I quit two years ago, but sometimes..."

I sat on the couch next to Peter and crossed my legs at the knee. "That's a long time. Would be a shame for you to break your streak."

"Two years, and you've made it through three hit attempts and all sorts of shit without lighting up." Peter seemed to be on an anti-smoking campaign. "Don't give up now."

"You're right." Nate sighed and nodded before dropping the pack into his top desk drawer. "Sabrina, you've met Peter, and this is David, his brother."

"Hi." I offered the big guy a small smile.

"Nice to finally meet you." Despite being delivered in a chilling baritone, the words were warm.

"I'm glad you're pleased." Nate leaned back in his chair. "I want you to start training her in self-defense."

"What?" David and I said at the same time.

"I already know self-defense," I protested.

"I don't think so." Nate's green eyes pierced me. "If you did, you would have gotten away from Dmitri."

Indignation rose inside me. "He had me by the throat!"

"Exactly." His gaze slid to the bruising at my neck. "You need to be able to get out of a choke hold. David can teach you that."

I snuck a look at the brooding giant. He seemed just as irked as I was about the training, his dark brows lowering over his light blue eyes. Scary with a placid expression, he was downright terrifying when he was pissed.

"Don't worry. He won't hurt you. Well, no more than he has to so that you can learn." Nate seemed to chew on the words as he said them, as if the idea of David and I sparring didn't taste very good on his tongue.

"Fine." I shrugged. It's not like I had any pressing commitments, and I wanted to be able to fight back if Dmitri or his minions every got their hands on me again. I flinched at the thought. "Did you get any more information about Dmitri? About what he said to me in the car?"

Nate shifted in his chair and took a long while before saying, "Dmitri wants to hurt you. From what we've been able to uncover, what he said about your father was true —he sexually abused Dmitri when he was his apprentice."

My stomach churned, and I almost felt sorry for Dmitri. But my father's actions weren't a valid reason for Dmitri's cruelty toward me or anyone else. "I didn't know anything about it. I was just a child."

"That doesn't matter to him." Nate shrugged.

David cracked his knuckles. "Someone has to pay. For him, that someone is you."

A chill seemed to drift through the room. I pulled my feet up and tucked them under me.

"But we'll protect you and kill him, of course," David offered in what he likely thought was a helpful tone.

"Guys, be ready for tonight. Let me talk to Sabrina alone for a minute." Nate's voice carried a weariness that hadn't shown during his earlier talk with his soldiers.

"On it." Peter rose and gave me a small smile before walking out of the room with his brother.

When the door shut behind them, Nate asked, "Did you enjoy the show out there?"

*Yes, it was hot.* I nixed that comment and went with, "Everyone seems on edge."

"Good. They should be. We've got a rat. Someone who told Dmitri where you'd be and when. I'll find him. And when I do..." He flexed his fists, his eyes blazing with barely contained fury.

"George." I thought back on how he'd looked at me, the questions he'd asked before Hargut and I had left. "It had to have been him."

Nate shook his head. "Not a chance. He's been with me since the beginning."

"He's sleazy."

"Yeah, but that doesn't mean he's a rat."

"He knew where we were going." I stood and walked around to the side of his desk, running my fingers along the smooth wood. "He was asking questions."

Nate followed my movements, his green eyes focused

on me in a way that heated my blood. "He's supposed to ask questions. He's security."

"I don't trust him."

"I do." He leaned back as I skirted around the edge of his desk and stood next to him.

When I perched beside him, his nostrils flared.

"How do you know he's not the rat?"

He sighed and placed his hands on the arms of his office chair. "Because his younger sister and I used to dick down back in the day. She got pregnant."

Jealousy twisted in my gut like a fish hook. "You have a kid?"

He smirked. "Not quite. I'd been careful, but when she had the baby, she'd told me it was mine. Of course, I'd requested a paternity test. Turned out, it wasn't mine. But she was desperate, didn't have money, no job, and the kid would have suffered, so I paid child support anyway. Still do. The kid doesn't know about me. But George knows what I'm doing for his family. And as long as they're safe and looked after, which they are, he's got my back. Mercy creates loyalty. Fear works too, but mercy is the long game."

I arched a brow. "Mercy creates loyalty, huh? Why can't you just admit that you wanted to help the kid? You're a softy at heart. It wasn't about ensuring loyalty."

"A softy?" His gaze drifted down my body. "I don't think so."

I licked my lips as a familiar pressure slowly built inside me. Just the nearness of him lit up every pleasure sensor I had, priming me for his touch. "You saved me because you're a softy. Same thing for the boy. You can't help but do good things."

"Good things?" He shook his head and gripped the chair arms. "I killed a man today, Sabrina. Shot him in the basement while you slept. Do you know why?" His words should have chilled me. They didn't.

"Why?" I breathed the word and edged closer to him until my knee touched his.

"Because he took you." His jaw tightened as he stared up at me. "Because he dared to think he could touch you."

"Because I'm yours." The words I'd longed to say to him slipped from my tongue in the easiest confession.

He closed his eyes, as if the words hurt to hear. "I'm going to protect you."

I shifted until I stood directly in front of him, both our knees touching and my ass pressed against his desk. "Because I'm yours." I'd say it as many times as I needed to so that he'd understand. I wanted him.

He opened his eyes and leaned forward, placing his palms at my waist. I shivered at his touch, the fire inside me threatening to consume all rational thought. His posture tightened, as if he were just a few threads away from unravelling.

"I swore to protect you. That's all." His touch didn't match his words. He squeezed, his fingers digging into me as he stroked his thumbs back and forth across the fabric of my t-shirt. "I'm going to keep you safe and send you off to college."

"I'm staying." I straddled him and sat in his lap, my ass resting on his thighs as he leaned back in his chair.

"We aren't doing this." Still, his hands never left me.

I rested my palms on his chest, feeling the rampaging beat of his heart. His hands slid lower, grazing along my hips, then circling around to my ass. When he squeezed, I curled my toes and leaned closer.

I hovered my lips over his, desperate to taste him. "I want you."

He groaned and flicked his gaze to my lips. "This can't happen."

"I've waited for you." I pressed my palms against his cheeks.

His pupils dilated as he slid his hands under my shirt and up my back. "What?"

"I've never been with anyone. Because I'm yours."

"Fuck." He bit the word as it left his lips.

I moved closer until I could feel the hard length of him against the seam of my jeans. Sensations flickered through me, my need for him so strong it verged on a sickness. He remained still, a silent war raging inside him.

"I'm yours. All of me. Whatever you want."

"This can't happen." He started to push me away.

I pressed my lips to his, tentative at first.

He didn't do tentative. With a low groan, he gripped my hair and took my mouth with a rough kiss that blasted away all expectations. Even though I was on top, he was in charge. Tilting my head, he slanted his mouth over mine, taking me just how he wanted. His tongue pressed against my lips, and I opened for him. Liquid fire flowed through my veins and pooled in my clit as he took over.

His low groan ricocheted through me as his tongue caressed mine. I answered, tangling with him as I gripped his shoulders. I'd wanted it for so long, imagined it so many ways—but the real thing was better than anything I could have concocted. Nate stoked my desire with his sinful mouth, promising me bliss with each artful stroke of his tongue against mine. Reaching around me, he yanked me forward until his cock pressed fully against me. I moved my hips, riding him despite our clothes. He gripped my ass harder, and my nipples ached as they pressed against his chest with each of my movements.

Running his hand to my hip, he squeezed. I squealed at the sudden shock of pain. He pulled back.

"Fuck, fuck, fuck." He blinked hard, then set me on my feet and stood.

I stepped toward him, wanting more of his touch.

But he held a hand up and stepped back. "No."

"What?"

"This is...you are...we can't..." He stopped and ran a hand through his hair as he tried to compose himself.

"I'm not a child. I'm eighteen—"

"Right." He nodded, perhaps at himself. "Eighteen. You're far too young. I'm your guardian. That's it."

Irritation, thick and acrid, welled up inside me. "I can make my own decisions. You aren't my legal guardian anymore."

He flexed his fists and then straightened his fingers. "Don't sass me."

"I'll sass you if I want to. I'm a grown woman. You're acting like a scared kid."

"Sabrina." His tone held a warning that I ignored.

"What? Are you afraid? Scared of me?" I stepped toward him.

He retreated. "I'm trying to do the right thing here, can't you see that? For once in my life, I'm trying to put someone else first. Put *you* first."

It sounded right, noble even. But it wasn't true. "No, you're protecting yourself."

"What?"

"You feel the same thing I do. You want this, but you won't let yourself have it. You're afraid." I wanted to move closer, but his wild eyes told me he'd bolt.

"No, no, no." He waved away my words. "You and me—it's wrong. I'm supposed to look after you. To send you off to college. Not"—he gestured at his chair—"not do that."

I tried a different tack. Running my hands up my body, I cupped my breasts. "Big tough mob boss can't handle the heat?"

His eyes flashed. "Sabrina, I'm warning you."

I was testing his control. But I didn't just want to test it. I wanted it gone. "Warning me?" I laughed and grabbed the hem of my shirt. "About what? What will you do? Run away because you're afraid?" I began to lift my top.

"Don't." He tensed, but watched every inch of skin I revealed as I peeled off my shirt.

When I tossed it on the floor at his feet and unbuttoned my jeans, his eyes darkened.

"That's enough."

"I don't think so." I unzipped my jeans and pushed them down my thighs.

Before I could finish the job, Nate grabbed me and sat in his desk chair, then flipped me across his knees. *Smack.* A burn ripped across my ass. *Smack, smack, smack.* I squealed and wiggled to try and get away from him, but he held me fast by pushing me down onto his knees with his left hand while he spanked me with his right. Over and over again, his palm came down against my backside, sending fire rushing along my skin.

"Nate!" I tried to push away from him to no avail.

"Teasing me." *Smack.* "Sassing me." *Smack.* "Showing me your fucking perky tits." *Smack.* "Grinding on my cock." *Smack, smack, smack.*

The more I struggled, the more he spanked me. The fire on my ass cheeks began to seep deeper into me, changing from pain to something warmer as he smacked me again then smoothed his hand over the burn. I moaned as he dipped his fingers down along my thong.

"Fucking wet." His voice was tight as he stroked me through my panties. "Fuck."

I whimpered and wriggled against his touch, wanting more. "Please."

My voice seemed to snap him out of his reverie, because he cursed in a creative litany, then yanked my jeans up to cover my stinging ass.

"Shit, I'm sorry. Shit." He lifted me to my feet. "Are you okay?"

Okay? I was fucking flying. I wanted more—more pain, more pleasure, more of his hands on me. Before I could vocalize all of that, he'd swiped my shirt off the floor and pulled it down over my head.

"I'm sorry," he repeated. "That won't happen again." His eyes were wide, as if he were horrified at what he'd done. He led me to his office door. "Just, ah, I'll see you later."

"I want to stay." I dug my heels in, but he easily overcame me and pushed me out the door.

"No. I'm sorry." He shut down, his eyes refusing to meet my own. "I shouldn't have done that. I'm sorry."

"It's okay. I want—"

He closed the door in my face, and I heard the click of a lock. The door handle wouldn't budge when I tried it. "Nate, let me in." I crossed my arms and stared at the door.

Silence inside. He'd given me the hottest moment of my life, then completely shut me out.

"Nate!" I slapped the door.

Low laughter met my ears, and I turned to see George leaning against the wall at the end of the hall. "Told you he was busy."

*Shut up* was on the tip of my tongue, but I ignored him and tried the handle once more. It didn't move. Hurt arced through me like lightning, and tears stung behind my eyes. I couldn't even begin to fathom the embarrassment that George's presence caused me.

He sauntered a few steps closer. "Your shirt's on inside out."

Glancing down, I saw he was right. *Damn.* To save what was left of my pride, I turned to walk past him and head back to my room.

The flick of a lighter caught my ear, and I stilled. After a few more moments, the slight acrid scent of a cigarette wafted from beneath the door. A grin spread across my face as I realized I'd driven Nate to smoke.

# CHAPTER SEVEN

NATE

I'D SPANKED HER. SPANKED. Her.

The SUV hummed down the road toward the dock as I glared out the window. How did I lose control so fast? One second, I had decided to show her out of my office, the next, she was in my lap grinding on my cock like the perfect little fuck toy.

I clenched my eyes shut to block the vision from my mind, but it only splayed wider on the canvas of my eyelids. Her blue eyes, the swell of her tits, the feel of her hot pussy against me. And then, when I'd laid her across my lap and spanked her until my handprints had reddened her tan skin.

"Fuck." I slapped my palm on my thigh.

Peter and David knew better than to say a word to me when I was like this. I should have been focusing on the weed shipment and the bloodshed that would happen in under an hour. Instead, all I could think about was how wet she'd been—her panties soaked—as I'd given her the spanking she'd been begging for ever since I'd seen her in the pool.

I'd broken. When she'd taken her top off, my cost/benefit analysis had short circuited. Taking her over my knee seemed the only response. And fuck, I certainly felt a benefit from it. The satisfaction of turning her ass crimson as she called my name and panted—there was nothing else like it. Oh, but the cost. The cost was going to bury me.

I longed for another cigarette as we pulled up to the abandoned dock. All the day workers were long gone, and I had an arrangement with the owner that my evening shipments would not be disturbed.

A gray trawler chugged up the Delaware, its outward appearance giving the look of a simple fishing setup. It carried a much more valuable cargo than simple cod, though. Some of the choicest strains of weed straight from grow operations in California and Colorado were onboard and represented a small fortune in street value. I kept my fingers constantly crossed that Pennsylvania and Jersey never got around to legalizing the stuff. It would wipe out my stoned clientele.

A handful of black SUVs were positioned around the dock, and I had shooters set up on rooftops and hidden in the few buildings along this stretch of river. The operation was simple—back up our 18-wheeler, load it, and kill anyone who tried to interfere.

The trawler edged up to the dock, the familiar captain visible through the windows along the front of the cockpit.

"We're ready to transfer. Cops have been paid. There won't be any boys in blue in this area while we're working." Peter peered out of the car, sizing up the scene.

"We've got lookouts along the highway. They'll let us know when the Russians show." David opened the door as the car stopped, and all three of us stepped out and walked onto the weathered dock. Pockmarked pavement turned to splintered wooden decking along the water. The trawler pulled up, and crewmen threw out its lines. My men secured it to the dock and waited for the gangplank to be set.

We worked in the dark, the only light coming from a sliver moon and a dull street lamp at our backs.

Peter kept a line of communication open with our men on the highway, his handset crackling. "Any sign of them?"

The reply came back, "all clear."

I motioned for the truck to back all the way to the dock. A cool wind whipped past, and the trawler bumped against the graying wood with a mix of hollow and thick thumps. My skin crawled, and Peter shifted from foot to foot next to me, the boards creaking beneath him.

"I don't like this." I peered at the water, then turned and checked the road. Nothing. "Where are our comrades?"

My men opened the back of the trailer and lined up on the dock, waiting for the trawler crew to drop the gangway. We'd use sheer manpower to make the transfer of drugs from the boat to the trailer. It took longer, but dicking with a crane would just draw unwanted attention.

"Something's wrong." David moved in front of me. "I can feel it."

"Call it off?" Peter asked. He scanned the waterline where the small waves lapped against the concrete and wood.

"Fuck no." I pulled my Glock from the holster under my arm. "Just keep your eyes open."

"What the fuck are they doing on the boat?" David walked farther out onto the dock.

Then I saw it. The captain wasn't moving. Hadn't moved at all since the trawler pulled up. Dead.

The Russians were already here.

I rushed forward and gripped David's shoulder, yanking him back. "They're on the—"

Gunfire ripped through the night, and three of my men along the docks fell. The Russians emerged from the trawler, swarming like ants with submachine guns. The rest of my men scattered as the shootout began.

David and Peter shoved me down behind a stack of railroad ties, the thick smell of tar the perfect accent to the thick, bloody violence going on around us. Shouts and gunfire peppered the night as I peeked around the wood to get a view of the battlefield.

At least two-dozen men had taken over the trawler, a planned ambush that went off flawlessly. We had no fucking clue. After their initial volley, they hid behind the thick metal rail and around the other side of the ship, only popping up to take well considered shots. Fuck that.

"Should I pull the guys from the highway to come help?" Peter popped up and fired off a shot. One of the Russians stumbled and fell over the railing, his body crunching on the gravelly shore.

"No, I get a feeling they'll be coming from that way soon. Tell them to be ready with the spikes."

"Got it." He spoke my instructions into the radio as I darted out and took out an asshole through the cockpit glass.

David's beefy hand grabbed my coat and pulled me back behind the ties. "Don't risk it."

"This is war." I sighted around the ties and took another shot, nailing one of the Russians in the arm. "Everyone fights. Even the general."

My men had taken defensive positions but continued firing back. It was like Whack-A-Mole. What seemed to be a well thought out ambush turned into shooting fish in a barrel. The Russians had nowhere to go. After half a dozen more of them went down, one of them got the bright idea to take off with the ship. But the morons had let us tie them off to the dock as part of the ruse.

The trawlers engine revved and strained to pull away from the dock. It held fast, but the wood creaked and groaned, some of it splintering as the pilot increased the power to escape.

"We can't let them get away." I peeked from cover. "There's only about ten of them left."

"Don't." David shook his head, his eyebrows drawing together. "Don't even think about it."

"Lay down covering fire for me."

Peter loaded a fresh clip. "Fuck that." He pulled out the radio. "We're going to rush the ship. If you've got balls of steel, join. If you don't, cover us." He tossed the radio down and clapped his brother on the back. "Let's do this."

"Fuck." David pulled his backup handgun from his second holster. "This is crazy shit."

I grinned. "I used to be known for some crazy shit, man. Don't go all pansy ass on me now."

The splintering sounds increased, and the trawler began to get a few feet of separation from the dock.

"Pansy ass?" David smiled—the scariest thing I've ever seen. "You did crazy shit, huh? Hold my beer." He rose and darted out from behind cover, both barrels firing as he rushed the ship.

"Holy shit." A surge of adrenaline powered through me as Peter and I rose and followed, a hail of gunfire sounding all around us as we bet it all on black.

# CHAPTER EIGHT

N ATE HAD BEEN GONE for hours, and I'd busied myself with shopping online for new room décor. Every time I heard the slightest noise from downstairs, I tiptoed out to the bannister to see if he'd come home. He hadn't. Was everything okay at the docks? I wanted to go downstairs and ask George if he knew anything, but I couldn't bring myself to approach him.

By midnight, my eyes were drifting closed as I searched through the Pottery Barn website. By one in the morning, I was fast asleep when a loud clatter from downstairs shot me awake. I rescued my laptop from the precarious edge of my bed, then rushed to the bannister.

Men were funneling through the front door, some supported between two others, some holding injuries.

"What the hell?" I hurried down the stairs and gawked as the men lay their friends down on the marble floor and inspected wounds. Fear walked across my spine like a spider. Where was Nate?

George still stood watch at the front door, though he helped some of the injured through to spots on the floor. A man wearing baggy khakis and a polo walked in, his wrinkled skin going extra-wrinkly as he stared around at the carnage. He carried a doctor's bag, the black kind from the movies.

"We need triage. Who's the worst off? I'll start there." His paper-thin voice barely reached my ears, but some of the men raised their hands and waved him over to the injured.

I hurried past the doctor as he said, "Phil's gone. Damn. Who's next?"

I tapped George on the shoulder.

"Yeah?" He stared out at the cars in the drive.

"Is Nate okay?"

He shot me a contemptuous look. "Afraid your meal ticket got popped?"

"What?" I wanted to shove him, but his rifle told me to keep my hands to myself. "What is that supposed to mean?"

"I'm busy." He turned his back and opened the door for another batch of bloodied men.

"Is Nate okay?" I wouldn't leave until he answered me.

"He took a slug in the arm." He didn't even turn to say it to my face. "He's on his way."

Relief swelled inside me as I backed away.

"You." The doctor pointed at me, though his eyes were focused on the young man lying in front of him.

"Put pressure on this wound." He pointed to the man's thigh where blood soaked through his jeans.

"I'm not trained or anythi—"

"Do it or Will's going to bleed out!" The doctor reached inside his bag.

I dropped to my knees and pressed my palms against the wound. Will, not much older than I was, winced and took a labored breath.

The doctor yanked up Will's shirt and shook his head at the bloody spot on his abdomen. It didn't look like much, though blood trickled from it.

"Keep pressure on him, I'm going to see if the bullet went straight through." The doctor eased his hand behind Will's back and felt around. He swore and pulled his hand away. "Came out up past his lung. Probably did all kinds of damage on its way through."

Will was pale, paler than a person ever should be. My hands began to shake, but I leaned harder on his leg, trying to stanch the flow of blood.

The doctor pressed a bloody hand to his forehead. "Everything's going to be fine." He smiled, exuding a sense of comfort I knew he didn't feel. "We'll have you patched up in no time."

Will nodded, his breaths becoming quick and shallow.

The word *no* played on repeat in my mind. I wouldn't let Will die. I didn't know him, had no idea what sort of man he was, but I wouldn't let him die. This wasn't happening. No. The doctor reached out to me and pushed me away. I fell back on my ass as Will's blood began pouring faster.

"Hey!" I struggled forward and replaced my hands on the wound. But it was too late. Will took a gasping breath. I waited for him to take another. It never came.

The doctor pointed at Will's leg beneath my bloody hands. "We were only prolonging his pain. Better to let him go." His voice still held comfort, but I didn't want it.

Someone yelled, "Doc Friar! Jimmy's hurt bad."

The doctor rose and attended to the next patient as I sat and stared at the dead man in front of me. Gone. Murdered by someone's—probably Dmitri's—bullet. I'd seen so much death that I thought I was numb to it. I was wrong. Will was no one to me, but his death still shook me to my roots.

"Sabrina."

I looked up. Nate stood above me, and I realized he'd been calling my name and grabbing my shoulder.

He glanced at Will, then the blood on my hands. "Come on. Let's get you cleaned up."

Tears spilled down my cheeks. "He's dead."

"I know." His tone gentled, and he knelt down. "Come on." He pulled me to my feet and walked me up the stairs. Turning into my room, he continued to the en suite bathroom and switched the water on.

"Wash up." He guided my hands under the faucet. Will's blood sloshed down the drain, leaving my hands until the water ran clear and the crimson was gone.

"Come here." He pulled me against his chest. The

smell of gunpowder, his cologne, and blood rested on him.

*Blood.* I realized he was only hugging me with one arm. Pulling back, I inspected his left arm, but couldn't see much for the suit jacket. "Take this off."

"It's okay. Really."

"No, it isn't." I ran my fingers along his shoulders and slid the jacket off. "Oh, god." Blood had soaked through his light blue dress shirt. "Off." I hastily unbuttoned his shirt as he offered some weak protests. Once he was bare, I inspected his arm. A small bullet hole along the front of his arm bled. Taking a note from the doctor's playbook, I lifted his arm and checked along the back of his arm for a matching hole.

"It went through." Nate hissed as I brushed my finger over the exit wound to get a better view. "Looks like a small-bore slug. Pretty clean, really."

"Don't play it off. You're *shot!*" I pushed him against the vanity and dug around in the cabinet beside the mirror. Alcohol, bandages, and a few other first aid items were in a box toward the back. I pulled it out and grabbed a washcloth. "Hold this on it."

He took the wash cloth and did as instructed with a bemused look. "I'm fine, really. This is like a mosquito bite to me."

I blinked and saw Will's too-pale face. I shot my hand out and grabbed the cabinet to steady myself.

"Whoa, whoa." He pulled me to his chest. "Just breathe. Everything's going to be all right." Stroking my hair with his right arm, he breathed steadily. His strong heartbeat thumped against my cheek as I inhaled his scent and reassured myself that he was going to be fine. "I'm sorry about Will," he said quietly.

"I didn't know him, but I wanted to save him. I-I tried, but I c-couldn't—"

"I know." He dropped a kiss on the crown of my head as my tears began anew. "It wasn't your fault. Shit got hairy at the docks tonight."

"Dmitri?"

He stiffened. "Yes. He was there. Escaped with his life, barely."

I'd never wished for someone's death before, but Dmitri was different. With him, either he would die, or I would. He'd made it clear that the two of us living in peace wasn't an option.

"I'm okay." I sniffled and took a step back. "I can clean up your arm."

"You don't have to. Doc Friar will get to me once he's done with the others."

"I want to." I glanced up and met his eyes.

He seemed to soften as he wiped the tears from my cheeks. "All right."

I uncapped the alcohol and ignored the slight tremor in my hand as I wiped the area clean, then used cotton balls to dab alcohol around the wounds. The blood had slowed down enough for me to get a good look at the entry and exit—both an angry red.

"You're doing great." Nate peeked at my work, then settled down while I bandaged both sides after applying some antibacterial ointment.

When I was done, he was all cleaned up with fresh white bandages.

"Thanks." He flexed his bicep and only winced a little. "It'll heal in no time."

"You're welcome." I stood in front of him, wanting to keep him here instead of letting him go back out into danger.

"I need to get downstairs, check on my guys."

"What happened?"

"Ambush. The rat told the Russians our entire game plan. But, with a little luck, we managed to turn the tide."

"How many." I cleared my throat. "How many dead?"

"Them, lots. Us, about six." His expression darkened. "They'll pay for ours in blood. I can guarantee you that."

"More killing?" I rested my palms on his chest, relishing the warm skin.

"Yes." He nodded and covered my hands with his.

At least he didn't lie to me.

"Stay here. I'll check on the guys. The doc should be almost done. He'll send the worst to the hospital. Otherwise, he'll fix the rest up downstairs."

"I can help."

He ran his hand down my cheek. "You've done plenty."

Worry bloomed in my chest, and I didn't want to let him out of my sight. "Can I stay with you?"

He rested his chin on my crown. "Wouldn't you rather stay up here, away from all of it?"

"No." I wrapped my arms around his waist. "I want to be wherever you are."

He sighed. "You're killing me, Smalls."

"What?"

"Nothing." He smoothed his hands down my arms. "You can come downstairs with me. Let me grab a shirt from my room."

I followed him past the carnage in the foyer and into his office. Peter and David were already there. Peter had a bandage wrapped around his head.

My eyes widened when I saw him.

"Bullet got a piece of my ear." He shrugged. "No big deal."

"You bleed like a stuck pig." David looked none the worse for wear.

"Shut up." Peter flipped him off and gestured at the seat next to him, inviting me to sit.

I walked over to take him up on the offer.

"Here, with me." Nate gave Peter a death glare and patted his lap as he sat behind his desk.

Sitting on his lap when we were alone was one thing. In front of his men? That was different. All the same, I walked over to him and sat. I couldn't turn down an offer to be close to him.

He adjusted me in his lap, turning me so my head rested on his shoulder. Once I was settled, he relaxed beneath me, as if the contact soothed his frayed soul somehow.

The brothers exchanged a look.

Nate didn't seem to be bothered by it in the least.

"Give me a status report." He drummed his fingers on the arms of his chair.

"We lost five, though we have a sixth that doc sent to the hospital. Carl Breenan's boy. We don't know if he'll make it." Peter gently pulled at the bandage on his ear. "We didn't leave any Russians alive. Just the few that managed to get away on the second boat."

Dmitri had shown up and sent more men into the fray but stayed on his speedboat, simply watching the carnage go down. Pussy.

"The weed?"

"Already in our warehouse, getting divided up for delivery to the dealers." Peter gave up at the bandage. "We should be well stocked for a little while, but it looks like we'll need to make some new transport arrangements for next time."

"It won't matter. The fucking rat will blow that plan up, too." Nate smoothed his palm up and down my back.

"We'll find him." Peter's face grew grim. "I've put out feelers with the few Russian contacts I have."

"And the Irish already know about our troubles. Not that they'll lift a finger to help us." Irritation edged Nate's voice. "We'll never seal an alliance with them until the rat is gone and Dmitri is decomposing."

"You want me to handle notifying the families from today?" Peter asked.

"I'll handle it. Just get me the numbers." Nate didn't stop running his hand up and down my back. If I were a cat, I would have purred.

"Will was Cindy Gardia's last son." David spoke up.

"Shit." Nate's caress stopped.

My heart sank, and I glanced to my hands. They were clean. But I could still feel the way Will's blood had poured out, the way his life ended far too soon just a short while before. I leaned into Nate, soaking up his strength.

"I'll go to her house to deliver the news. She deserves at least that much." Nate paused for a few moments, thinking. "And set up the usual fund for her, for all the wives and mothers, but make it double our standard pay."

"Double?" Peter's eyebrows shot up.

"They earned it." Nate's tone was certain, final. "Make it happen."

Peter pulled out his phone, taking notes. "Sounds good. I'll get that all sorted out."

"When's our next shipment. Two weeks?"

"Yeah, supposed to be coming in on the river again." David eyed me.

Nate noticed. "She's already neck deep in this mess with Dmitri. There's no point shutting her out. Not now. It's too late."

David didn't seem convinced. "Maybe, but she doesn't need to know our operations."

"I'm sitting right here." I met David's eyes. "I'm not a rat. And I will do everything necessary to make sure Dmitri goes down. My life depends on it."

He frowned, but didn't reiterate his objection.

Nate pulled me back to his chest. "Tell everyone the shipment will go on as planned at the river. But I want you to set up the real delivery at the private airfield south of the city, the one near that old farm."

"Yeah, I know the one you mean." David rubbed his chin. "Shouldn't be a problem."

"Keep the airport location amongst yourselves. Let the rat tell them we're going the river route again. Throw them off the scent."

The authority in Nate's voice seemed like such a change from a few years ago when wisecracks were his main weapons. I shifted in his lap, wanting to get even closer. Was it wrong that his power was a turn-on?

"Airport. Got it." Peter nodded.

"One more thing."

"Yeah?" Peter was still tapping away on his phone.

"Send your mom on up to my room tonight. I'm feeling all antsy."

Peter's fingers stopped, and he glowered at Nate. "You're a prick, you know that?"

I hid my smile in Nate's chest. He may have changed, but the wisecracking smartass still lived beneath his surface.

"I'm aware." Nate resumed stroking my back.

Peter and David stood and shuffled to the door.

"I'll see you in the morning." David shot me a look. "Training, bright and early."

I gawked at him. "It's already two in the morning."

"Better get to bed then." He shut the door behind them.

Nate dropped his head back and let out a long breath. "David's right. You need to sleep and to train."

"You need to sleep, too."

He huffed out a low laugh. "You offering to sleep with me?"

*Yes, please.* "Well, you did spank me and all. I figure it's only fair."

He groaned. "I'm sorry about that."

"Don't be." My ass was sore, but butterflies swirled and dove in my stomach as I thought about how it felt to be draped over his knees, his hand between my legs.

"I mean, it's more of a sorry, not sorry." His hand slid down my back and skirted along the waistline of my jeans.

"I figured."

He cleared his throat and dropped his hand. "But it can't happen again. This"—he scooted me out of his lap so I stood facing him—"can't happen again."

Ice pricked my heart as I stared into his eyes. "Why?"

"You're eighteen. You have your whole life ahead of you. College and a real chance outside of this fucking mess." His tone gentled and he took my hands in his. "I know you have this idea of me as some sort of savior, good guy type. I'm not. I kill people. I take. I'm not what you think."

"You don't know what I think." I pulled my hands away and crossed my arms over my stomach. "You don't ask me. All you do is tell me what can't happen."

He scrubbed his shadowed jaw. "Let's not do this right now. We've both had a long night. Okay?"

"No, not okay. You can't kiss me one minute, then tell me no the next. I don't work that way." I had tried to brush off the repeated rejection, but it was starting to burrow deeper inside me, leaving me with a newfound bitterness.

Weariness washed over him, aging him a few years. "I can't be what you want, Sabrina. I'm not that man. I kept you away from here so you could live your life without having to look over your shoulder. That's what a life with me would be like. You have to understand that once I've killed Dmitri, you'll have to go. It's for your own good."

"That's for me to decide." Anger flared more quickly than usual, fatigue and the events of the past few hours giving me a shorter fuse. "I know how old I am. But that doesn't mean I don't know what I want." I leaned down and pointed my finger at him. "You don't tell me what to do or how to feel. And you can deny this thing between us all you want, but I know it's real. I've known it for years. If you want to be a pussy and hide from it, that's on you." *Holy shit. Did I just call the head of the Philly syndicate a pussy?*

His nostrils flared, and he grabbed my wrist. "There you go with that bratty mouth again."

I smirked. "I know you like it." I made a show of looking down at the erection bulging against his zipper. "I know you want to spank me again."

He squeezed my wrist. "Don't push me, Sabrina."

I yanked my wrist away. "Why? What'll you do? Cry some more about me being eighteen?" Turning on my heel, I marched away from him. Just as fast, he'd yanked me back and held me in front of him, his rough grip on my waist.

"Do you want to know what sort of man I am?" His dangerous tone slithered around me, seducing me. With his dark hair mussed, a five o'clock shadow on his square jaw, and a delicious fire burning in his eyes, he looked just this side of lethal. "Because I can show you. Right here. Right now."

Did I? I'd been throwing myself at him, but what would happen when he finally took the bait? My heart stormed in my chest as I stared into his eyes. But I wouldn't back down, not now.

"Yes." The word slipped from my lips.

His eyes darkened. "On your knees."

I lowered slowly between his legs, but he gripped my shoulder and shoved me down, making it all too clear what he wanted. Nervousness crept into my stomach. I'd never done anything like this before. What if I wasn't good at it?

He flicked the clasp on his pants open and unzipped, then set his hands on the arms of his chair. "Take my dick out." His voice was rough and dark.

A thrill coursed through me and settled between my legs. It was finally happening. Nate and me, the way I'd dreamed about. But mixed with the burst of adrenaline was fear. This was new territory, and the worry of not doing it right, or displeasing him in some way, fought with my desire.

But I wouldn't be deterred. Not now. I leaned forward and pulled his pants lower on his hips, then flipped down the waistband of his boxers. *Oh, my.* His cock was smooth and olive-toned, the head darker and swollen. I ran my hand down to the thick base and looked up at him.

He gripped the chair. "Lick the head."

Okay. Easy enough. I touched it with the tip of my tongue, then came back with a full lick as if it were an ice cream cone, two scoops.

He groaned. "Put it in your mouth."

I opened wide and slid my mouth down on it, then closed my lips around the shaft right above where my hand gripped him. A slight salty taste tingled on my tongue as it pressed against the tip.

"Suck me." His voice had turned into a deep rasp as I moved up and down on him.

I pressed his cock deeper, but gagged and had to back away for a second. My eyes watering, I looked up at him.

"Fucking hell." He grabbed my hair and guided me back to his cock.

I took as much in my mouth as possible.

"This is the man I am." He gripped my hair tighter, tiny pinpricks stinging against my scalp as he pushed me down on his cock. "I don't go easy. I don't fit into some fairytale. I'm not a hero. I'm an asshole who likes to get his dick sucked."

I gagged again, but he didn't release me. Instead, he thrust his hips up, fucking my mouth as I dug my fingers into his thighs. His grunts reverberated through me, making wetness pool between my thighs. Gripping his base, I squeezed and stroked in time to his thrusts. He let up just enough for me to catch my breath through my nose before pushing me back down onto him. I laved my tongue across his head and down his shaft.

"Fuck, that's it. Look up at me."

I turned my teary eyes to him as my mouth made sloppy noises around his cock. He held my gaze as he thrusted into my mouth, each stroke hard and certain.

"I'm going to come," He gritted out. "You're going to swallow every drop."

I didn't know if I could, but I would try. I sucked, hollowing out my cheeks as he groaned and thrust in rapid succession. His come filled my mouth in warm spurts, and I swallowed, then swallowed again as he relaxed into the chair, his hard cock still throbbed in my mouth. I ran my tongue around his head, licking him clean, before pulling back.

He released my hair and simply stared down at me. "See what kind of man I am? One who'll use you." He was even sexier breathless. "Not the sort of man you should be hanging around with. Let that be a lesson for you."

I leaned forward and licked him, enjoying his groan. "Can we go again?"

---

# CHAPTER NINE

W HEN I WAS A horny teenager, sometimes I'd wake up and find myself humping the ever-loving shit out of my bed. The night after Sabrina's blow job? Same. Only it wasn't some big-titted porn actress I was fucking in this particular scenario. When I woke up, I had only one thought on my mind—Sabrina.

I called off the sexual assault of my mattress and rolled over onto my back, my hard-on saluting the morning with a stiff wave. *Can we go again?* Her voice played over in my mind, her swollen lips and teary eyes stamped in my memory. *Jesus.*

I gripped my cock, already on the verge of exploding. With a few quick strokes and the mental image of her lips wrapped around my shaft, I came all over my stomach. But it didn't stop my need for her. Right then she was probably asleep in her Hello Kitty palace. Lying on her back. Maybe with her legs spread just enough for me to get a peek. But if I got a peek, I'd want a taste, and if I got a taste, I'd want a fuck, and if I got a fuck, I'd want another. I'd be trapped in the "If You Give an Asshole a Cookie" scenario, and I'd always want a glass of milk.

Instead of creeping on her, I showered and dressed, then headed downstairs. The sun was barely up when I found Peter standing in the hallway staring out the back windows toward the pool.

"What's up?"

"Training."

I followed his gaze. David and Sabrina circled each other on the square of grass next to the pool. Sabrina's hands were up, her knees bent. She'd braided her hair down her back and wore a sports bra and athletic shorts. Where was her t-shirt? I resisted the urge to slap my hand over Peter's eyes.

"How's your arm?"

"It's nothing." I shrugged it off. "It'll be healed up in no time." Thanks to Sabrina's doctoring.

David lunged for her. She wasn't prepared for it. He got her into a choke hold with ease, though she tried to throw her elbow back into his ribs. After a few moments, he released her and coached her. She put her hands on her hips and cocked her head slightly to the side, listening and learning.

"She's already doing better than she was fifteen minutes ago."

My eyes narrowed. "You've been watching her for fifteen minutes?"

He chuckled. "She's yours, boss. Don't worry."

*Yes, she is.* "No. She's not going to be part of this life. She's going to college, getting away from here."

He turned to me, his lip twitching in a smile. "It didn't look like that when she was sitting in your lap last night."

I waved a hand. "That was just to comfort her. She'd tried to save Will, so she was, you know, sad and shit."

"Right." His tone told me he wasn't convinced.

And I wasn't about to elaborate on what further activities went on in my office after he left. It was time for a subject change. "Heard any word from your sources?"

"Not yet. It's early, though. Things are bound to be shaky today. And the Russians are definitely hurting, given last night. I might have to wait for it all to settle before I can start pushing again."

The kitchen door opened behind us, and Opal shuffled out with a coffee decanter. "Morning, boys."

"Morning," we chimed in unison.

"Breakfast will be up in half an hour." She continued into the dining room as George approached from the foyer.

"House is quiet." He glanced past me at Sabrina who was, once again, caught in David's beefy arms. "I just walked the drive to the gate and back to be sure. Everything's in order."

"You didn't stay up all night, did you?" Peter asked.

"No. Tony was on the door. I'm just here to relieve him for the day shift." His eyes wandered to Sabrina again.

"Get to it, then," I barked.

His eyes met mine, then he dropped them in deference. "Yes, sir."

Once he'd walked out of earshot, Peter's irritating chuckle met my ears again. "Nobody's after your girl."

"George needs to stop looking at her." I slowly unclenched my fists, trying—and failing—to relax.

His chuckle grew into a laugh, his shoulders shaking.

"What's so fucking funny?"

"George isn't interested in Sabrina."

Not possible. I studied her through the glass, the sun in her hair and the plump ass beneath the light blue gym shorts. No man in his right mind wouldn't want her.

Peter clapped his hand on my shoulder. "George may be a general skeeze toward women, but he only has eyes for you."

My mouth went dry. "What?"

"Come on, you know." Peter gave me a wink.

"No, I don't."

"Really?" He grinned. "George swings both ways, but he sends you these longing looks all the damn time. Even David's noticed."

I glanced at George in the foyer. He looked away quickly. *Oh, hell.* Back in the day when I was banging his sister, he *did* seem to hang around more than was normal —saying hi to me and shit while I was trying to sneak out the back door. Still, I couldn't believe I hadn't noticed. "You're shitting me."

Peter shook his head. "Nope."

I smoothed my hand down my suit jacket. "I mean, it makes sense. Look at me, for Chrissakes. You probably fantasize about me just as much as George does. Always wanking off to thoughts of me. You can't help it when you have to be around this fine package all day. Did I tell you about that time I suspected ol' killer Conrad had gone gay for me?"

Peter shook his head. "I'm glad you haven't changed."

"Your mom is too."

He punched me in my good arm before turning and heading toward the front door.

"What's on your agenda for the day?" I asked.

"Resupply. We went through a shit ton of ammo at the dock. I'm going to hit up Sam at the garage. Get some more bullets, and see if he has any new toys for us to use against the Russians." Sam was an old hand at the mafia game and ran a legit garage that hid a not-so-legit chop shop and a gun smuggling enterprise. "I'll be back before Colum and his boys show up for the meeting this afternoon."

"Right." I hadn't forgotten the Irish were coming to visit, but with all the craziness, it wasn't in the forefront of my mind. My spirits sagged at the thought of them lording around my office, pretending that they were the belle of the bullshit ball. "They'll want to hear all about last night."

"And they're going to be hardasses about the rat."

"I don't blame them there. We need to solidify our organization before we can expect anyone to join forces with us." I rubbed my temples.

"Right." He buttoned his suit coat. "Fucking sucks, though."

"No shit." I re-focused on Sabrina. She was dancing out of David's reach, but she almost tripped over her own feet.

"Later." Peter's footsteps receded as I watched Sabrina try and fail to escape David. Her balance was off, she wasn't anticipating his moves, and she needed to get lower.

I slid my coat off, tossed it on the back of the couch in my office, and unbuttoned my cuffs. The cool morning air hit me as I pushed through the glass door leading to the yard and pool. The grass was still damp with dew as the pool sparkled under the first rays of light.

Sabrina was caught in a choke hold, David laughing as she clawed at his arm. "Asshole!" She stomped his foot, but he didn't move, just kept her steady as she struggled and ultimately gave up.

"Let me give it a shot." I finished rolling up my sleeves.

David let her go and she whirled to face me. Her cheeks were pink from the exertion, and a sheen of sweat covered her forehead.

"Have at it. It's too easy for me." David smirked and strode past me as Sabrina gave him the finger.

When he disappeared into the house, she asked, "What about your arm?"

"It's fine." It ached, but when I'd changed the bandages after my shower, the wound was already scabbing over. "You need the handicap. Though you'll still lose."

"Is every man in this house a cocky asshole?" She put her hands up and circled me.

"I think you know I'm the cockiest." I grinned and feinted toward her.

She stumbled back, then got her feet beneath her again and shot me a scowl. "Cheap."

I shrugged. She jumped.

"You need to relax."

"Relax?" She shook her head.

"Yeah. You're on a hair trigger. You'll exhaust yourself, jump at the wrong things, and wind up hog tied by Dmitri."

She flinched.

"Sorry." I held my hands up. "I want to make sure that doesn't happen. So let's work on it, all right?"

Shaking her hands out, she nodded.

"You need to be relaxed but aware, if that makes sense. Watch everything, calculate, figure out what your opponent is doing before he does it. Look for tells." I put my fists up. "A lot of the time, he'll lean whichever way he intends to go. It's simple, but it works. Watch the body language. Are his hands in fists? Then you need to splay your fingers to try and block or slap his arms away. Are his hands open? Then he's going to grapple you. Like this." I darted forward, grabbed her arm, and flipped her over my hip.

She landed on her back, all the air whooshing out of her. Her scent mixed with the smell of fresh grass. Glaring, she got back to her feet.

My arm stung like a son-of-a-bitch, but I'd be damned

if I'd let it show. "Watch me. See if I telegraph anything."
I backed away a few steps and put up my fists.

She opened her hands.

"Bend more at the knees. Get lower. It'll help you be
more explosive."

"I'm low." She watched my hands.

I feinted right, then ran hard left, punching out and
missing her face by a few inches.

"You missed."

"On purpose. I could have knocked your teeth out." I
ran a hand through my hair. "You need more practice."

"It's my first day." She put her hands on her hips.

"Right." I stood straight and still. "Take my knee out."

"What?"

"You want to take a man down, the easiest way is to
take out a knee or go for the crotch. You need to focus on
those areas." I waved her toward me. "Break my knee."

She cocked her head to the side. "What if I
hurt you?"

I laughed. "Not a fucking chance."

She scowled and took a big step, bringing her right
foot up to crush my knee.

I sidestepped and pulled her to me, her back to my
front, my good arm locked around her waist. "Too slow." I
wanted to lick the sweat from her neck.

She threw her head back. Stars bloomed in my vision
when she made contact with my chin, jarring me. I let
her go.

Grinning, she backed away. "David taught me that

one. Apparently, most people have a nerve in their jaw that, when hit, can knock them out."

I rubbed my chin. "Glass jaw."

"Right." She bounced on the balls of her feet, her breasts shaking with the movement, her nipples hard beneath the fabric. "Want more?"

*I want it all.* My cock agreed, going from semi to full mast with a single pump of my heart. *No, no, no.*

"Come at me, bro." I tweaked my nose with my thumb.

She stepped forward, feinted right, and kicked out toward my crotch. Missed by a mile, thank god.

"Not bad, but you have to move faster."

She wiped a stray hair from her face, then rushed me when she was halfway through the movement.

I dodged, laughter bubbling in my chest. "Misdirection. I like it."

She made a grrrr noise and wrinkled her nose. "You move too fast."

"That's what all the girls say. Then they drop their panties."

She roared and charged me. Her small fists thunked against my chest until I grabbed them and wrenched her arms behind her back.

"You can't act out of anger. It makes you sloppy, unfocused. Plan ahead."

"I can't when you talk about other women you've fucked!" Her eyes glistened as she yelled into my face.

"Hit a nerve?" I let her go.

"What if I changed my mind about saving it for you and got on my back for the next guy I see?"

*Daaaaaamn.* My hands balled into fists at the thought of another man touching her. She rushed forward and shot her knee toward my junk. I backed away just in time.

"*Anger makes you sloppy*," she parroted, a little smile of triumph playing across her lips.

I lunged forward and captured her in my arms. She squealed and grabbed a handful of my hair, yanking as I lifted her off her feet and pushed her up against the stone side of the house. Her legs wrapped around my waist, and before I could reason with myself, I kissed her. Hard and rough, the cost/benefit analysis nowhere in sight, I plunged my tongue into her mouth—owning her as she melted against me, her arms wrapping around my neck.

Reaching between us, I flattened my palm against her pussy. She was burning up for me, her body open and wet. I removed my hand and ground my cock against her.

I told myself to stop, to put her down, to keep my dick as far away from her as possible. But I didn't listen. Instead, I dry fucked her against the wall.

She made small noises that I devoured, each thrust of my hips had her rubbing against me, chasing a burst of pleasure that I wouldn't give her. Not like this.

# CHAPTER TEN

I CLUTCHED HIM TO me, wanting every bit of contact between his body and mine. He obliged, pressing me against the cool stones and kissing me until I couldn't form a coherent thought. I ground against him, my clit buzzing and my stomach tightening with each stroke from his hard length.

He tore his mouth from mine and turned, dropping to his knees on the grass and laying me on my back. His hands roved my body as he took my mouth again, his tongue sure and erotic against my own. With a hard pull, he yanked my sports bra up, revealing my breasts. He palmed one, squeezing and kneading as he kissed down to my neck.

I'd never been touched like this, and now that it was happening, I wanted it all at once. Arching my back, I pressed my breasts closer to him. He accepted my offer and took one nipple into his mouth. I moaned, the sound low in my throat as his teeth grazed me. The sensation was far more intense than anything I'd been able to create with my own fingers and imagination. Nate set me on fire with his mouth. When he moved to the other nipple, I tugged at his hair, wanting more and more as he ground his cock against me.

Kissing down my stomach, he grabbed the waistband of my shorts and my panties and yanked them to my knees.

"Someone might see," my voice came out breathy as I glanced up at the windows along the back of the house.

"Let them. I want them to hear you, too, calling my name when you come all over my face."

"Nate!" I squealed as he fastened his mouth to my pussy while keeping my knees pressed together.

He darted his tongue between my folds, his touch sending me to erotic heights I'd never known existed. "I'm the only one who's ever tasted this?"

"Yes." I tried to open my legs, but he kept them closed, the tip of his tongue flicking against my clit.

"It's mine?"

"Yes!" I bucked my hips, pressing my pussy to his face as he groaned and licked deeper.

"Then give it to me." He yanked my shorts and panties down and shucked them off past my tennis shoes. Opening me wide, he stared at the most intimate part of me. "So pink." He licked, long and slow, my toes curling in my shoes. "All mine." Pressing his palms against my inner thighs, he spread me as far as I could go, then sucked my clit between his teeth.

I squeezed his hair between my fingers. Drunk on the

sensation of his mouth, I rocked my hips, no longer caring who might see. He licked and sucked, then moved lower. The pressure of his tongue inside me ripped a moan from my lungs.

He pulled back and slowly licked around my clit. "Just me. Only me. Say it."

"Only you."

He dove back down, focusing on my clit with relentless strokes. My legs began to shake, and he dug his fingers into my skin, holding me steady as he fucked me with his tongue. Everything spiraled out of control, and my hips strained and locked wide open. I froze and then came in a blinding rush, my pussy contracting as waves of pleasure rolled through my body. I moaned his name. Over and over, there was nothing else but "Nate" on my tongue as he continued licking me even though my legs were shaking out of control. Should I have been embarrassed at how fast I came?

When the last of the tremors subsided, I tried to scoot back, the intense feel of his tongue too much. He growled and held me in place, kissing up and down until finally sitting up and licking his lips.

He grinned. "Breakfast of champions."

"Th-that was..." I let out a long breath as he rearranged my sports bra, then shimmied my shorts and panties back up my legs.

"I know." His self-satisfied smirk tried to pull an eye roll out of me, but I was too blissed out to retaliate. Never in my life had I come so hard. And this, after countless nights of touching myself while thinking of him. How could there be such a night and day difference?

I took his hand, and he helped me to my feet. My knees felt like jelly, but I managed a step akin to a newborn fawn. "You just did that on the grass. In the back yard." I looked up at the house and cringed. Who had heard me crying Nate's name?

"Yeah." He slapped my ass, hard. "If you don't get inside, I can't promise that it won't happen again."

"Holy—" I hurried inside, my oversensitive clit begging for reprieve while also crying out for more.

Nate followed and closed the door behind us. He put a hand on my shoulder and turned me around to face him. "Listen. Now that we got that out of our system—"

"Out of our system?" I tilted my chin up and met him head on. "Is that what you're going to call it?"

He carefully unrolled his shirt sleeves. "Yes. Now that it's done, we need to put the brakes on all of this."

"Oh, so after you eat my pussy on the back lawn, it's time to cool it?"

He put both hands on my shoulders and squeezed. "If we take this any farther, I don't know that I'll be able to stop." A naked sort of honesty colored his voice. "And that's not what I want for you."

The sting of rejection aside, I was beyond tired of him telling me what *he* wanted for me instead of listening to what *I* wanted for me. "I don't want to stop."

He closed his eyes and let out a labored sigh. "We have to."

"You know what." I stepped out of his grip. "Fuck you."

His eyes snapped open and narrowed on me. "What?"

"I said go fuck yourself," I hissed. "This is some high school bullshit. You know that? You got what you wanted and now you're just going to break it off? Actually, that isn't even high school. That's *junior* high."

He gaped, wounded pride flowing out of him. "Are you fucking kidding me?"

"No, I'm not. You keep telling me I'm eighteen, but it's crystal clear I'm the mature one here."

He sputtered. "I am not junior high anything and you—"

"Yes you are. Running like a scared little boy. Well, I'm tired of chasing you. If you don't want this, then that's fine. Stay away from me. We're done here." We weren't done. I'd never be done with him, but I was at a total loss of how to deal with his bullshit. He wanted me. I wanted him. What was so wrong about that? Why couldn't he stop pushing me away?

"Don't do that." He stepped toward me.

I moved back. "Don't do what? Tell you that you're full of shit? Tell you that I know you want this as much as I do? Fine. I won't. I guess you got what you were after— the first taste. Good for you. Go ahead and add that notch to your bedpost."

Hurt flashed across his eyes, but that wasn't going to stop me. He wasn't the only one in pain.

"You want this to end? Then I agree. It's over.

Thanks for the fun on the grass." I turned and rushed down the hall, my eyes stinging with tears I refused to shed in front of him.

"Sabrina, wait." His footsteps echoed behind me.

"No. Leave me alone." I shot up the stairs and to my room, then slammed the door and locked it.

Hello Kitty mocked me as the tears rolled down my cheeks. He stood outside my door. I waited for him to knock, say something, *do* something. He didn't. He just stood there for long minutes before I sensed him walk away, heard his shoes on the stairs, and then the front door slammed.

# CHAPTER ELEVEN

NATE

"YOU DON'T UNDERSTAND, MAN," I said into my phone and took a swig from my IPA. Gilly the bartender gave me a disapproving look. Was I drinking at ten in the morning? Yeah. Did I give a shit? No. I owned The Slaughterhouse, a dive bar in Fishtown, so Gilly had to serve me even if it was God o'clock on Rapture Sunday.

Conrad cleared his throat on the other end of the line. "I understand perfectly." The cold killer was the only one I could talk to, even though he was officially dead. He and his woman, Charlie, had settled in a little town out west and made a new life for themselves. The tinkling laughter of a little girl in the background made me smile. "Tell my niece that I've got some real heavy shit to discuss over here, but that I miss her."

"She knows. All three of them keep asking when you're coming to visit."

"Not anytime soon." I took another swig. "I'm

meeting the Irish this afternoon. I've got a rat. I've got a Dmitri. And, the worst part, I've got a raging boner for Sabrina."

"You could have left the boner part out." His low smooth voice conjured familiar images of late nights spent doing the old boss' dirty work. Those days were simpler, back when I had no idea how difficult being in charge was. It looked so easy. You gave an order, your soldiers followed it. The parts I didn't see—dealing with the cops, money laundering, accounting, thieves, rival organizations—came crashing down on me as soon as I took the reins.

"The boner was the best part."

He grunted in disapproval. "Look, it's obvious to me that she wants you for the long haul—"

"No, she just *thinks* she does."

"The fuck does that mean? You don't say that stuff to her, do you?" The last sentence was delivered with a hint of alarm.

"Well, yeah, I told her she doesn't know what she's talking about when she—"

A rusty laugh crackled through the phone, which then turned in to a full-throated guffaw. "You told your woman that she doesn't know what she's talking about?" He howled with laughter as I downed the rest of my beer, then ordered a whiskey.

"Ah, shit, Nate. I knew you were dumb, but you're really outdoing yourself over there."

Charlie's voice whispered in the background. Conrad relayed what I'd told him, and then I heard a low whistle.

"Charlie's not pleased, I take it?"

"She just said you're lucky Sabrina hasn't kneed you in the nuts."

"Fuck." I drank half the whiskey in one burning gulp. "So what do I do?"

"Do you want her?"

"Yeah, she's the fucking sun. Hot, smart—she got a full scholarship to Temple, for chrissakes—caring, has this amazing smart mouth on her. Jesus, the things she says."

"I hear all that. I do. But is there more? Do you just want to hit it and move on, or what?"

The thought was—and I admit this was odd—*abhorrent* to me. Even being away from her for this impromptu bitch session with Conrad was making me itch to get back to her, to take back what I'd said. "No, not with her. She's different." And wasn't that a sobering thought?

"Different." He chuckled. "Yep. I had an inkling that day when we found her. She looked at me like I was the boogeyman from her nightmares—and I'm pretty sure I was—but when she saw you, it was over."

"What do you mean?"

"I mean that she loved you on some level then. As much as a thirteen-year-old can love, anyway. Now that she's grown, she's totally fallen for you." He paused. "I don't see why. You're such a son of a bitch."

"Love?" I sat back in my chair and finished my drink before holding up two fingers. "Make it a double."

"You drinking?"

"Yeah."

"Meeting with the Irish this afternoon?"

"Yeah. But they're piss drunk half the time. We'll get along famously."

"Keep your wits about you, *boss*. Sabrina's got you turned every which way. Getting trashed when you've got business to attend to will only make shit worse."

"Right." I downed a big swallow as I held the phone away from me. "Got it. Don't you think this is...I don't know. *Soon*? She's too young. I'm too...too *me*?"

"I can't really weigh in on that. The second I saw this sexy little piece through her shop window, I was a goner.

I nodded, though he couldn't see me. "True."

"Look. She's had five years to think about this, and it sounds to me like she spent the whole time in love with you."

"In love with the *idea* of me—" I corrected him. "As something I'm not. I'm not a good guy like she thinks."

Charlie's voice murmured in the background. Con laughed. "Charlie says you need to stop trying to play the heavy and just be yourself. That's what Sabrina loves."

I pinched the bridge of my nose. "Why would she love me?"

"No clue. Ow!" Con laughed again. "Lay off me, woman! Charlie says you're very loveable."

I grumbled, no real words forming.

"My advice—apologize and quit telling her she doesn't know what she feels. That's a sure path to losing a nut. If you feel the same, then say it. If you don't, you need to say that too so she can move on. But don't ruin this thing just because you know deep down that you're a shitcake who doesn't deserve a beautiful, college-bound, amazing woman."

The truth in his words burned almost as bad as the cheap whiskey. "Damn, since when did you get so insightful?"

"Since I married a woman who"—smack noise and then a squeal from Charlie—"gets me on every level."

"Hey Con, don't pork her in front of the kids."

"Good point. Lock the door, baby."

I drained my glass. "On that note, I'm out."

"Call me anytime, asshole. I still owe you bigtime."

"And don't you forget it."

"Go get her. And don't let her go." The call ended, and I ordered one more drink. I had a lot of thinking to do, and I always seemed to get my best ideas when I was toasted. Right?

———

Peter was slapping me in the face. Why the hell was Peter slapping me in the face? I tried to focus on him when he smacked me again.

"Cut it out!" I blocked his next attempt.

"Finally. Jesus Christ, man." He slumped back against the seat. We were in a car. When did we get in a car?

"What's happening?"

"*What's happening*?" He glared at me. "What's happening is that you got so trashed at The Slaughterhouse that Gilly called me to come and get your ass.

We're supposed to meet with the Irish in half an hour, and you aren't even coherent!" He turned to David in the driver's seat. "Step on it."

"I'm going as fast as I can. Don't jump all over me. This isn't my fault."

"Just fucking go."

David grumbled as my eyes closed.

*Smack.*

"Jesus! Stop hitting me!"

"Wake the fuck up! Here." Peter handed me a cold Gatorade.

Hope flared. "Got any liquor in it?"

"Fuck no." He unscrewed the cap for me. "Just drink it."

"Where's Sabrina?"

He pinched the bridge of his nose. "Drink. It."

"Tell me where Sabrina is and I'll drink," I said to one of the two Peters.

"She's at the house, probably still up in her room crying over some asshole who's been trying to break her heart. Now drink the goddamn Gatorade." He thrust the bottle toward my face.

I grabbed it and took a few sips.

"Nuh uh. More than that." He tipped the bottom up, and I swallowed slowly.

Sabrina was crying? Over me? I certainly wasn't worth her tears. Not a chance. She deserved better.

"Crying?" I swallowed a few more gulps.

"Yeah."

"Shit."

"Pull your head out of your ass. You have much bigger problems. The Irish are going to crush our nuts into a paste if you aren't on your game."

I nodded as if I agreed. But I didn't. Sabrina was more important to me than all of the Irish mobsters in the world. What had I done? Wait, did he say *crush our nuts into a paste?*

"A paste?"

"Yes." His glare helped me focus the two Peters into one.

"That's fucking brutal, man. Way to kill my buzz."

The vein in Peter's temple bulged. "Can we just throw him out of the car and split the operation between us?" He thrust the Gatorade back into my hands.

David grunted a laugh from the driver's seat. "We could. But that would be a lot of work. Would really cut into my murder schedule."

I snickered into the bottle. "I'm supposed to kill you two for that, right? *I know it was you, Fredo.*"

"He's quoting *The Godfather*. We are fucked."

"Everything's fine." I sat up as the car slowed and stopped in front of the house. "I'll talk to her and smooth things over."

"I'm not talking about Sabrina!" Peter climbed out of the car. "The Irish will be here in ten minutes!" He slammed his door, then gave a Hulk-roar of frustration and beat on the roof.

"You really pissed him off this time." I could hear the scary smile in David's voice.

"He loves me." I burped and elbowed the door open.

The sun was extra bright as I stepped out of the car and wobbled toward the front door.

"You're such a dick." Peter slung one of my arms over his shoulder and helped me into the house.

George blanched when he saw us. "You okay, boss?"

"I'm good. Great. Thanks for anal. I mean asking." I tried to wink, but all I did was blink really hard.

Peter hustled me through the foyer and into the back hall, finally depositing me at my desk while yelling for Opal to bring water.

"I'm fine."

Opal hurried in with a bottle of water in each hand. "What happened?"

"He got trashed."

"But the Irish?" She handed me a bottle.

Peter took it, opened it, and handed it to me. "They're still coming."

"Oh dear. I'll fetch some bread to help soak up the alcohol."

"We have it all under control. The Irish. The shipment to the airport. The Russians. All of it." I drank the water. "The only thing I don't have under control is Sabrina."

"Wrong. The thing you don't have under control is yourself." David lingered in the doorway. "I'll have a chat with George and Tony, make sure they've got the extra security handled for the meeting. You sober up."

"I'm already there." I propped my feet up on my desk.

"Right." David shook his head and stalked into the hall.

My thoughts returned to Sabrina. Maybe I had time to go up to her room and apologize before the Irish arrived. A glance at Peter told me that wasn't happening. His angular face was all sorts of angry-crumply, the lines making him look ten years older.

Opal returned with a plate of bread and butter. I ate under Peter's watchful eye.

After what seemed like all of thirty seconds, David appeared in the doorway. "They're here."

I stood and schooled my features.

"Crumbs." Peter pointed at my lapel.

I brushed them off and walked around my desk to greet the Irish. Colum's security guy, Sully, walked in first and checked the room.

"We're hiding the bombs under your car right now." I smiled. "But this room's clean."

Peter's eyes widened. "He's kidding."

Sully squinted at me, then marched out of the room toward the parking area.

Peter glared at me. "What the hell, Nate?"

"Oh, come on. You know it was funny."

He rubbed his brow with two fingers. "It'll be a fucking miracle if we make it through this meeting without a shoot-out."

Colum strode into the room, his son Angus behind him and his second in command, Leary, following. The Irish boss was a classic ginger with flaming red hair, freckles, and gin blossoms on his nose from a life of good drink.

He gave me a bear hug and clapped me on the back. "About fecking time we got together again."

His son, Angus, was the spitting image of his father, though trimmer and with some good looks thrown in from his mother. Leary was around Colum's age, late fifties, with beady eyes and a wicked business sense.

"What did you do to Sully? He hot footed it out the front door like he had a bee up his arse."

I shrugged. "I may have joked that we were planting bombs under your car."

Colum pulled back and stared at me, the tension in the room ratcheting up to smothering levels. My inner alarm bells cut through my drunken haze as Colum eyed me.

Peter edged closer to us, his hand hovering at his stomach, ready to grab his piece if shit got real.

Then Colum's face crumpled into a grin. "Jaysus, I bet he's out there right now on his back under the Escalade, checking every little thing." He laughed so hard tears glistened in his eyes before settling down. "Oh, feck me, that's good shite."

Peter let out a sigh of relief and motioned for the Irish to have a seat on the sofas as I walked around my desk and sank into my chair.

"Anybody want a drink?" I smirked at Peter.

"I just had a little nip in the car, so I'll be good for a bit. Now, let's get down to business, shall we?" Colum sat next to his son while Leary stood off to the side, staying alert.

"The merger." I nodded, the drunken cobwebs slowly clearing.

"Let's not get ahead of ourselves." Colum relaxed into the sofa, his portly stomach protruding over his khaki pants. "You've got problems to solve before we can even begin to talk about marriage again."

"The rat." I leveled him with a hard stare. "That's going to be taken care of in short order."

"Know who it is, do you?"

"Not yet."

Leary shook his head.

"You got something to say?" I fired off at him.

He focused on me but kept his mouth shut.

"Don't mind Leary. He's just a little skittish seeing as how the Genoas killed his Da all those years ago, and here we are talking about alliances with what's left of that organization."

"What's left?" I leaned forward and wove my fingers together on the desk. "What's left is the biggest, fastest-growing, and most robust organization this town has ever seen. We've doubled our legit operations since I started, cut back on the shit that brings the most trouble, and have collected record profits. The Genoas had a family business. We have an empire."

Angus glanced at his father. Clearly, the son was interested in what I had to offer despite the old man's reticence.

"I'm not doubting you." Colum held up a hand. "Not a bit. But this problem with the Russians, that could lead to a war we want no part of. We're like you, trying to get some more solid businesses to front the rest of our operations. It's a slow process, but Angus has been spearheading those efforts." Pride gleamed in his eye. "Got a business degree from Yale and came right back to the family to use it."

"Then we're on the same page." I would keep trying to woo him. The Irish had the capital and the means to solidify our grip on the city. The Russians wouldn't have a foothold once we'd joined forces.

Both of us knew that the Irish would stand to gain greatly from an alliance. But Colum was smart—he wasn't betting on a horse until there was a clear winner. Once I beat out the Russians, the deal would be as good as closed. But if the Russians somehow managed to stumble into a win, he'd ally with them in a heartbeat.

Colum stayed cagey. "We are on the same page, but like I said, I can't get involved in this Russian mess. Once you clean all that up, we'll be happy to meet you at the altar."

"I'll need a pre-ceremony blowie, as is custom."

Colum belted out a belly laugh. "Jaysus, this guy."

"What about the last shipment of weed?" Angus kept his voice low, but asked a pointed question.

I turned my attention to him. "What about it?"

Colum scratched his chin. "Angus brings up a good point. If we ally with you, who's to say these ambushes won't continue? Maybe if other organizations see you as weak, they'll start coming, too."

Anger rode me, but I kept a lid on it for once. "Weak?" I smirked. "Did you tally up the body count from our little Russian interlude? Dmitri took a solid hit. He'll take more and more if he tries to fuck with my shipments."

"But he will." Colum leveled his intelligent gaze on me. "He'll be back for more. Word on the street is that you have something of his. Something that he'll happily spill an ocean of blood to get back."

My stomach churned. He was talking about Sabrina. The word was out about her, which made the threats swirling around us infinitely more complex. Dmitri wasn't just playing a private game anymore—he'd opened up the table. If the Irish knew, then so did everyone else.

I hadn't heard about a bounty, but I wouldn't put it past Dmitri to offer serious cash for anyone who could bag her and bring her to him. I'd have to keep her close, under lock and key. Despite the crush of dark thoughts, I kept my poker face. "What I have is my business. If Dmitri feels somehow slighted and wants to run his organization into the ground over it, that's his downfall." I drummed my fingers slowly on the desk. "I'm more than happy to help him accomplish that goal."

Colum stayed silent for a few beats, the earlier tension slipping back into the room through the crack under the door. After a while, he said, "Messy. I don't like messy." He shrugged. "But things always are when a woman is involved."

He rose, the others following his lead. "We'll reopen this discussion again soon."

I didn't like the heavy-handed way he ended the meeting. He needed to know who had the big swinging dick in the room, and it wasn't one of the guys from team Lucky Charms. "You know, Colum. Once I destroy the Russians and take all their shit, I'll be even bigger." I stood and walked around my desk. My height gave me an advantage as I stared the old boss down. "I'd become the largest game in town by far. So, instead of worrying about others trying to take me down, maybe the real worry should be that I won't be happy with most of the playing board. Maybe the real worry is that I'll take it all."

His eyes narrowed, all hint of amusement gone. Despite his façade, he was a shrewd man. One that knew how to play the game.

"Let me show you out." I gestured toward the door. The dismissal was clear.

Colum shuffled out, followed by Angus and Leary.

He paused in the foyer and turned to me. "I'll tell you what. Though we can't seal the deal right now, I'd like to do a little exchange to show my good will."

I liked his new tone—deferential, but not kiss-assy. "Exchange?"

"Yeah. One of your guys for one of mine." He glanced at his son. "Angus is a huge asset to my organization, and he'll give you a good idea of what we bring to the table. Let him stay here for a few weeks, get the lay of the land, and maybe I could reconsider helping with the Russians. No promises, though."

I turned my focus to the son. "You cool with that?"

A frown ticked at the corner of his mouth. "I'm not sure—"

"Oh." Sabrina stood halfway up the stairs, book in

hand, wearing nothing but a white bikini. She dropped down another step, her breasts jiggling, her mouth-watering body on full display to all the assholes below. "Sorry. I thought the meeting was finished." She slid her gaze to mine, a sly smile playing across her lips.

She must have wanted another spanking. But she couldn't hide the slight puffiness around her eyes. She'd been crying just like Peter said. The regret socked me in the gut and danced with the jealousy already tangoing there.

"Nice to meet you, young lady." Colum stepped forward and held out a hand, luring her closer.

Sabrina hesitated, but then walked down the steps and shook. "Sorry," she said again.

"Don't be. We were just finishing up. I'm Colum. And you are?" He knew damn well who she was.

I stepped forward, cutting in front of Colum and blocking his view. "This is my—" *My what? My ward, my sort of niece, my new obsession, my spankbank superstar?* "This is Sabrina."

"It's my pleasure, Sabrina."

"Thanks." She had to look over my shoulder to meet his eyes. "I was just on my way to the pool. I didn't mean to interrupt."

"Don't you have a t-shirt or something?" I hissed.

Her light blue eyes found mine. "I have lots of them." With that, she sauntered off toward the back hallway, her plump behind swaying in the bikini bottoms that cut up her ass cheeks in a small rectangle.

Spanking. Oh my god, the spanking I'd give her.

"Nice to meet you." Colum called after her.

"Lay off." My voice was low as I turned back to him.

He smiled. "I can see why she's such a bone of contention. Now, Angus, about the swap. I think you'd do well to—"

"I'll stay here. Sure." Angus's gaze was glued to the hallway where Sabrina had disappeared. "I'm sure I could learn a few things about going legit, so I'm in if that's what Da wants."

*Oh, fuck no.* I didn't need this horny schoolkid around Sabrina. But I couldn't turn down the olive branch from Colum. Blowing the deal between us wasn't an option, especially when I might need to lean on him for help against the Russians. Would it blow the deal if I punched the ginger in the mouth for looking at my girl?

"It is exactly what I want. And who would you be sending over to us?" Colum glanced at Peter.

Not a chance. "Go get Tony," I called to George at the front door.

He walked out and came back in a few moments with a guy about Angus's age.

I motioned him over. "This is Tony. He runs security around here." Not a total lie. Technically, George was head of security, with Tony as his second in command. But I wasn't going to give up any key players when we were on the verge of all-out war with the Russians.

"Tony?" Colum sized him up. "Sounds good to me."

Tony shot me a confused look.

"You'll be interning with the Irish for a few weeks. Be on your best behavior." I had no doubt Peter would show

Tony the finer points of spying and relaying information back before he left for his Irish assignment.

"Okay." Tony was smart enough to keep his questions to himself.

"We can swap this afternoon. I assume they need to get some things together before the exchange," Colum said.

Angus shot another look down the hallway toward the pool. "I'll be back this afternoon."

The booze had mostly worn off, but I'd never let sobriety stop me from being an ass, and I wouldn't start now. "Sabrina is off limits."

"Come now." Colum clapped me on the back. "Angus will mind his manners. Won't you, son?"

"Of course." He snapped his gaze back to mine. "You have nothing to worry about, Mr. Franco."

At least the kid had the sense to address me with respect. I'd give him that. "Good. I'll see you back here this afternoon. The housekeeper will prepare a room for you."

"Thank you."

I showed them out, everyone having a laugh at Sully who leaned against the Escalade, dust on his pants and an oil stain on his shirt.

"No bombs, eh?" I waved.

He glowered.

Once they were gone, George closed the door, and I turned abruptly and headed toward the pool.

"Hey, we need to talk about what went down with the Irish." Peter dogged my heels.

"Later."

"Nate—"

"I said later." Nothing would keep me from Sabrina. Not now.

He made a frustrated sound and stopped as I continued down the hall and out into the sun. Sabrina swam beneath the water's surface, her long blonde hair flowing out behind her as she shot along the bottom.

I stopped dead when I saw her white bikini lying on the concrete at my feet.

## CHAPTER TWELVE

I WASN'T GOING TO waste another second crying over Nate Franco. Instead, I let the water flow over me, washing away the tears from the morning. Maybe he was right. Maybe we were over. My heart ached at the thought, and I didn't believe it. I could be pissed all I wanted, but I knew that Nate was it for me. I just wish he felt the same way.

Hitting the wall, I flipped and shot out toward the other side. A huge splash, then rough hands on me had me sputtering to the surface.

"What the—"

"You're naked!" Nate draped his soaked suit jacket around me and pulled me to him.

"So what?" Indignation wrapped my words in a stranglehold. "You didn't have a problem when I was naked out here earlier."

"That was different."

"How?" I swiped the wet hair from my face and glared at him.

"Because then I was between your legs and you were screaming my name." Water dripped down his face and rested on his dark lashes like round crystals.

"Get off me." My cheeks heated at the memory.

"No." His arms tightened around my back.

"Why do you care?" I yelled in his face as he spun me and floated us toward the side of the pool. "You think I'm just some dumb kid who doesn't have a clue."

"No, I don't." His wet hair stuck up at funny angles. He looked younger, just like the Nate I'd fallen in love with. "I'm sorry about what I said. I didn't mean to—"

"Completely discount my feelings and treat me like a child?" I supplied.

He swallowed hard. "Yeah, that."

"Why the sudden change of heart?"

"I-I had a few drinks."

I scoffed. "You had to get liquored up to come to this conclusion?"

"I do my best thinking when I'm lit." He seemed completely serious.

I wanted to hit him and kiss him at the same time. "So now you're sorry?"

"I'm sorry for not listening to you. For all the stupid things that came out of my mouth."

"Are you sorry for what you did to me on the grass, too?"

He blinked as if I'd slapped him. "Hell no. I'll never be sorry for that."

A little spark of heat fizzed to life in my heart. "So this is another sorry, not sorry. Like you did when you spanked me?"

"No." He shook his head. "I mean yes? I'm not sure. I'm sorry about what I said, I'm not sorry about what I did. So, sort of?"

I leaned my head back against the side of the pool. "You sound confused."

"I am." He swiped some wet hair from my forehead. "That's what you do to me. Turn me every which way. Ever since I first saw you down here, I..." He seemed to wrestle with what he wanted to say next.

I wrapped my arms around his neck, his jacket sliding off my shoulders and floating around me. "Keep going. And tell the truth." A glance at his lips had me warming even more.

"Shit." He shook his head a little. "When I first saw you down here, I wanted you."

*Cue the inner fireworks.*

"But I didn't know it was you. I thought maybe one of the guys had brought their chick by. That didn't bother me. I still would've..."

"Would've what?" I leaned closer, peering into his expressive green eyes.

"I would've gotten what I wanted, no matter who you belonged to."

I wrapped my legs around his hips. "Is it normal to be jealous of myself when you thought I was someone else?"

He laughed, his Adam's apple bobbing. I wanted to lick it.

"But then I realized it was *you*. The shy, sweet girl I'd found and taken care of. And I refused to see you as anything else. Because you're so young. And so innocent."

"Oh, come on." I squeezed him between my legs. "Innocent?"

"You are." A wrinkle formed between his brows. "You've never been with anyone. You have this amazing future. You deserve the best. Not some... some mafia capo asshole with a smart mouth and a short life expectancy." He absently ran a finger on the scar along his jaw.

My heart melted more and more as he spoke, his words halting but sincere. It hadn't occurred to me that he didn't think he was good enough for me. It all began to make more sense as I considered him. He thought I would have this amazing life. I hoped he was right. But it included him. It always had.

I pinned him with a hard look. "This isn't about *deserve*, this is about *need*. I don't know what I deserve, but I know I *need* you. Not just out of some hero worship from when I was thirteen, either. It started there, and if that had been the extent of it, it would have died while I was away at school. It didn't. I thought about you every day." I thought I was done crying for the day. I was wrong. Tears overflowed, mixing with the water on my cheeks. "Every. Day. I hoped you were safe and happy. And I wanted to get back to you more than anything. But you wouldn't let me. And I knew—no matter how hard it was for me—that you kept me away for a reason. So I didn't come back. Not until I was ready. And now I'm here. I want this amazing future you've painted, but the part you don't understand is that you've always been in the picture right there with me."

"You're even poetic." He smoothed his palm along my cheek and wiped my tears. "You going to major in books or something?"

I smiled and rubbed the tip of my nose against his. "Pre-law."

"Oh, shit." He pulled back. "Lawyer?"

"Yeah."

"Not the prosecutor type, right?"

I shrugged, teasing him. "Maybe. I might decide to take down the entire Philly underground. Really clean up the city."

He smirked. "I could talk you out of your plan."

"Yeah?"

"Well, maybe not *talk*, but I'd definitely be using my tongue."

Sparks ignited in my veins.

His gaze turned serious, his jaw tightening. "I don't deserve you. Not even a little. I'm an asshole. You need to know things about me before we do this."

I didn't know what he meant by "this," but I wasn't about to stop him from telling me about himself.

"I'm a bastard first thing in the morning. Like, if you wake me up, I might want to strangle you, and I'll definitely fuck you rough. I can't stand any music created by boy bands. I have a weird habit of counting things in fives. I just like five. I don't know why. I'll try not to smoke anymore, but I can't make promises with you around." He pressed his forehead to mine. "One more thing. I want you."

My stomach flipped.

His grip on me tightened. "I want you so bad that I can't fucking think straight. But we don't have to rush. I won't push you to give me anything you aren't comfortable with." He gritted his teeth, but put conviction in his words. "I can wait."

"Fair enough. A few things about me—I have to have coffee in the morning or I'll lose my mind. I love boy bands. I have tickets to see a K-pop boy band this fall."

He gave me a quizzical look.

"Korean boy bands are the best," I explained. "My favorite food is strawberry Laffy Taffies. I giggle every time I try to get a pedicure. And I've fantasized about you every night for years. So, while you may be happy to wait, I'm not." I leaned forward and caught his bottom lip between my teeth.

He didn't hesitate, pressing his mouth against mine in a possessive kiss that sealed the shaky truce we'd just arranged. I molded my body against his as he pressed me to the side of the pool. His hands cupped my face, and his tongue delved inside, taking as I opened myself to his onslaught. He tasted like whiskey and mint, and I became lost in his kiss. When he edged his hips forward, his hard cock teasing against my spread legs, I gasped.

With a mumbled curse, he wrapped his coat around me and carried me from the water.

"Where are we—"

"I'm going to do this the right way." He pushed open the door to the house and carried me, dripping wet, through the hall and up the stairs. I ignored George's pointed stare and clung to Nate, my heart racing as he hurried down the hall to his bedroom, then kick-slammed the door behind him.

Carrying me through to his bathroom, he set me on the warm tile and opened his glass shower, twisting the knobs.

I held the jacket around me and shivered from the cool air that circled my bare legs. I'd gotten naked and jumped in the pool to spite him, but now, when we were at the brink of doing something I'd never experienced, a nervousness shot through me.

He held his hand under the spray. "It's warm now."

I glanced at the rain shower. "Okay."

He unbuttoned his shirt, inch after inch of toned muscle revealed as he freed himself from the wet fabric. Stripping down as if I wasn't standing there gaping at him, he shucked his boxers, his hard cock pressing against his lower stomach.

"Eyes up here, Sabrina." He smirked as I tore my gaze away from his body.

My face flamed. "Sorry. I just—I never. You know. I never, um..." I stopped talking, mainly because I wasn't saying anything anyway.

He pulled me to him, then slid the soaked coat off my shoulders. It dropped to the gray tile floor with a watery splat.

Naked. Totally naked with Nate. Every nerve ending

on my body hummed as he slid his hands down my upper arms.

"You're beautiful." He framed my waist with his palms, then ran his hands around to my ass and squeezed.

I squeaked and went onto my tiptoes, pressing against his body. His cock rested along my stomach.

"Scared?" He tilted my chin up, our eyes meeting in the closest thing to soul-to-soul contact possible.

*A little.* "No."

"Right." He smiled, slow and wicked, then pulled me into the warm shower.

The heat was soothing as he lathered me up with clinical attention to detail. I sighed as he soaped my breasts, his finger grazing my hard nipples again and again.

"Going to come for me already?" He dropped to his knees and turned me around, soaping my ass, his fingers touching all my most intimate places.

I gasped as he slid a finger along my clit. "Nate!"

"What? I was just being thorough." He drew his soapy hands down my legs, then stood.

I trembled, the need building up inside me and dancing with my uncertainty. As I rinsed off, he soaped up and followed suit, then hustled me out of the shower and into a towel. His erection hadn't waned the entire time we'd been together, and I gawked at it as he quickly dried off.

Drawing my eyes away, I started to fasten my towel around me.

Nate grabbed it and pulled it away. "Get on the bed."

Goosebumps raced across my bare skin as he devoured me with his gaze. His eyes burned with an intensity that heightened my fear, but also my need for him. Gorgeous, smooth skin, except for scars here and there, lean muscle, and a face I could draw with my eyes closed—he was everything I wanted.

Turning, I walked into his bedroom, the cool wood floors a contrast to the heat of the bathroom. Was I supposed to be on top of the covers or under? Shyness crept up my spine, so I pulled back the navy comforter on the king size bed and slid between the sheets. The fabric was soft, but it felt like thorns against me—especially my nipples. My skin was on high alert, and I couldn't look away from the bathroom door. I was rewarded after only a few seconds as Nate stalked out, his hungry eyes on me.

"Don't hide from me." He grabbed the sheets and yanked them back. If the sheets felt like thorns, the rush of cold air was daggers. "I want to see all of you." He climbed between my knees and spread me.

I dug my nails into the mattress as his eyes darkened and traced every line and curve of my body. Starting at my throat, he ran his hands across my collarbones, down my chest, along my quivering stomach and to my hips.

"Don't be afraid." He bent his dark head to my stomach and dropped light kisses there.

"I don't want to be. But I don't know what to expect."

"Expect to enjoy every second of what we do together." His gentle touches unwound my anxiety, and as his mouth warmed the underside of my breast, I arched my back. He moved up and pinned my nipple between his lips, then opened his mouth wide around it. When he sucked, I dragged my fingers through his hair.

Slow, so slow. Each caress erased my fear and replaced it with desire. His kisses multiplied, fanning out across my breasts and up to my neck. When he nibbled at my ear, I had a brief vision of flipping him over and sinking down on his cock. My whimper drew a quiet laugh that rumbled from his chest to mine.

"Impatient?"

"Yes." I wrapped my legs around his hips. "I want it."

"And you'll have it." He took my lips, ravishing my mouth with his wicked tongue before sinking down my body and placing a wet kiss on my pussy.

I jerked, but he held my hips in place as his tongue swirled and flicked. He grabbed my ass with greedy hands and lifted me to his mouth. Digging my heels into his back only spurred him to lick me faster, his tongue mastering my clit as I tried to quell the pleasure that threatened to overcome me. My legs shook, everything in my body going tight as he groaned against me, the vibration sending me to a level of arousal I didn't know existed.

"If you don't stop, I'm going to—" Too late. My mind blanked, and fireworks fizzed behind my eyelids. "Nate!" He kept the pressure on, making sure I was drawn under the tidal wave of pleasure. I happily sank beneath the water, relishing the rolling waves, each one gentler than the last.

He licked and sucked, his mouth covering me and wringing every last bit of release from my body. With one last kiss, he said, "That's my girl."

Those words added to the warmth already twirling in my chest. He climbed up my body and kissed me, the slight taste of myself an erotic treat. When he'd gotten me breathless again, he pulled back and reached for the drawer on his nightstand.

"Are you..." I would rather club a seal than continue with the question, but I had to ask. "Are you clean?"

"Yes." He peered into my eyes. "I always wrap it up."

I shook my head. "I want to feel you."

His jaw tightened, and I realized just how tense he'd been this whole time. He was on a hair trigger, one I wanted to pull.

"Are you sure?"

"Yes. I've been on birth control for a year."

"Why?" He returned to me, lying between my thighs, his heavy body weighing me down deliciously.

"Just helps with my period, and"—embarrassment crept into my voice—"and I've been hoping for this day for a long time."

His gaze softened, though the rest of him was rock hard. "Have I mentioned that I don't deserve you?"

I smiled and pulled his face to mine, kissing him with my whole heart. He ran a hand through my hair, his other hand sliding down to my hip. Careful not to squeeze the bruised spot, he moved his hand around and palmed my ass.

When his cock pressed against me, I tensed.

He pulled back. "I need you relaxed. That's the only way you'll be able to take what I'm giving you."

"Okay." I let out a long breath. "I can relax."

He kissed down my jaw. "Do you need to come all over my face again? I'm happy to oblige."

I grabbed his shoulders. "I'm ready. But maybe I can touch it some first?"

"My pleasure." Sitting back on his knees, he pulled me up with him.

Wrapping my hand around him, I swallowed hard. I'd never put anything inside myself wider than a tampon. Nate was *much* wider.

"It'll fit." He smirked. "Barely."

A bead of moisture at the tip drew my eye. I ran my thumb across it and licked.

He groaned and grabbed my knee. "You trying to kill me?"

"No." I ran my finger down his abs and grabbed his cock again. "Just trying to see how this is going to work. Porn isn't as informative as you'd think."

"You want to see, huh?"

I nodded.

"Spread your pussy lips. Two fingers." He took my hand and slid it between my thighs. "Open your fingers. Perfect." His eyes fixed on where I spread myself for him. "How am I going to last?" He seemed to be speaking more to himself.

"How long do you last?"

His cocky smirk returned. "As long as you need me to." He moved closer and ran his cock head between my fingers, up and down my slick skin.

I jolted as he made contact with my clit.

"Keep watching that pretty pussy."

I leaned forward and followed his strokes, the whole image of him touching me like this sending flames licking along my body. It was obscene and addictive.

He pressed his head against my entrance. "You ready?"

Was I? After this, Nate would own me, body and soul. I wouldn't be able to get enough of him. If he changed his mind about me, I'd be destroyed.

He tipped my chin up, our eyes meeting. "You can trust me."

"I always have." I lay back, and he followed me down, his hands entwining with mine and pinning me to the bed.

Kissing me again, he pushed lightly with his hips. I let my legs fall open. A flame burned inside me, small but hungry. He pressed again, and his tip slid past my entrance.

I froze beneath him.

He broke the kiss and pressed his forehead to mine. "You okay?"

I forced myself to relax. "Don't stop."

Pushing forward again, he sheathed himself halfway inside me. Everything seemed to stop. It was just the two of us, joined in a way that I couldn't describe. All I knew was that I didn't want it to end. I wanted to feel all of him, to savor the illicit pleasure that I'd wanted from him for so long.

His arms shook, a fine sheen of sweat on his body as he waited for me to adjust. "I'll be gentle. I'll do it soft."

I moved my hips a fraction of an inch. "Who are you trying to convince?"

"Fuck." He pushed all the way in.

I gasped and squeezed his fingers. "Nate."

"Okay?"

"I'm good." The foreign sensation of being filled melted away, and something far more delectable sprang up in its place. "I want to move."

He groaned and dropped his head to my shoulder. "Yes." Pulling back, he surged forward, filling me again. This time, I rocked my hips up to him. The friction on my clit told me this was just a taste of the ecstasy waiting for me.

"More." I dug my heels into the backs of his thighs.

He ground against me, then pulled out to his tip. Looping one hand behind my neck, he pulled me up. "Watch as you take every inch." He eased his slick cock inside me, and my pussy throbbed around him. I watched him disappear, the sight its own aphrodisiac.

"Oh my god." I gripped his biceps as he lay me down and began long, slow strokes.

Wrapping his arm around my back, he pulled me toward him and buried his face between my breasts. When he took a nipple in his mouth and kept the same smooth rhythm, I arched for him. He took the hint and began to move his hips faster as he kissed first one breast and then the other. No more teasing, he nipped and sucked at me until all I could concentrate on was the building pressure where we were joined.

He pistoned even faster, each stroke jarring and

perfect. My breasts bounced as he lay me back down and kissed my neck. The illicit smacking sound of skin on skin only added to the symphony of sex, and Nate was the maestro.

"Just looking at you is going to make me shoot my load." His gravelly voice scraped past. "But I won't, not until you're coming on my cock."

Licking his thumb, he snaked it between us and pressed it against my clit. I made a strangled cry that he took with a rough kiss. He was still holding back, his muscles trembling, but he was on the verge of losing control. I wanted him just as gone as I was. Running my hands through his hair, I dropped my palms to his back and scratched my nails down the hard muscle.

He bit my lip, his thrusts growing harder, faster. His thumb was making it difficult to concentrate, but I took the only other step I had available to make him lose it. I pulled back from his kiss. "Nate?"

"Yeah?" He slowed. "Did I hurt you?"

I gripped his waist. "I want you to coat my pussy with your come."

His eyes rolled and his movements because harsher. "Oh, fuck."

"All over my pink." My breathless voice landed the final blow.

He gripped my ass, yanking me up to him as he plunged inside me.

I pressed my hands to the headboard as he claimed me. The fire inside me spiraled out of control as his thumb flicked past my clit again and again. Catching his gaze, I opened my mouth in a silent cry as my orgasm exploded through me. Flames sizzled through my blood as everything in me combusted. My breath came back, and all I could say was his name in the midst of moans.

"Fuck yes. Fuck." He gave me a few more punishing strokes, my body greedy for every last bit of him. His cock hardened even more, stretching me farther than I thought possible. Then he pulled out. I stared down at his cock as ropes of come shot against my swollen flesh. He marked me, coating me with him just as I'd asked. Erotic was too mild a word for the look of it, the filthy perfection of Nate's come all over my pussy.

He sat back, but couldn't pull his gaze away from the mess we'd made. "You sure don't talk like a virgin."

I smiled up at him. "I've had a lot of practice talking to imaginary Nate."

His chest puffed up. "Imaginary Nate has nothing on me."

"You can't get jealous of your own imaginary self."

"You got jealous of your pool self." He rose and walked to the bathroom, his hard ass a treat to look at as he went.

"Touché."

He returned with a warm washcloth. After we'd cleaned up, he pulled me to his chest and kissed the top of my head. "Was it like you thought it would be?"

I ran my fingertip around his nipple. "Yes and no."

"Better, right?" So damn cocky.

I smacked his chest. "It was..." I hated to feed his ego,

but I didn't want to lie, especially not after what we'd just shared. "Amazing."

He squeezed me closer. "Same here."

"Really? You're not just saying that?" I tried not to think of his past, of the others.

"I don't just say shit." He laughed. "I mean, I do. But not to you. Not about this." He gripped my upper arms and pulled me on top of him so we were face to face. "I'll swear on whatever you'd like that you gave me something sweeter than I ever thought possible."

"Swear by thy gracious self."

He cocked his head to the side. "Is this the book smarts thing? That's what this is, isn't it?"

A smile pulled at my lips. "You act like you never even went to high school."

He kissed my forehead, as if he couldn't go for too long without pressing his lips to some part of me. The thought sent a thrill racing to my achy spots.

"I went to some school, yeah. But I cut class, didn't pay attention for shit, and I'm pretty sure they just graduated me so I'd quit terrorizing the students and flirting with the younger teachers."

I ran my finger down the harsh line of his jaw, the scar smooth next to the unmarred skin. "Sounds about right."

"I'm not educated. Not like you. I won't be able to keep up with the smart stuff you've got going on up here." He tapped my forehead.

It was as if he were looking at himself in a funhouse mirror. I saw something completely different than what he described. "Do you think an idiot could run the biggest criminal syndicate in Philly? Do you—"

"I—"

"Let me finish."

His mouth clapped closed, though his eyes narrowed. *Meow.*

"Do you think that a man could be the youngest boss this town has ever seen and be a total moron? Is that what you think? Because, let me tell you. You're dead wrong. And I'm the smart one, remember? So I don't want to hear any more of this nonsense about you not being good enough. *I* decide who's good enough to get between these thighs. You made the cut."

His eyebrows lowered. "No one else is going to make the cut."

My heart did a backflip. "You saying you want an exclusive?"

He gripped my chin. "I thought I already made that clear."

"I don't know. You didn't actually say the words." I cut my eyes away from him. "And I'll have to check my calendar—"

"I wasn't going to." He shook his head and sat up, taking me with him. "I really wasn't, but that smart mouth of yours." He pulled me over his knees.

"Hey!" My protest was loud, but the kitten inside me purred and stretched.

"But after that stunt you pulled in front of the Irish, and then again in the pool, and right now teasing me with some bullshit about other men." He rubbed my ass and kept me steady on his knees as I made half-hearted attempts to escape. "Tell me you're mine."

"I don't know—" *Smack*. That one. Burned. So. Good.

*Smack*. I squealed at the second hit that landed in the same spot as the first. Wriggling against him, I could feel his growing erection pressing into my side. *Smack*.

"Okay." I scratched his ankle with my nails. "Okay!"

*Smack*. "Okay what?" He soothed the burn with a steady circular rubbing motion.

"Okay it's only you."

"That's right." Satisfaction dripped from his words. *Smack*.

"Hey! What was that for?" I craned my head around.

He peered down. "For the Irish." Raising his hand again, he brought it back down with a crack. "And that's for the pool."

"Asshole." I tried to kick my leg out and roll away, but he yanked me back and added another smack.

"Have any more sass for me?" He grinned and slipped his finger between my legs, probing my wet entrance. "I could do this all day, Sabrina."

I bit my lip, torn between wanting more and needing some time to recover.

"Good girl." He pulled me up and snuggled back on the bed, pulling the sheet over us.

I bit his neck. "You're mean."

His low laugh curled my toes. "You ain't seen nothing yet."

# CHAPTER THIRTEEN

## NATE

S HE FELL ASLEEP ON my chest, her light breaths
tickling along my pec. The late afternoon sun
tinged her hair in gold, and her skin practically glowed in
the light.

Fucked. I was so fucked. The angel in my arms had
rocked the world off its axis, and I was barely hanging on.
One minute, I'd decided to stay the hell away from her.
The next, she was underneath me where she belonged. I
would have groaned if it didn't run the risk of waking her.
My cock was already hard and ready, the feel of her soft
breasts pressing against me giving me no reprieve.

Lack of impulse control? Check. Addictive personal-
ity? Check. A bombshell that no man could turn down?
Check. Mix all that up and what do you have? Me. In
desperate need of a cigarette, but even more in need of
another taste of Sabrina.

I couldn't let her go. No matter how hard I'd tried to
turn my back on her, I couldn't. Now, after this? She

wasn't going anywhere. One hit and I had a habit. Some-how, I knew it would be like this with her. Maybe that's why I tried to so hard to avoid it.

While I was busy being an introspective pussy, she stirred in my arms.

She blinked up at me, her blue eyes almost electric in the light streaming through my windows. "You all right?"

"Yeah." I ran my fingers through her silky hair. "Just thinking."

"About what?"

"You."

"So you're staring at me while I sleep and thinking about me?" A little smile played on her pink lips.

"That's not creepy or anything."

"Not at all." She pressed her cheek to my chest.

Silence crept into the space between us. But it wasn't the sort that chafed.

"Do you remember that night?" Her voice was so quiet, I barely heard it.

Trailing my fingertips up her back, I drank in the feel of her soft skin. I knew what she was asking—did I remember the night I found her. "Yes. Though I wish to god you didn't."

"I can't forget it." She snuggled closer. "Never will. I'd been terrorized, promised horrible things by my captors. I couldn't breathe, couldn't even have a thought that wasn't tinged with the ugliest sort of fear. Every word, every touch, every shadow—all of it hurt because I didn't know what was going to happen."

I wanted to take all the ugliness away. To lock it up

inside me where it couldn't harm her anymore. But it was too late for that. All I could do was hold her and listen.

"My nightmares had come to life. And I thought I'd be torn apart by them. Until I saw you." She looked up at me, tears swimming in her eyes. "You took me in your arms, and for the first time since I could remember, I felt safe. Even though we were surrounded by bodies, by blood—I knew that if I was in your arms, nothing could touch me."

Fuck if I didn't have a sudden attack of heartburn. "You were glued to me."

"I couldn't let you go. Even when I showered off the blood, I had to have you in the bathroom with me. You sat facing the wall, but just knowing you were there made it bearable. And then I begged you to stay with me for the night. You wanted to go, to help your friends clean up the mess. But you didn't. You stayed with me. Held me until I fell asleep."

"Every night for two weeks." I remembered. Her terrified eyes, the way she watched me, as if she thought I might up and disappear on her. She didn't know that it was impossible for me to leave her. I wanted so badly to help her, to heal the broken parts that cruel men had left behind. But I was just a bumbling asshole from the shit side of Philly. Thing was, even though I'd felt helpless, and worse, useless, she hadn't looked at me that way at all. She looked at me as if I was something—like I was someone who was worth more than a bullet and a shallow grave.

"You're a good man." She put her finger to my lips. "I

know you want to protest. Don't. You have a great heart, Nate Franco. I don't care about the things you have to do in your business or how tough you act. I know the real you, the one who held a scared, crying girl night after night. The one who gave me a room full of Hello Kitty. That's the real you."

And what about the guy who'd just taken that same girl's innocence? I couldn't reconcile the two. Guilt pricked at my mind, but I had a hard time feeling bad about being with Sabrina. She had a good head on her shoulders, one that I wanted to know more about. A tiny voice in my mind warned me that once she truly got to know me, she'd run. She'd find someone who suited her better. Thing was, I'd kill any man who thought he could take my place. From the second she'd come back into my life, I'd been on a crash course with this exact moment—her in my arms as we talked about our bloody, intertwined past. We spoke to each other on a level no one else could understand. Our souls had met five years ago and whispered about each other ever since.

"What are you thinking?" She kissed my shoulder.

"Just some cheesy shit that I'll never let come out of my mouth."

She laughed and threw her knee over my thighs, brushing against the base of my cock. "Wow."

"That's always the correct response." I flipped her onto her back and kissed her, giving her the full feel of me against her warm pussy.

She ran her fingers through my hair, pulling as I made out with her like I was seventeen again. Would I ever get enough of her taste, her soft lips? I needed her again, needed to know this was real. But I would never hurt her.

With a groan, I pulled away and sat back.

"What?" She was breathless, her eyelids at half-mast. Spread out before me like a feast, I wanted to take my time and lick every bit of her.

"I'll take you again if we keep this up."

She made an "mmm" sound, and her gaze slid down to my cock. "That doesn't sound so bad."

"Aren't you sore?"

Her lips formed an adorable pout. "A little, but—"

"I can wait." I backed off the bed and pulled on my shorts.

"Always trying to protect me." She wrinkled her nose.

"Look." I prowled over her and captured one of her nipples in my mouth before releasing it with a pop. "I don't want to wreck you with this monster cock, okay?"

She giggled.

"What's so funny?" I claimed the other nipple, adding a slight bite.

"Nate." She squeezed my shoulders.

"All I'm saying is that I intend to do some nasty shit to you as soon as possible, and I want you ready."

Her eyes sparkled. "You promise?"

My cock kicked at the devilry in her gaze. This girl was going to be the death of me.

## CHAPTER FOURTEEN

### SABRINA

THE NEXT MORNING, I awoke to Nate's head between my legs. After wringing two orgasms from me, he pulled me to my feet and hustled me downstairs for breakfast.

"Can't we spend a little more time in your room?" I took the steps haltingly. The memory of him inside me wasn't enough. I wanted to feel him again.

"Be patient." He goosed my ass. "If I don't talk to Peter this morning, he may beat the door down when I'm inside you. The next time you're beneath me, I'm going to take it slow."

"When?" I couldn't stop the pout in my voice.

"If you're a good girl, tonight."

I cut him a look over my shoulder as we walked into the dining room. "What if I'm a bad girl?"

He gripped my shoulder and whipped me around. "Sooner." Pressing his lips to mine, he backed me into the wall next to the door. His hands roved my body, cupping my breasts as his tongue slid against mine.

Breaking the kiss, he pressed his lips to my ear. "I will bend you over this goddamn table."

"Promise?" I ran my hand along his erection.

He groaned and sank his hand down my shorts, past my panties, and eased a finger inside me. "Fuck."

"I'm ready for more." I dropped a kiss on his neck. "Though you might not be able to handle it since you're, what, forty?"

"You know good and damn well I'm not forty." He added another finger, pushing deeper inside me as I panted. "Sassy brat."

"I should probably start calling you Daddy."

He hissed and gripped my ass hard with his free hand. "I'm going to shove my fat cock so far inside this hot cunt that you'll—"

"Nate?" Peter walked into the room, the door hiding us for a moment.

Nate yanked his hand from my panties, then pressed his fingers into my mouth. "Just you wait." His whisper sent pin-pricks up and down my spine as I licked my own taste from his fingers.

Pulling away, he walked toward Peter. "What is it?"

Peter whirled and did a pretty good job of pretending he hadn't known we were getting frisky behind the door. "Oh, I didn't see you there." The bandage around his head was gone, but the top of his ear seemed to be held together with some rough stitches.

Nate straightened his slate gray suit jacket. "We were just..."

Peter gave Nate a bored look. "Right. We need to talk about the Irish, the next shipment, the books, and a few discipline issues in the lower ranks."

Nate pulled my chair out for me. I walked to it, my cheeks burning as I sat, and I was grateful that Peter continued on with business without giving me a second glance. Morning light streamed in from the high windows banked with deep emerald curtains.

"We also need to discuss our new guest."

"Guest?" Nate sat and draped his napkin across his lap as Opal bustled in with coffee.

"Angus." Peter sat across from me.

"Shit. Yeah. That guy."

"Who's Angus?" I thanked Opal for the coffee.

"Our new exchange student from the Irish." Peter glowered and piled his plate with eggs, sausage, and a couple of pancakes.

"We'll just keep him out of the way. I'm not too worried. Did you have a chance to chat with Tony before we sent him off to his new Irish digs?"

"He'll report back regularly."

"Good."

"Why the Irish?" I crunched a piece of salty bacon.

"What do you mean?"

"Why ally with them? Seems like if you unseat Dmitri, the Bratva would be open to new management, and that management might want to deal with you. Don't they have a bigger operation?"

"See?" Nate forked a big piece of scrambled egg. "She's smart, like I told you."

"I never doubted it. The only dumb thing she's done is hang out with you." He gave me a sly smile.

"Dick," Nate grumbled into his coffee.

Peter continued, "The reason is that the Irish are already entrenched in the same business areas where we'd like to expand. They're smaller, but they are ripe for growth right along with us. Bratva aren't quite as forward-thinking. They still deal in the harder drugs, women, and even information—espionage against the U.S. government. We don't want to partner with a group like that."

"Women?" I cringed at the thoughts that brought to the surface. I didn't know much about my mother, other than that she was a mistress for several of the Bratva captains, but that she'd come from a small town in Chechnya. Her sad eyes haunted my dreams, but I couldn't remember her face. Not really. Had she been trafficked into serving the Bratva and then killed? My father had always told me she was with the angels.

"Not just running hookers either." Nate scowled. "They sell girls—many of them younger than you—mostly runaways or victims of the foster system. When I destroy Dmitri, I'm going to crush that side of his business and take the rest."

Peter and Nate's shared disgust of human trafficking warmed me. For being such "bad men" as they painted themselves, they certainly set out to do a lot of good.

"I'm glad." I didn't need to say more.

"Now, about the delivery."

"Is there a problem already?" Nate sighed.

"No, I'm just letting you know the score. I've arranged it all. The shipment will be at the airport, and I've hired another trawler to ride to the dock as our decoy. I've kept it close to the vest, hiring only people I know we can trust. It won't leak."

"Finally some good news." Nate held up his coffee cup in a mock toast as Opal refilled the decanter. "Now, what was this about discipline problems in—"

"Morning." A young, copper-haired man strode into the dining room. I'd glimpsed him briefly in the hallway the day before but hadn't actually met him. He was fit with sharp blue eyes. Whereas Nate and Peter always wore suits, he wore a light blue Polo and khaki pants.

David followed him into the room and took a seat at the table. He shot Angus some not-so-subtle looks that verged on threatening, but perhaps were intended to be more stern. Like a warning not to fuck with any of the people in this room.

"How'd you sleep?" Nate waved him to a chair next to Peter.

"Great, thank you." Angus shook Nate's hand before sitting. "Thanks for having me." He shot me a sidelong glance.

Nate's forehead wrinkled, then mischief twinkled in his eyes. "David, I'd like for you to give our new friend here a tour of the grounds this morning."

David took a sip of his scorching black coffee. "The grounds?"

"Yeah." Nate sat back, the epitome of relaxed. "Show him the pool, the kitchen, all that. Then take him downstairs."

David, the tank of a man, stopped mid-chew. "The basement?"

"That's what I said." Nate grinned. "Give him an idea of how our operation works, especially when it comes to our enemies. That's important, Angus. You need to know how your friends will treat the people that wrong you."

Angus nodded. "Yes, sir."

David pinned me with a hard look. "We'll still need to train afterward."

"Okay." I'd already dressed in a t-shirt and athletic shorts. Maybe I'd be able to defend myself instead of getting put into a submission hold every time David came near me.

"Great, so that's all settled." Nate picked up his fork.

"Can I go too? On the tour?" My voice sounded soft compared to the low, gruff voices of the men in the room.

"You already know where the pool is." Nate stared daggers at me.

"I know." I took a careful sip of orange juice. "But I want to see the basement."

"Why?"

"Why not?" I couldn't voice my real reason, not in mixed company. I didn't want him to hide the ugly parts of his world from me. To know all of him, I'd need to see what he kept hidden, no matter how bad it got.

Nate drummed his fingers on the table, then gave an amenable—if fake—smile. "Sure."

I wished I could explain it to him, but a storm brewed in his eyes as we finished our breakfast.

"Peter, let's get to work." Nate tossed down his napkin and strode from the dining room, not giving me so much as a glance.

I fidgeted and wondered if I'd made the wrong choice.

"Maybe we can start with the basement, then?" Angus rose and gave me a warm smile. He didn't have the swagger of Nate's crew, but he was handsome all the same.

"Yes." David finished his coffee and stood, buttoning his coat as he led us from the dining room and into the hallway at the back of the house.

A few turns later, and we stopped in front of a heavy door. David swung it open to reveal a dark staircase with steps made from roughly-hewn stone. Flicking on a light switch, he gestured to me. "Ladies first."

I could have sworn I saw a spark of amusement in his eyes, but that couldn't be right. David never cracked his cold exterior, much less laughed.

Stepping forward, I halted as cool, dank air hit me. It smelled like earth and rust and something I couldn't name, but felt deep in my bones. Death. My instincts screamed at me to go back, but I wasn't going to look away. I had to see it all for myself.

My foot wobbled on the uneven stair, but Angus grabbed my elbow. "Looks like that first step is a doozy."

"These stairs were built a hundred years ago right along with the rest of the house." David followed us down, closing the thick door with a resounding clang.

The air seemed to grow colder as we descended, though I wasn't sure if that was real or my imagination. Once I hit the packed dirt floor, David flicked on another light that illuminated a large area ahead of us. Rows of shelves held paint cans, tools, and all manner of household odds and ends.

The light didn't radiate far enough to show what lay beyond the shelves, and there were no windows to help with sunlight.

"Yep." Angus hovered at my elbow. "Looks like a basement."

David grunted and walked away from the stairs and the shelving, disappearing into the stuffy black interior.

"Something tells me that I should be glad I'm down here of my own free will." Angus peered into the darkness where David had gone.

I nodded. "I'm right there with you."

"I'm Angus, by the way. I don't think we've had a chance to officially meet."

I turned to meet his gaze. His youthful face reminded me of the boys I went to school with. "Sabrina."

"Nice to meet you." He smiled. I bet most girls melted for him at that point. Not me. I'd much prefer to get glowered at and spanked by my brooding mob boss upstairs. The thought had my cheeks heating.

Angus's smile broadened. Maybe he thought my blush was for him?

"Come." David's harsh voice cut through the gloom, and a light flicked on in the back of the basement.

My feet didn't want to move.

Angus went first. "I'll check it out."

"No, I'll come too." I straightened my spine and followed him into a separate chamber off the main storage area of the basement.

A tremor shook me inside and out as I peered around. The floor in here was far darker than the rest of the packed earth, especially in the center where a single metal chair sat beneath a bare lightbulb. The copper smell of what I'd thought was rust surrounded me, but it wasn't rust. Not at all. I stepped back, not wanting to tread on the blood that had soaked into the floor —now dried.

Tools were laid out on two wide tables at the back of the room. They were clean, but I knew they weren't always that way. The saw, the screwdrivers, the multiple sets of wire cutters—all of them were coated with blood. I just couldn't see it. I glanced at my hands, then crossed them over my chest and stuffed them under my arms.

"This is where we handle business." David seemed to expand with pride. His own private torture chamber filling him with a sense of accomplishment.

I kept my mouth shut. Part of me wanted to run, while the other part wanted to ask what got people a ticket to this room. I already knew one way—try to take me from Nate.

"Is this where Dmitri's man..." My voice failed, but I

started again, "The one who tried to kidnap me. Is this where Nate..."

"Yes." David looked at the gunmetal-gray chair.

I leaned against the door frame, my knees going wobbly.

"Good." Angus, unafraid, strode around the room. "We would have done the same if anyone dared to take one of ours."

David's face gave nothing away, though he seemed to give a small tip of his head in agreement.

"We have something similar, though we can't lay claim to the Butcher's expertise."

*Did he just refer to David as the Butcher?*

Angus bent over and examined the blow torch. "But these days, thank god, we rarely ever have to use it. Keeping our guys happy is key. And we've come up with new ways to do it."

"Oh, and what are those?" Nate's voice wrapped around me, and I turned to find him at my back.

He pulled me into his arms. "You look pale."

"I'm okay." But I sagged against him. "I didn't know you were coming."

He whispered into my ear, "I couldn't stay away."

Angus looked everywhere but at Nate and me. "We've actually started a new online gaming operation."

"What about the justice department?" Nate asked, still holding me close.

"They shut our first operation down in the big fiasco a few years ago—"

"Black Friday." Nate's words rang a bell. I'd read a

news headline about online poker games going dark when the justice department pulled the plug.

"Right. But they can't stop the games on the dark web. Bitcoin has made those games more and more profitable as time goes along, especially given that the currency has no official government oversight. Not to mention, we're revamping our website with an eye toward a favorable Supreme Court ruling coming in the summer term this year. They're taking up the case. We've hired the best intellectual property lawyers in New York to file amicus briefs and get the whole thing overturned."

"So you'll be the first ones out of the gate if the ruling goes your way." Nate let out a low whistle. "Smart, kid."

"Thanks." Angus didn't object to being called a kid, but something told me he wasn't particularly fond of it.

Nate smoothed his hands down my arms, then rubbed my skin. "You're cold. Let's go upstairs."

"I think I've seen enough." I shot one more glance to the torture implements, then turned and let him lead me back to the staircase.

Once the morning sun hit me, the heavy mood of the basement lifted. I made a mental note to never, no matter how long I stayed in this house, go through that door again. Knowing what Nate had to do for his business—hell, to stay alive—was necessary, but I hoped that no one else, other than Dmitri, ever got shown to the dungeon.

"Angus, there's the pool." David pointed outside. "Now, if you'll excuse me, I have to train Sabrina."

"I can help." Angus strode up to the wide glass windows looking out onto the backyard. "I've been prac-

ticing with some MMA trainers. Nothing bigtime, of
course. Just some basics with striking and grappling, but I
have a few moves."

Nate made a low noise in his throat, almost a growl,
but then coughed into his palm to hide it. "I'd like you to
help me go over some numbers, if you don't mind. With
that business degree, I'm sure you can assist me with
untangling a particular accounting knot that Peter's
discovered."

Angus glanced at me, then smiled reluctantly. "I'd be
happy to help."

"Great." Nate clapped him on the back and steered
him toward the office. "Oh, almost forgot." Nate returned
to me, slid his palms along my cheeks, and kissed the
ever-loving stuffing out of me. Surprised at first, I melted
into his kiss, giving him free rein of my mouth as his
hands roved to my waist and pulled me against him,
lifting me off the floor. After a few breathless moments,
he set me down, his eyes smoldering.

"What was that?" I held onto him.

"Just so everyone knows who you belong to." He
didn't look at Angus, but the intent was obvious. Leaning
closer, he pressed a kiss to my ear. "And you're going to
get it later."

"Promises, promises."

He stepped back, his cocky grin firmly in place.
"We'll see what you say after tonight."

# CHAPTER FIFTEEN

## SABRINA

A FTER A MORNING OF training that saw me on my ass more often than not, a lunch filled with accounting talk, and an afternoon of summer reading, I was tired, sore, and ready for bed. But no matter how long my day was, I couldn't quell the excited buzz that rippled through my system. Nate had been sending me smoldering looks all day and took every opportunity to touch me, even if it was only to graze my hand with his as he walked by. Each little touch was like a shot of lighter fluid, and by the end of the day I was soaked and ready to blaze.

Snuggled in a leather chair in the corner of Nate's office, I'd been reading the same paragraph for five minutes when he walked over.

"Let's go up." He held out a hand.

I took it, and he pulled me to my feet.

"Night." Angus gave a small wave and walked into the hall. He and Nate had been crunching numbers and discussing the many illegal uses of Bitcoin for hours on end.

Peter still sat at the side of Nate's desk, a calculator in front of him and a pencil behind his ear as he surveyed a printed sheet of ledger paper.

"We can look at it tomorrow. Fresh eyes."

Peter squinted. "I still can't reconcile the data, and it's pissing me the fuck off. Someone is skimming cash. But I can't tell where. It's not the drugs." He sat back. "But it *has* to be the drugs. There's nowhere else the money could be coming from that makes sense."

"Tomorrow." Nate pulled me along with him.

"Fine." Peter rose. "I'll go pick a fight with David to take the edge off."

"Last time you did that, I had to buy you two new teeth." Nate's steps grew faster as we left the room, practically hustling me through the hall and to the stairs.

It appeared I wasn't the only one who'd had a tough go of waiting for bedtime. Peter responded—with something sarcastic, no doubt—but we were well up the stairs, and Nate didn't seem to care.

We'd just made it inside his room when he slammed the door and pushed me against it, his mouth on mine, his hands pulling at the hem of my shirt.

I was happy to help, yanking my top off and working Nate's buttons off one by one.

"Do you have any idea how hard you made me today?" He rolled his hips toward me, the hardness in his pants a testament to his words. "Any clue how fucking sexy you look when you're playing the little miss studious game? Over there with your book?"

I shrugged as he kissed to my neck, sending chills all over me with his wicked lips. "I was just doing my schoolwork."

He reached behind me and unsnapped my bra. "Like a good schoolgirl?"

"Yes."

"Wrong." He stripped my bra off and fastened his lips around my nipple, licking as he shoved my jeans and panties down to my knees.

I bumped the back of my head on the door as he bit down, his hands gripping my ass hard enough to leave a mark.

"You're not a good girl." He sank to his knees and licked my pussy. "You're the worst girl. You need some fucking discipline." He snaked his tongue between my folds, pressing against my clit as he kneaded my ass with his palms.

My gasp turned into a moan as he gripped the backs of my thighs and pulled them apart just enough to get his tongue inside me. I grabbed his dark hair, squeezing the soft strands between my fingers as he fucked me with his tongue.

"Not getting off that easy." He sat back, his eyes stormy, then rose and tossed me over his shoulder.

"Nate!" I pressed my palms to his back, but he threw me onto the bed. The air whooshed out of me as he yanked my jeans and panties the rest of the way down, then tossed them aside.

"Get on your knees." He pointed to the bed.

The command in his voice lit up the erotic centers of my mind like a pinball machine. I scrambled onto my stomach, then pushed up onto all fours.

He rubbed my ass, then reared back and landed a stinging slap. "You knew I didn't want you to go down to the basement."

I craned my head around to catch his gaze. "I needed to see."

*Smack.* I arched my back at the flash of pain.

"You sure it wasn't because you wanted to stay close to Angus?" *Smack.*

"No!" I tried to sit back, but he gripped my hips and held me in place.

His hands rubbed my aching ass. "You sure?"

"Why?" I held his gaze. "You jealous?"

*Smack.* I yelped at the fresh sting, and then the next, and the next. Why did I have to be a brat?

"Yes, I'm jealous." The sound of his zipper sent a shock of desperate need through me. "I don't want him anywhere near you. But I don't have a choice in the matter. You have to be here, and he has to be here. But"— he kissed the spots where his hands had warmed my skin —"I do have a choice in his room selection."

"What?" I raised an eyebrow.

Nate dropped his voice. "He's right next door." The bed shifted, and Nate's thick head pressed against my wet entrance.

"He'll hear!" I hissed.

Nate laughed, low and delicious. "That's the idea." He pushed forward, nudging his head inside me.

I moaned at the fullness and the slight sting.

"I want him to hear every orgasm I give you." He eased farther inside, my walls expanding for him as my body hummed with the need for more. "Every time you call my name." He pushed all the way, and my eyes rolled back.

"You're bad." I let my head hang as I ate up all the sensations.

"Yes." He pulled back and plunged all the way in with a skin-on-skin slap.

He was still dressed for the most part. Why was there something so hot about that? Gripping my hips, he pulled back and slammed forward harder, then did it again, and again. I began to shove back to his rhythm, driving him farther. He moved a hand to my hair, grabbing a handful and pulling it. I arched to relieve the pressure, then gasped at how deeply he sank inside me. His balls slapped against me with each rough stroke.

The pressure of his hand on my hips disappeared, and when it reappeared at my ass, I tried to turn my head to look at him, but he kept his grip on my hair.

"Nate, that's not—" My protest died as he pressed his wet thumb around my asshole, rubbing the forbidden spot and sending dazzling sparks shooting through me.

"Not what? Not mine?" He growled. "Wrong." He massaged my hole, never delving inside but rubbing in a circle as my pussy clenched tighter and tighter around him. "I'll be taking this hole with all the rest, Sabrina.

Soon. And you'll love it." He released my hair, then reached around with his other hand and stroked my clit.

I couldn't escape his touch, and I didn't want to. My hips rocked back to him, each movement increasing the tension in my clit as he played every bit of me with his fingers. My hard nipples brushed against the sheets, adding to the cacophony of sensation that washed over me. I couldn't stop. Nothing would keep me from that sweet release. Almost there, my hips began to seize. Then Nate pulled his thumb from my asshole and slapped my ass harder than ever. The jolt of pain rocketed through me and exploded between my legs.

I came on a scream, the sound strangled in my throat as my body locked and my orgasm blasted through me. Over and over, my pleasure expanded and contracted until I was floating along, boneless and overcome with the sweet peace that only Nate could give me.

"You almost made me shoot, Sabrina." He rubbed my ass, soothing me as he thrust in and out slowly.

I'd melted to the bed, my ass still in the air but my shoulders against the mattress.

"Almost took it all from me. But I'm not done yet." He pulled out and flipped me onto my back. Ripping his shirt off, he tossed it to the floor, then shucked off his pants and boxers. Covering my body with his, he pressed kisses along my throat as he eased inside me.

I wrapped my arm around his neck and guided my lips to his. He kissed me deeply, each thrust of his tongue matching one from his cock. One palm on my breast, he twisted my nipple slowly, igniting the same fire he'd already brought to a roaring climax only moments before. He was unhurried, taking his time and owning my body with each sure stroke. His mouth pressed to mine, our bodies entwined, even our breath mingling as he languidly made love to me. That's what this was—making love—each of us sharing more of ourselves than we'd ever thought possible.

He pulled back and stared down at me, my world contained in his eyes. "This is so good." He thrust for emphasis. "You're so good, so fucking right." He dropped a kiss on my lips.

The three words that would change everything danced on the tip of my tongue. I wanted to say them, hoping that he'd treasure them. Whether I said them or not, they were true. I loved Nate Franco from the moment I saw him. There was no one else, not a soul on this earth that could ever take his place in my heart.

Something warmed in his gaze, lust mixing with an emotion that mirrored my own. Could he see it in my eyes, somehow sense the truth? Maybe that kind of love couldn't stay hidden. Not forever.

He kissed me again, and I let myself go. Gave myself over to him, not wasting the moment worrying about whether he felt it too. Even if he didn't, I had enough love for the both of us, and I would be happy to share it for the rest of our lives.

His movements grew more frenzied, passion lacing his kisses as our sweat-slicked bodies glided against each other. I angled my hips toward him, trying to catch each movement, each sliver of contact against my clit. With a devilish grin, he reached between us and massaged the spot. Wrapping an arm around my back, he melded our bodies in perfect fusion, his hips pounding as our eyes locked. Everything inside me wound to a feverish height.

"I can't hold out. Not with you." He grunted with each stroke, his arm shaking from strain, but he didn't let up. His fingers rubbed my clit in a smooth circle, pushing me to the edge. "Take it all." His brows drew together, and his groan shot through me as his release hit.

"Nate." I tried to catch my breath, couldn't, and came as his cock pulsed inside me. My filthy mind pictured his come, how it would coat me and mark me as his. I moaned my release, reveling in him as we both flew to the clouds and floated back down like feathers on a lazy breeze.

When the only sound in the room was our breathing, I realized how loud we'd been.

"Oh my god. I think the whole house heard." How could I blush when he was still inside me?

"Good." He kissed my nose, my chin, and finally my mouth. "You know I don't mind giving a performance, especially when it's as top notch as the one we just put on."

"You're terrible." I couldn't stop my smile.

"You're wonderful." He thrust once more, his semi sending tingles along my overheated skin.

Those three words whispered through my mind again, clamoring to get out. I wouldn't let them. Not yet.

———

"What's that?" Nate leaned over to look at my laptop.

Wearing one of his white t-shirts, I sat against his headboard with my laptop and logged onto my student account at Temple. "I have to register for classes. They just opened up at midnight. If I don't get on it, I'll miss it."

"Miss classes?"

"Not entirely. I mean, I won't get the ones I want, so then I'll have a weird schedule or teachers that aren't rated as highly."

"Huh." He stared at the screen, his brow scrunched, then scooted next to me and pulled me so I sat between his spread legs. Looking over my shoulder, he watched as I opened the class roster. "Why does it say you're an undergraduate? Aren't you a graduate since you graduated high school?"

I was glad he couldn't see my smile. "No, I'm still an undergraduate. Graduate school is—"

"Oh, yeah." He shook his head. "Sorry. I've heard you say grad school before. So that's after undergraduate, like advanced degree stuff, right?"

"You catch on quick. Maybe you're the one who should go to college." I leaned back and kissed his cheek.

He grabbed my chin and kissed me on the mouth until I'd almost forgotten about registration. With a final bite of my lip, he turned my head back to the screen. "Hurry up. I don't want you getting the shit classes. Though, I can always send someone to open up a spot for you in one of the good ones."

I clicked through the literature courses. "Did you just threaten to kill a classmate so I could take their seat?"

"Naaahh." He rubbed his palms down my thighs and rested his chin on my shoulder. "Maybe," he whispered.

I pointed at my screen. "I get to skip freshman composition since I have AP credit, but I still need three credit hours of English for the semester."

"Skip? I knew you were smart, but damn." He whipped my hair over my shoulder and nibbled at my neck. "So, why law?"

Though his lips made it hard to concentrate, I chose a British fiction course and moved on to Western Civilization classes. "I think maybe that—okay, this may sound dumb—it would be the sort of degree that would make me feel empowered?"

"Empowered?" He stopped mid-nibble. "Like what do you mean?"

I'd never voiced my insecurities out loud, mainly because I couldn't tell anyone *"Hi, I'm Sabrina. My drug importer father was murdered in front of me by a hitman, my adoptive parents were also murdered—oh, and then I watched a mafia death match happen right in front of me while I cowered."* But Nate was different. I didn't have to explain with him. He knew my path as well as I did, so maybe he'd understand why I'd want to choose a different direction. "I just feel like I've been a victim for most of my life. First with my father, then with his killer, then when you found me. I don't want to feel that way anymore."

"Hmm."

I leaned back against his chest. "I pour my heart out and all I get is 'hmm'?"

"Look, I get it. You want to feel in control. Because there were so many times in your childhood when you had zero control. But, the thing is, you've never been a victim to me. You're strong, Sabrina. So fucking strong. To get through all you have, then to be a star student, to get into a great college. The world gave you a shit sandwich, and you threw it back in its face. I'd say you're a lot more badass than you think."

I'd never thought of it that way. Maybe because I didn't have a habit of coming up with shit-sandwich metaphors, but all the same, he'd given me a new perspective. One that I appreciated. One that made me fall just a bit farther, as if I needed another reason to dive deep for Nate Franco.

He cleared his throat and guided my hand back to the scroll pad. "So you have to take some sort of advanced English, and history, and"—he watched me click through some more rosters—"algebra, French, and Introduction to Law?"

I clicked the last class on my list and sighed. "Thank god I got all the good ones."

"That's a ton."

"Sixteen hours. Not so bad." I shrugged. The course load wasn't all that different from boarding school. "Plus, the study time I'll need for each, it'll probably total out to twenty-five to thirty. And I plan to get a part-time job for another ten or so."

"Whoa, whoa." He wrapped his arms around my waist. "A job?"

"Yeah." I ran my fingertips down his arms, the soft hairs tickling as I went. "I can't just laze about by the pool all the time."

"Yes, you can. You class up the joint." He smoothed his palms up my shirt and cupped my breasts.

"It would just be, I don't know, as a barista or something at a Starbucks, or maybe even tutoring—"

"No way." He squeezed. "One on one with college boys who have a constant hard-on? No, thanks." His thumbs brushed against my nipples.

I wiggled against his growing erection. "Don't trust me?"

"I trust you just fine. Them, not a chance. I remember me when I was that age. If I'd seen a girl like you..."

"Yeah? What would you have done if you'd met me when you were twenty?"

He yanked my shirt over my head, pulled me back against his chest, then pinched my nipples. "I'd have fucked you raw every chance I got and twice on Sundays."

"Who's to say you can't do that now, even though you're an old man and all?" I ground my ass against his cock.

"You're a little brat." He twisted my nipples and bit down along my jugular.

"Going to spank me again?"

"No, you like it too much." His right hand delved

beneath my panties, his index finger pressing against my clit. "Already wet just from thinking about it."

I lowered my voice to a purr. "Maybe I'm wet from all this talk of college boys."

He growled. I barely got my laptop closed before he tossed me face down on the bed and yanked my panties off. But he didn't spank me. He sank his teeth into my ass. I howled as he bit me and slid two fingers into my slick pussy.

Holding me in place with his fingers inside me, he bit my other ass cheek hard enough to bring tears to my eyes. Then warmth covered the spot, his tongue pressing against the grooves made by his teeth. Sliding his fingers out, he circled my clit slowly. Pulling wetness from my pussy, he used his thumb to massage my asshole, each stroke sending goosebumps racing along my legs.

He left more bites—these gentler—along my skin as his fingers worked me over. When he plunged his thumb inside my ass, I tensed.

"Relax." His kisses feathered along my lower back.

I let my muscles go, and he slid his thumb in and out, his fingers still on my clit. The sensation of his thumb was almost too much, but at the same time, I wanted more.

Rocking back against him, I turned my head and met his gaze. "Make me come?"

"Anything you want." His eyes sparkled. He removed his thumb and walked me closer to the foot of the bed. Then he lay on his back, guiding me to sit on his mouth.

When his tongue met my clit, I jolted, and when he pressed his finger into my ass, I moaned. I gripped the footboard and stared down at him as he ate my pussy, his tongue flicking my clit and making wet noises as I rode his face. My thighs clenched, and I didn't care that I was grinding on his face and pushing back to get more of his finger in my ass. I wanted everything from him. He groaned his approval as I gave up all modesty and spread my legs even farther, pressing my pussy to his mouth.

He opened wide and tongued me until I gripped the footboard like a lifeline and came in a rolling wave of abandon. I chased every last tendril of release until I was spent, then fell over on my side.

Nate rose, adopted a stern expression, and shook a finger at me. "Now, let that be a lesson to you, young lady."

After my giggle fit subsided and we snuggled into bed, I passed out in his arms.

# CHAPTER SIXTEEN

## NATE

"I T HAS TO BE somewhere else." Angus drummed his pencil on the desk and stared at the ledger.

"There is nowhere else." Peter glared at the paper. "I know it's the fucking rat. I just know it."

"They're connected?" Angus scratched his chin.

"Have to be, but I can't figure out how." Peter flung his pencil onto the desk. "Fuck!"

"I thought you were good with numbers." David smirked from his seat on the couch.

Peter stood and advanced on his brother. "Hey, meathead, why don't you come over here and figure it out if you're so smart?"

"I'm not the one who claims to be smart." David shrugged, more than happy to light Peter's short fuse. "You're the one who tells everyone he's a member of Menstrual."

I choked on a laugh.

"It's MENSA, you dumbass." Peter unbuttoned his sleeve and began rolling it up.

Angus shot me an amused look. Surprisingly, he seemed to fit in well around here. After his night next door to my room, he didn't give Sabrina any more longing looks—which was good for his life span—and he seemed to get along well with my guys.

"That's what I said. Menstrual." David grinned. He must not have had enough exercise at his morning sparring lesson with Sabrina.

"Outside." Peter jerked his chin toward the door.

"What if I don't feel like kicking your ass right now?" David cracked his knuckles. "I'm a busy man."

"Shut the fuck up, you overgrown turd, and get outside so I can beat your ass."

Angus dug around in his wallet and slid me a twenty. "On the Butcher."

I sized up the brothers. On any given day, David would be the obvious pick, but Peter was riled up just enough that he might be able to win it.

"I'll take it." I nodded at Angus as we all rose and walked outside.

Sabrina sat in a chair by the pool, her legs in the sun, but the rest of her in the shade. Thank god she was wearing a t-shirt and shorts. If she'd been in a bikini I would have either had to fuck her in the pool shed or wrap her in a towel. Or, possibly, wrap her in a towel and then fuck her in the pool shed. *Tomayto, tomahto.*

"What's going on?" She rested the book in her lap and eyed us with intelligent apprehension.

"I'm about to drop a beat down on Frankenstein here." Peter shook out his hands, then brought his fists up.

"Name calling isn't nice." David shook his head in mock disapproval.

"Then you won't like this next part at all, you dickless piece of chickenshit pie."

"Jesus." I laughed and circled around them to stand at Sabrina's back. I massaged her shoulders as the brothers eyed each other.

"Why is Peter so pissed?" She rolled her head around on her neck as I loosened her up.

"He gets frustrated when he can't figure shit out with his super smart dork brain. This is a good way to work it off and get him refocused. It's like a pressure valve."

"So you're saying David's trying to help him?" She didn't sound convinced as Peter barely missed getting socked in the face by David's left jab.

I pressed my thumbs into the tense spots along her shoulders. "Yeah, but David also enjoys beating the shit out of people, so it's really like group therapy."

Peter landed a vicious punch to David's midsection, but the big guy answered with a backhand to Peter's jaw.

I watched as Peter staggered back, then resumed his stance. "That's going to leave a mark."

She laughed and dropped her head back, giving me a nice view down her shirt. "Can't you tell them to work it out like adults?"

"What's the fun in that?" I leaned down to kiss her forehead.

A bullet shattered the umbrella stand just to the left

of where my head had been. The canopy dropped onto us as the crack of the shot finally made it to my ears.

"Up, run!" Tossing off the umbrella, I yanked Sabrina from the chair as another shot whizzed by and exploded into the stone side of the house.

Shielding her with my body, I pushed her ahead of me and toward the house. David and Peter had their pieces out, but it wouldn't do any good.

"He's far. Too far. You'll never get a chance. We need cover." I pushed Sabrina down behind the bushes that lined the house's foundation, but it was shitty cover at best.

David kicked over a patio table, which was about as useful as a lemon meringue dildo. We were out in the open, the nearest trees too far to help. We could have jumped in the pool, but it would only take a second for one of us to come up for air and get a brand new mouth through our forehead. Fucked, so fucked. We had to get inside.

Angus yanked at the back door. "What the hell? It's locked." He banged on it.

David dove in front of me, two layers of protection for Sabrina. Or maybe he was protecting me. I didn't give a shit, as long as Sabrina would walk out of this alive.

A *thunk* drew my eye to the window at my right. A large-caliber slug lodged there, and the window rattled, the bullet-proof glass barely able to contain it. The crack of the shot followed soon after.

"We have to move." I eyed the side of the house, but the door finally opened, George standing just inside.

I shoved Sabrina into the house and kept my body between her and the gunfire as Angus, Peter, and David hurried in and slammed the door.

"Are you okay?" I ran my hands along Sabrina's body, her wide blue eyes telegraphing fear and ripping my heart open. I never wanted to see that emotion there again. She'd already spent too much of her life in terror.

"I-I'm fine." She patted around on my chest. "You?"

"I'm good. The shooter won't be, though." The distress in her eyes was a powerful motivator, and I swore to myself that the shooter would pay with blood.

I turned to the handful of men who crowded into the hall, word already spreading through the house. "Get out there and find him. Now." The bite in my voice could have snapped a diamond in half. "He's in a tree to the Northwest. Probably high-tailing it to his car right now."

George pulled out a radio and began relaying my instructions to the men at the gate.

"He's only 100 to 150 yards away, but the mother-fucker has a fifty cal and he knows how to use it. Go!"

The men scattered, with Peter rushing out with them. David stayed at my side. Protocol. Whenever shit went down, at least one of the Raven brothers served as my personal bodyguard. But that was about to change.

"Sabrina, baby." I smoothed the hair off her ashen face.

"You could have died." Her eyes watered. "You *almost* died."

"I'm alive. Don't worry." I pulled her close and wrapped my arms around her. What if that bullet had hit a foot lower? Had hit Sabrina? I swallowed hard, resolve solidifying in my gut. "I need you to go to your room with David and lock the door until you get the all clear, all right?"

"Where are you going?"

*To find the asshole who tried to take me out and gut him.* "I'm going to help secure the place, okay?"

"Please don't go." She grabbed my hand.

"I have to. But David will stay with you."

David's thick eyebrows lowered. He wanted to protest and stick with me, but he was a good soldier. He'd do what I said.

"Trust me." I kissed her on the crown of her head.

"I do. I always will." Her chin trembled. "Promise me you'll come back." She was a woman, one with more strength than I ever imagined. But in that moment, she reminded me of the lost little girl who'd stolen my heart. And I vowed again to protect her for as long as I drew breath.

I cupped her face in my hands. "I'll come back." I kissed her, far longer than I had time for, but Sabrina was worth every second.

Breaking the kiss hurt me on some gut level, but I needed to make an example of the man who put her life in danger. One that the Russians would never forget.

"David." I nodded at him. "You know what to do."

"I'll protect her with my life."

"Stay in the room. Don't trust anyone. Someone locked the door while we were outside. Someone knew about the shooter." I glanced at George who had his phone up to his ear and was giving rapid instructions. "When I find the rat, I intend to roast him slowly."

David grunted in approval.

Turning back to Sabrina, the worry in her eyes for me, the sheer depth of emotion that she showed with her whole heart, moved me to tell her the truth—to tell her I'd fallen for her. But I couldn't. She didn't deserve the weight that the love of a man like me carried. Who was I to love anyone? A selfish asshole who wasted half his life drinking, whoring, and working for whatever boss would have me. My love would only bury her slowly until she suffocated under the pressure of all my mistakes, each flaw another shovelful of dirt on top of her.

I kept my mouth shut and strode away, never looking back despite the crushing need to do just that.

———

"Take off the hood." I flipped open my lighter and raked my thumb over the wheel to light it up. The orange flared in the darkness of the basement. We'd caught him about two miles away from his shooting spot, speeding like the devil was after him. And I was.

He'd killed the retired couple who lived two streets over and used one of their oak trees as his perch. They'd been dead for a couple of days, their bodies left in the kitchen where it appeared they'd been sitting down to breakfast. Unchecked fury lit my veins at the sheer butchery of it, but more so at how the shooter had been sighting down his barrel at Sabrina, waiting for his chance to take a shot at me.

David's heavy steps on the stairs reassured me that the house was all clear—all except for the piece of shit in the basement. Sabrina was safe, and now it was time for payback.

The bulb overhead flickered on, and Peter yanked the shooter's hood away to reveal a battered and bloody face. He could have been anywhere from forty to sixty, judging from the gray hair and the busted cheek bones, but I recognized his eyes.

"Karilev, isn't that right?" I spat on the blood-stained floor and flipped my lighter shut, plunging us into darkness. Scuffling sounds behind me told me my men were getting set up. Low light shone from a laptop on the table at my back.

The Russian smiled, blood in his teeth. "You've heard of me? Good."

"I've seen you before. At Vince's house. You came for a bounty, carried the body in over your shoulder."

"Many times." He shrugged. "Can't remember any in particular."

"It was a woman."

He swallowed, his gaze shifting away from me.

"You remember now?"

"Just a job. Like this one. Taking you out. Just a job."

"Wasn't she Vince's mistress? Pregnant with his kid, right? She already had a kid, married to one of the Irish, if I remember correctly. But you killed her anyway, then brought him the body."

"Money is money."

I nailed him across the cheek with a right cross. The crunch of bone under my knuckles burned, but it was more than worth it to hear the fucker squeal.

Pulling back, I straightened my lapels and ignored my bloody knuckles. "Maybe so. But payback is a bitch." Turning to my men, I asked, "We ready?"

David flipped on the overhead light.

"Good to go. Skype is set up." Peter adjusted the laptop so the camera captured the scene.

I pulled a long, thin filleting knife from my coat pocket. "Let's give our old pal Dmitri a call, shall we?"

# CHAPTER SEVENTEEN

SABRINA

T HE DOOR TO THE basement was shut tight. David had left my room ten minutes before, right after getting a call from his brother. The immediate danger was over, but David wore a glare that told me his work was just beginning. I'd crept down the stairs and along the hallway to Nate's office. Deserted. Only George stood watch at the front door, and I could hear Opal working in the kitchen.

They were here. I'd heard several sets of footsteps downstairs when David had left. There was only one other place they could be—the basement. I stared at the heavy door, wondering if I had the nerve to push it open and find out what was going on in the bowels of the house.

"Hey."

I jumped and whirled, my hands up in defense.

Angus stepped back and held up his palms toward me. "Whoa, tiger. It's just me."

"Jesus!" I crossed my arms over my middle. "You scared the life out of me."

"Sorry." He glanced at the door. "Are they down there?"

"Yeah."

"They got the guy. I guess he's down there right now. No telling what they're doing to him." His jawed tensed. "Good."

"God." I clenched my fingers into my sides. "This is real."

He nodded and took a step toward the door. "You make a move on a boss or his woman, there's hell to pay. That's the way it's always been. Otherwise, it would be a free-for-all—anyone who wanted to be king of the mountain would make an attempt. There have to be consequences, steep ones, for an attack like this."

So much violence. I thought I understood Nate's world, but the brutality of it was something that went beyond anything I'd ever experienced. Even Angus, who'd been kind in the short time I'd known him, was clamoring for blood.

"Are you going down?" My voice quavered.

"Yes." He grabbed the door handle. "You should stay here."

I should. He was right. But I wouldn't. If this was the life I was choosing, then I needed to see all of it, to understand my choice on every level. Nothing could scare me away from Nate.

"I'm coming." I stepped up behind him.

"Are you sure?" He looked at me over his shoulder,

concern crinkling the skin next to his eyes. "It'll be brutal."

"I know." I took a deep, shaky breath. "But I need to see it."

"This is a bad idea." He opened the door anyway, allowing me to follow. "I would hold your hand, but Nate would take my arm off."

A small laugh bubbled to my lips, but the sound was drowned out by a scream that had to belong to the shooter.

My knees tried to buckle, but I didn't let them. I followed Angus down the stairs, the heavy door closing behind me and sealing the tomb.

"—next time you send someone to do the job, I'll send him back in pieces." Nate's voice.

"Why do you think I sent Karilev?" Dmitri's voice slithered through the air.

How did he get here?

"Dmitri." I gripped Angus's shoulder as my eyes searched through the dim basement for the Russian. "That's his voice."

If he was here, surely Nate had him hog tied?

"You send dickless wonders to kill me because you're an asshole." Nate was in the back room. "Next question."

Another scream from the captive chilled my blood.

Angus and I followed his voice. When we got close, Angus whispered over his shoulder, "Dmitri's on a video call. He's not here."

I couldn't relax, exactly, but there was a small

measure of comfort in knowing he wasn't in the same room.

"I sent Karilev because he's expendable." Dmitri's cold tone verged on bored. "I've rather been enjoying this little snuff show you're putting on for me. Keep going. But, might I ask a favor?"

"Only if it involves me putting a bullet in you."

"No, this one is a bit more, shall we say, personal. Could you put my *kukla* on the video? I haven't seen her since she was sunning herself this morning."

My hands and feet went numb, and I couldn't seem to draw a breath. Angus reached back and put a hand on my waist, keeping me behind him. He stood in the doorway to the back room, his wide back blocking my view.

"So beautiful, my little doll. I prefer it when she wears the white bikini, you know. I imagine pulling it off her with my teeth. How she'll purr for me once she's trained and—"

An agonizing scream, one that went on and on, curdled my blood and cut off the far more chilling sound of Dmitri's voice. When it finally died to a quiet gurgle, I knew its owner was dead, too.

"Well, well. I rather liked the way you looped the guts around his neck like that."

"Yeah?" Nate's tone held murder in its timbre. "I'll be sure to do the same to you."

Dmitri's slimy laugh coated the air. "I do hope you'll wait until after I've enjoyed my doll. She's so smooth and perfect. I bet her skin will scar beautifully. By the time

I'm done with her, she'll look like a whole new canvas covered with my art."

"You aren't touching her." The clang of instruments being thrown down rattled through the air.

"We'll see. Thanks for the show, Nate. I only wish I'd had popcorn to go with it."

"The same thing will happen to the next guy you send, and the next, and the next. If you want to keep wasting your resources, go right ahead."

"Don't worry about me. I've got plenty of cannon fodder to spare. Give my best regards to my *kukla*, and tell her I'm coming for her soon."

I gripped the back of Angus's shirt so I could stay on my feet. Something shattered in the room beyond, and I got the feeling Nate had wrecked the laptop.

"We are moving forward with our plans to hit his shipments," Nate's dark command whipped through the air. "Tonight."

"The heroin?" Peter asked.

"Yes. I want all of it intercepted and dumped out at sea, right along with the Russians."

"I want in." Angus found his voice.

"Your father wouldn't like that."

"What he doesn't know won't hurt him."

"Who's that beh—"

I peeked around Angus's arm, keeping my eyes away from the shooter's body. Nate was covered in blood—his shirt soaked and streaks of it on his face.

Wild and lethal, he stared me down. "You shouldn't

be here." His irritated gaze flickered to Angus. "Why'd you bring her?"

"I didn't. She wanted to come." Angus shrugged.

"I came because I'm a part of this now." I stepped from behind Angus and met Nate's gaze. "There's no point trying to hide what you are or what you do from me."

Nate glowered. "You think you can handle watching me kill a man?"

I still couldn't look down, couldn't take in the full horror of what Nate had done to the man who'd been alive only moments before. But he'd done it to protect me, to exact vengeance for an attack on the both of us. He sent a clear message to Dmitri even though Dmitri seemed too sadistic to heed the warning.

"It's not something that I want. I don't want you to have to hurt anyone, but when it's necessary..." I finally dropped my gaze to get a glimpse of the dead man, his gray entrails wrapped around his neck and his blood staining the floor. "I don't want you to hide it from me." It was a relief that I couldn't see the shooter's face.

Peter and David exchanged a look, one that was perhaps more shocked than anything else.

Nate flicked his hands, the blood spraying in small droplets, and shook his head. "I need to get cleaned up. Wait for me upstairs."

I wanted to continue this discussion, but not in front of his men. Turning my back on the grisly scene, I trudged upstairs to his bedroom. I flopped on his bed and tried to erase the dead man's image from my mind. I didn't judge Nate for what he'd done. How could I? I felt safer now that the shooter was dead. But I would never feel truly safe until Dmitri was in the ground.

A shiver raced through me and punctured my heart when I recalled Dmitri's words about watching me sunning myself by the pool. Though I would feel like a prisoner in this house, I wouldn't go outside until I knew there were no unwanted eyes on me.

I burrowed into the navy-blue duvet as the sun streamed through the parted curtains. The bed smelled like Nate's soap, clean and masculine. I rubbed my cheek against the smooth fabric as my thoughts continued to race.

After another few minutes, heavy footsteps on the stairs told me that Nate was approaching. I sat up and crossed my arms, waiting for the confrontation. He burst in, his hair darkened with water. Shirtless, fresh from a shower, and with no trace of blood on him, he stalked to the bed, grabbed my ankles, and yanked me down. Prowling over me, he gripped my wrists and pinned them above my head.

"That wasn't for you to see." The anger in his voice mixed with the concern in his eyes. "You shouldn't have to deal with shit like that."

"I can handle it." I met his gaze. This wasn't the time to back down.

"I know you can." He squeezed my wrists, then let off. "But that doesn't mean you have to, okay? It's part of what I do. I've done horrible things, and I'll do a lot more to keep you safe and to keep this operation running. My men and their families depend on me. I won't let them down. Not when I've brought them so far out of the old ways and into the new." He shook his head and put a gentle hand to my cheek. "I'm trying to get away from that shit—the killing, the turf wars. That's why I'm allying with the Irish, why I've had Peter focused on gaining more legit businesses. We either modernize or we die. But the Russians are part of the old way. I have to fight this war before we can reach the peace on the other side."

"I understand."

"You do. You're smart. But that still doesn't mean I want you anywhere near the war that's about to go down. The things I'll have to do..." His eyes darkened. "I don't want you to see me like that. I never want you to be scared, especially not of me."

I leaned up and whispered my lips across his. "I just saw you covered in blood."

He winced.

"But I didn't see anything but *you*. Being strong. Doing what you had to do. No matter what, I always see you."

He let out a breath, and I could have sworn his eyes watered, but he claimed my mouth with such sweet intensity that I simply reveled in the feel of him. No more thoughts, no more reassurances—just the two of us coming together exactly as we were meant to.

# CHAPTER EIGHTEEN

## NATE

"I'M SO FUCKED. So, so fucked." I itched to light up a cigarette. "She saw it all."

Peter snorted. "She's tougher than you think."

We sat in the back of a speed boat, gently rocking on the Delaware as we waited for a particular tugboat to appear—one that carried heroin straight from Afghanistan to the Russians. Other boats dotted the river, some seemingly docked for the night, their lights off, giving no clue as to the dozens of men with guns inside.

"I think she's tough." My hand reached for a phantom pack of cigs in my suit coat pocket. "But this life isn't for her."

"No, you don't want it to be for her." Peter gave me a knowing look. "That's not the same thing."

I wanted to punch him, if only to release some of the tension. "Did you and Con get together or something? Have a reach-around sesh and talk about my love life?"

Peter grinned. "If the stone-cold killer gives the same advice as I do, then you know it's the gospel truth."

Fuck if he wasn't right. "It doesn't matter. She's young, and she's already been through enough. We're rough. A bunch of assholes, really. She's not like us."

"I could teach her some torture techniques. Not just defense." David kept his gaze downriver.

Peter let out a hooting laugh, but I wasn't entirely convinced David was joking.

"So now we're offering an immersive course in mafia affairs?" I rubbed my eyes. "That's not on her agenda. Temple is. Law school is."

"You're going to have to let her in." Peter leaned back, his elbows on the silver railing.

"That's the problem. I already did. She's all in here." I pointed to a random spot on my chest. Just happened to be my heart. Coincidence.

"We know that." David grunted and stared toward a distant boat approaching on the black water, only a tiny sliver moon giving any light. "You love her. Obvious."

"Obvious?" I gawked at the meaty motherfucker.

"Yeah." Angus's voice floated up from the stern of the boat. "You two are done. May as well set the date."

"Mind your own business, Irish! Shouldn't even be here. Your dad is going to lose his shit when he finds out." I turned to Peter. "And since when did you know shit about women? I haven't seen you or Frankenstein over here with a woman in forever."

Peter opened his mouth to protest.

"Your one-night chicks don't fucking count," I cut in.

"Just because I don't have it for myself doesn't mean I can't call it when I see it. You two are the forever sort of thing. Me? I haven't found the right one yet." He smirked. "Doesn't mean I don't have try-outs at least once a week, though."

"You mean with your hand?" I did a jerk-off motion. "Can't decide if your true love is the left or the right?"

Peter grinned. "Oh fuck off, Nate."

I turned to David. "What about you, NeckBolts?"

Peter cleared his throat as David stared across the water.

"David doesn't talk about her," Peter said quietly.

*Oh, shiiiittt.* David had a lady? What happened to her? Peter could have nailed me in the face with a two by four, and I wouldn't have been more surprised than I was at that moment.

Peter's handheld crackled to life. "Two speedboats, one in front and one behind. The tug has at least a dozen men, maybe more, onboard."

"Looks like it's going to be a party." I snagged my submachine gun from the bow of the boat.

Peter loaded up with two pistols and his favorite Uzi. David wasn't dicking around, either. He pulled out our newest asset, which took up half the space in the boat, a rotary minigun capable of firing 5,000 rounds a minute. The deck was stacked with ammo canisters, and the plan was for Angus to pilot the boat around the heroin-laden tug while David went Rambo with the gun. It would be a miracle if he didn't tag one of our own guys in the coming melee.

I took the handheld from Peter and clicked it on to broadcast to all my men. "Game faces, gentleman. Tonight, we strike back. Our number one priority is taking the tug. If shit goes south, we'll sink the fucking thing. But we will not let the Russians get their filthy paws on that product. We are going to take their futures and make them ours. We will build our empire on their bones and dare any fucker to try and take it from us. Let's get to work." I clicked it off and tossed it back to Peter.

He raised an eyebrow. "That was actually hella inspiring."

"Why are you so fucking surprised?" I palmed my gun and peered into the gloom, the low hum of a speed-boat bouncing across the water.

"I don't know." He shrugged. "You just seem different these days. More, I don't know, *bossly* or something."

"Bossly?" I shot a glance to David. "You get a load of this guy?"

"He's right." The meathead nodded. "It's Sabrina. She makes you better."

*I know.* The speedboat, sleek and white, appeared from the shadows, the tugboat not far behind. A smat-tering of gunfire pierced the night, barrels flashing on the west shore. As we'd planned, the boats veered away from the danger, hugging the eastern side of the channel. They returned fire, but my guys were well-protected on the shore.

Peter held the wireless at the ready. I held a hand up, waiting for the right moment to strike. The boats increased their speed away from the shooters, racing toward the finish line with their load of smack. They didn't notice the other tug boat near the west bank. Why would they? It was dark, seemingly anchored for the night.

I dropped my hand, and Peter spoke into the hand-held. "Now."

The tugboat roared to life, its engines already warmed up. At full blast, it pushed toward the shore, and behind it, a hundred feet of metal cable rose from the water, the other end bolted to a steel dock. Snapping tight just above the waterline, the wire groaned under the tension.

The first speedboat didn't have a chance. It rammed the wire, which ripped it apart, cut through the wood and fiberglass like a blunt knife in the hand of a killer. Only a splintered husk remained, the dual engines sputtering as they sank. The Russians' tug slowed and began to turn, seeking to escape.

"Let's go." I spun my finger in the air.

An armada of boats powered into the river, forming a floating wall down and upriver from the tug and the second speed boat. They had nowhere to go. The speed-boat tore a circle around the tugboat, the men onboard firing indiscriminately outward.

As it approached, I glanced at David, who held the rotary gun at his hip. "Light it up."

The gun whined as the carbine began to spin. Then David put the hammer down. Slugs cut through the dark river, sending up a small jet of water. When his aim found the boat, he sliced through it almost as surely as the cable had cut through the other one. Round after round, he destroyed their hull as the other boats fired on the men aboard. It only took seconds for it to become a lifeless hulk floating in the cold water.

Only the tug was left, floating in a sea of killers, the way blocked.

"Hello?" A thick Russian accent marked the voice. "You in the boats there?"

I whirled. It was coming from the onboard radio.

"Hello, I'd like to talk. Okay?"

Peter looked at me and shrugged.

I stepped over and picked up the mic. "Yeah."

"You want the shipment, yes? Okay?" Banging sounded in the background.

"Yes."

"I'm not with Dmitri. Okay? I drive boat. Okay? That's all. Okay?"

*"Why does he keep saying okay?"* Peter mouthed.

I cocked my head to the side. "Okay."

"I told Dmitri's people maybe we should give up. They try to kill me, so I'm locked in cockpit. But, I can help you. Okay?" More banging and yells that I could hear on the radio and over the water.

"Sure. What's your plan, buddy?"

"Yuri. I am Yuri."

"Yuri, what's the deal?"

"I saw the cable on the water. I ram cable. I hold on tight. But Dmitri's men go flying. Okay?"

I pressed the mic to my chest while I thought it over.

David frowned. "But I want to use the Rambo gun." He hefted the rotary killing machine higher on his hip.

"You can still use it. Just not as much."

"Eh, but you must promise you let me go. Okay?" Gunfire had been added to the yelling and pounding. "And decide quick."

"What could it hurt?" I clicked the radio back on. "You've got a deal, Yuri."

"Okay."

Peter spoke into his handheld. "All the boats near the cable need to clear out. And our tug needs to pull as hard as possible."

The ships dispersed as more gunfire erupted around the captain's door on Yuri's tug.

"Yippee ki-yay, motherfuckers!" Yuri yelled over the radio as his tug's engine roared to life, the boat shooting forward. Our tug's engine matched the sound, pulling the cable taut as the bolts holding it to the decking across the river whined under the pressure.

"This is going to be epic." Peter leaned over the side of our speedboat as Angus piloted us in reverse away from the cable. If it snapped, it could whip us right in half.

The tug picked up speed, men flying off the back and into the churning wake. It ate up the fifty feet between it and the cable in a heartbeat. It jerked violently against the metal, men and machinery flying off the deck as the tug listed sideways, almost capsizing from the momentum.

The cable finally gave up and pulled free from the

steel dock. It lashed out and around toward our tug but slapped into the water before reaching it and doing any damage. The ensuing chaos had all of us gripping the railing as waves and calamity rocked through the water. Once the biggest wave passed, Angus motored us toward the tug as David peppered the deck with bullets. It was unnecessary; there wasn't a soul in sight. But he was having fun, so I let him keep at it.

I pressed the button on the mic. "Yuri?"

Silence except for the rapid fire and thunk of bullets into metal and wood.

"I think the fucker did himself in."

Peter rounded up our men, forming a boarding party. We needed to get control of the tug and get downriver fast. All the noise would be sure to bring attention, and the police would have to do something despite their payoff.

I was about to give the go-ahead when a voice crackled over the radio.

"Okay?"

# CHAPTER NINETEEN

### SABRINA

N ATE WALKED INTO THE bedroom. He'd already
pulled off his shirt and was yanking off his pants
as I sat up.

Relief swelled inside me, but I tried to play it cool.
"How'd it go?"

"Better than I expected. Things went right for once."

"The heroin?"

"Let's just say there are some whales out in the
Atlantic who are currently developing a taste for the
finest heroin ever produced in the poppy fields of
Afghanistan."

"Good." I wanted to go to him, to check him for
injuries or any hurt, but I forced myself to stay put, to
show that I could accept the danger inherent in his life
without freaking out all the time. "You're okay, right?"

"Yeah." He smirked. "I know you want to inspect me.
Quit being coy."

I jumped at the opportunity. Okay, so maybe I wasn't

as good at playing it cool as I'd hoped. Running my fingers over his torso, I said, "You came away unscathed this time. That's an improvement. Maybe you're finally learning how to do your job right."

"Sassy woman." He grabbed a handful of my hair and walked me back to the bed. "When did you get such a smart mouth?"

I gripped his cock through his boxer shorts, the hot length of him coming to life in my palm. "Maybe when I figured out how much you like it."

"I do like it." He shoved me down to my knees, my back against the side of the mattress. "But I *love* it when you use it to suck my cock."

I licked my lips as he pulled himself free from his boxers, the fat head glistening in the low light. Not waiting, I took him deep in my mouth, rubbing my tongue along his shaft as I went.

"Fuck." He groaned and tossed his head back as I sucked.

Wrapping my hand around the base of his shaft the way he liked, I worked in tandem with my fingers to touch him from base to tip. Wet noises bounced around the room as I moved back and forth. He thrust his hips in time with my rhythm, almost gagging me a few times. When I looked up at him, he groaned at the tears shining in my eyes and one rolling down my cheek.

After a few more deep thrusts with his hips, he pulled me up and pushed me back on the bed. With a yank, he removed my panties while I peeled his white t-shirt away.

"How did you get so good at sucking my cock so quickly?"

I gave him a sweet smile. "I've been practicing on TicTacs."

He stared, his eyes going wide before a laugh rocketed from his lungs. "You goddamn sassy girl."

I tweaked my nipple. "What are you going to do about it?"

He growled and dove between my legs. His mouth, hot and wet, sealed to my pussy, and his tongue delved deep inside me as I arched off the bed and gripped the duvet. He knew just what to do, working my clit and bringing me to the edge of ecstasy in an embarrassingly short amount of time.

I dug my fingers in his hair and called his name, but he didn't intend to get me off so easily. He climbed up my body and pressed his thick cock head against my entrance. I was wet and needy, but I still gasped as he thrust inside me. All the way to the hilt, he stayed still as he stared into my eyes.

The words that had been bubbling inside me for so long turned into an undeniable roar that I could no longer ignore. "Nate." I put my palm to his cheek. "I love you."

His eyes clenched shut as if he were in pain. Though I was full of him and my need for him, in that moment a great emptiness settled inside me. Even though I knew there was little chance of him saying it back to me, it still hurt.

I dropped my hand. "You don't have to say it back.

It's okay." The good thing about internal bleeding was that no one else could see it.

He opened his eyes, that deep green meeting me half-way. "I'm not an easy man to love. I'm not the man for you. You deserve so much better than anything I can ever offer you. But I'm still a selfish bastard. And I've never been able to do a cost-benefit analysis. When it comes to you, all I ever see is benefit."

I stopped breathing. I stopped thinking. My entire world ground to a halt as I hung on to each of his words.

His gaze never left mine. "I've never loved anything in my life. Not like I love you. When I first saw you, something inside me broke. Not just broke, it shattered into more pieces than I could ever collect again. You were young. You'd been hurt so badly. And for the first time, I wanted to fix something instead of destroy it. And that knowledge is what broke me. Because I couldn't fix you. I couldn't make it all go away. And even though I was a failure, and I sent you away, and I continued down my destructive path, you came back to me. I think we were both broken and we were the only ones who could make each other whole again."

My heart swelled until I feared it would burst from my chest. Tears welled in my eyes and rolled down, tick-ling my ears. "Did you just say you love me?"

The side of his mouth ticked up in a smile. "After I say the most poetic shit I've ever said in my whole life, all you can think of is the part where I said I love you?"

"That was the most important part."

"Well, in that case, I love you. I've always loved you in one way or another, from the moment we met."

"I was 13, you creeper." I giggled.

He narrowed his eyes. "It wasn't like that."

"For you, maybe. But I've been masturbating to thoughts of you for years."

He shook his head. "Are you trying to kill my boner, jail bait?"

I angled my hips up, rubbing his cock deep inside me. "I think it's safe to say your boner isn't going anywhere."

"You're a bad girl. You know that?" He pulled back and shoved, hard and sure.

I batted my eyelashes. "I guess I need someone to punish me."

"You came to the right place for that." He slammed into me, jarring the bed.

My toes curled, and I wrapped my arms around his neck. "Do your worst."

He started a hard rhythm and never broke eye contact. "I love you. I love you so much."

How many times had I hoped to hear those words from his lips? They were euphoric. It was as if everything clicked into place. All it took was for him to stop fighting it, but he had always been a fighter. So it wasn't surprising that it took him this long to come to terms with the fact that we were always meant to find each other, to be strong for each other, and to love each other.

"I want you to use me to get off." He rolled over and took me with him, settling me on his hips. "Show me all of you."

I leaned forward and braced my hands on either side of his head. He grabbed my wrists and positioned my palms on his chest. "Use all of me." He surged up, spurring me onward.

Sinking down, I took him all the way inside then lifted up and pushed back down.

He nodded. "That's it."

His hands wandered to my breasts, cupping and kneading them as I rocked back and forth. When I ground down on him, I discovered it gave my clit a delicious rush of sensation. So I kept doing it as he leaned up and claimed a nipple in his mouth. A line of flame traced from my breasts to my pussy as I rode him. All modesty abandoned, I stroked my clit against him again and again, each burst of pleasure building on the last.

He worshiped one breast and then the next as his hands wandered to my ass and squeezed. When he slapped one ass cheek and then the next, I moaned his name.

"That's who owns this pussy. Say it again."

"Nate. It's yours."

"Fuck yes it is." He slapped my ass again, sending me higher and higher.

My body moved to its own rhythm, my hips grinding down until everything inside me tightened into that one little spot. I threw my head back as Nate feasted on my breasts. With one more delicious bit of pressure between my thighs, I came, moaning to the ceiling and filling every corner with Nate's name. I rode him, letting my hips guide me down the cascade of pleasure. Nate laid back, his gaze on me as my orgasm began to subside. He thrust up three times, his body tense, and he grunted—that deep and masculine sound that was so particular to him—as he came inside me.

Sated, I dropped onto his chest and lay there trying to catch my breath. He ran his hands up and down my back and cooed about what a good girl I was. I loved his praise. I couldn't help it. Wrapped in his arms, and joined in the most primal of ways, I was home.

———

I spent the next morning trying to evade David's bear paws during a sparring match in the foyer. After being taken to the floor three times in a row, I missed the softness of the grass. But not enough that I would risk Dmitri getting a look at me.

"How did he do that, anyway?" I circled around to David's right.

"Do what?" He eyed me warily, looking for some sort of trick to divert his attention.

"How did Dmitri get a video camera on the property?"

"He didn't." David stopped circling. "Not exactly anyway. We checked all of the electronics on the property and looked for any additional video cameras, but there weren't any. Peter also did a check of neighboring properties as well, but there weren't any there either."

I tried to keep my gaze up, though I was analyzing

how many steps it would take me to kick out and hit his knee. "So how?"

"Drones."

"You've got to be kidding me."

"No. We suspected, but now we know for sure. We have a man permanently staked out on the roof here with a sniper rifle. Late last night a drone flew over the house. Our guy spotted it with his night vision scope and took it out. We have a day shift guy and a night shift guy until this is all over."

I rushed forward and kicked hard at his knee. Only an inch away from making contact, he managed to swipe my leg away. But I stayed on my feet and bounced back out of his bear paw grip.

"You're getting better." David took up his fighting stance and focused on me again.

"But I'm still not good enough."

"When you've been fighting as long as I have, we can compare notes. But for now, you're getting better, and improvement is what we're after."

I jabbed with my left hand then feinted right. "We've been spending all this time together fighting, but I've never learned much about you and your brother. Where did you grow up?"

"No." He dropped and shot out his leg, sweeping my feet out from under me.

I fell on my ass, the marble floor giving me an unwelcome bruise. "What do you mean no?"

He helped me to my feet. "I don't talk about the past."

*Shut out.* "You know all about my past. Why can't I know something about yours?"

He ran both hands through his dark hair, his muscles flexing beneath his thin gray t-shirt. "Your past is tinged with blood. My past is drowned in it. Maybe one day I'll tell you more, but not today."

I tried to go for his throat, but he caught me with ease.

"You telegraphed that from a mile away. Work on it in the mirror, and we'll practice more tomorrow."

I put my hands on my hips and glared at him. "I ask you one little question about your past and you shut down and ditch on training?"

"Training was over half an hour ago. You need to work on paying more attention to your surroundings." Without another word, he strolled out of the foyer.

"Is there anything I *don't* need to work on?" I grumbled to myself.

"Your bedroom skills are spot on." Nate walked up behind me and dropped a kiss on my neck.

"I'm all sweaty."

He growled in my ear and bit the lobe. "I'd lick you all over."

A shiver went through me as he ran his hands down to my hips.

"Too bad I have an interrogation to carry out."

All the blood drained from my face and the tips of my ears went cold. "The basement?"

"Not this time." He hesitated and seemed to be

having a silent argument with himself based on the way his eyebrows pulled together.

"What is it?"

He gave a small shrug as if admitting defeat in his mental disagreement. "You said you want to be a part of this, and I'm done trying to tell you what you should and shouldn't do. So, if you'd like to sit in, then you are welcome to."

I couldn't stop the grin spreading across my face. "Really?"

"Yeah."

"Can I shower really quick and change first?"

He slapped my ass. "Yes, but hurry up before I change my mind."

Ten minutes later, I was showered and sitting on one of the couches in Nate's office, a legal pad and a pen in my hand.

Nate sat at his desk and took me in with a long look. "If you'd add some heels to the outfit, we could play naughty secretary."

I glanced down at my white button-up top and gray skirt. "You guys are always dressed up, so I figured I would fit right in."

"Come sit on my lap. I've got something for you that will fit right in."

I bit my lip as footsteps echoed in the hallway. Nate schooled his features, trading his cocky grin for an expression of stone.

Peter walked in with a stranger. The man was tall and thin, possibly mid-forties, with scraggly dark hair. He wore a pair of jeans and a simple t-shirt with a "Dandy Tuna" logo on it. Despite his bedraggled appearance, he gave me a wink.

Nate stood and pointed to the single chair that had been set in front of his desk. "Yuri, have a seat."

Yuri obeyed, sighing as he sank into the wooden chair. I wrote Yuri's name at the top of my legal pad.

Peter stood in the doorway, his right hand resting on his belt. I'd quickly learned that this stance allowed him to reach for his weapon with lethal quickness.

Nate sat. "Would you like something to drink?"

"No. I already had a good breakfast thanks to you."

"You're quite welcome." Though his sentiment was polite, Nate resembled a shark with a tasty piece of meat in front of it. "Let's talk about Dmitri."

Yuri scratched his head. "To be honest with you—"

"Let me stop you right there. Whenever someone says 'to be honest with you,' the next words out of their mouth are often a lie." Nate's smile was cold. "I don't want to start off on the wrong foot with you. And I'm sure you want to make a good impression. My friend Peter over there?" He gestured toward the door where Peter pushed back his jacket to reveal the black butt of his pistol. "He's particularly good at figuring out when someone is lying. And he doesn't like liars. Not one bit."

Peter tapped the butt of his gun for emphasis.

"So let's start this over again, shall we?" Nate drummed his fingers on the desk. "Tell me about Dmitri."

Yuri rested his hands on the arms of his chair, but he couldn't hide the tremor that shook his fingers. "I'll tell you what I know. Okay? I was hired by Dmitri over a year ago. I come from a long line of tugboat captains in Russia. My brother and I came to America as teenagers. He's in the Coast Guard, and I'm well known on the waterfront. I have a lot of connections with the shipping people. Dmitri found out about all of that, and he came to me with an offer. Okay?"

Nate leaned forward. "What was the offer?"

"Either I started working for him to bring heroin into the city, or he'd murder my entire family including my five-year-old daughter." His voice cracked on the last words. After a few moments, he continued, "That was when I first started working for Dmitri, and I've been bringing his shipments into Philadelphia at least once a month since then. Okay?"

"What can you tell us about his operation?"

"He has an office down by the water."

Peter leaned against the door frame. "The storage warehouse?"

Yuri nodded. "Yeah, the front looks like individual storage units, but the rest of it just houses his guys, and they store drugs and guns there."

"Is that where Dmitri stays?"

"No. He's rarely there. Okay? Only to do a little business here and there. He mainly stays in his high-rise in the city. It's some sort of penthouse. I don't know where."

"You sure you don't know?" David pushed past Peter into the room.

Yuri shrank under his cold gaze. "I swear. I've never been there. Okay?"

David sat behind Yuri, intimidation from every angle.

Nate held up a hand. "I believe you. What do you know about the rat he has in my organization?"

Yuri shifted uncomfortably in his chair. "I've heard talk that Dmitri has your rat by the balls. And that the rat is close to you." He glanced to Peter. "Very close."

Peter stiffened. "The fuck did you just say?"

"Calm down." Nate held Yuri in his hawk-like gaze. "Do you have any idea who it is?"

"No. Okay? No. Only Dmitri knows. He doesn't tell anyone. Except for maybe the *shlyukha*. She's the only one he talks to, because she's the only one who'll never repeat what he says."

A wrinkle formed between Nate's eyebrows. "The what now?"

"Whore," Peter supplied the translation. "He said the whore."

"Who do you mean? He has a woman?" Nate asked.

"No. It's not his wife, and I don't think they have a good relationship. He does things to her..." Yuri trailed off and glanced at me.

"You can say it in front of her." Nate slammed his hand on his desk. "Eyes on me, Yuri."

Yuri's head whipped around. "I mean to say that he hurts her. The *shlyukha*. That's what he calls her. They say he keeps her chained. They say he likes to cut her. They say he forces himself on her in front of others."

My horror grew the more he spoke, and I couldn't keep the question from leaving my lips. "Who is she?"

"I'm sorry." He turned his head slightly, but not

enough to meet my eye. "I didn't want to say those things in front of you."

"Who is she?" I repeated. Dmitri's words from his kidnap attempt resurfaced in my mind. He'd said he'd already ruined my father's other toy. Could he have meant—no. I shook my head. No.

"I can't say for sure. She's Russian. A little older. Some of the men that worked on the boat from time to time when I had shipments gossiped that she was once a rare beauty who was shared amongst the generals of the Bratva. One of them crossed Dmitri very badly, so he took her as payment and punishment."

The legal pad and my pen slid from my hands and slapped on the floor.

Nate rose and pointed at Peter. "Watch him."

"What is it?" Nate knelt in front of me and took my ice-cold hands in his.

The words didn't want to leave my lungs. If I said it out loud, it would be real. And I didn't want it to be real. Not like this.

"Baby, please tell me what's wrong."

"It's her." Tears burned in my eyes.

"Who?"

"My mother."

# CHAPTER TWENTY

## NATE

S ABRINA STAYED IN OUR bed for the rest of the day. I wanted to help her, to reassure her that I would do everything in my power to free her mother. But the truth was I wasn't sure what I could do. We knew the building where Dmitri was holed up, but we also knew that it was well fortified and nearly impossible to raid. On top of that, I had no evidence that it truly *was* her mother.

I didn't give Sabrina those details, just held her through her silence and tears. She'd never known her mother, but that bond was still there. Her pain was my pain. And I would do everything in my power to make this right for her.

In the late afternoon, her breathing evened out as she finally fell sleep. I rose and padded down the stairs.

George gave me a short salute from his post at the front door as I passed. "We got two more drones this morning. Both of them equipped with cameras. Peter and

David went in search of the operator, but they didn't turn up anyone. We'll keep trying. But they could be somewhere more remote."

I nodded my thanks for the report and strode to my office. Sinking behind my desk, I cradled my head in my hands. Word was already traveling about our heroin heist the previous night. Pretty soon, the Russians would be riled up like a nest of hornets and looking for somewhere to strike. It was all part of the plan. They would expend their energy attacking our next shipment, which was due in three days. Hopefully, the rat already told Dmitri about it and directed them to the river where I could set a trap, while the actual shipment came in via the airport to the south.

I was tap dancing through a minefield.

"How's she doing?" Angus walked into my office and dropped onto the couch across from me, dark circles under his eyes from our late night on the river.

"About as well as you could expect. Finding out that the mother you thought was dead is actually in the hands of a fucking psychopath, who takes every opportunity to torture her, doesn't sit so well." I flexed my fists and wished for a simpler time when I could solve all my problems with a right hook and some well-placed body shots. Those days were gone. I was over here playing chess when I was just a hood rat who'd only been marginally good at checkers. "Tell me something, Angus."

"Sure."

"Does your dad ever get tired of this shit? Does he

ever tell you that being the boss is a huge pain in the ass? I guess what I'm trying to ask is, does your dad keep it real? Because, I'm here to tell you, being boss comes with lots of bells and whistles and some really cool shit, but it also comes with the sort of responsibility that keeps you awake at night."

Angus crossed his ankle over his knee. "My dad started out as a low-level enforcer back in the day. He would go to Irish businesses that didn't pay the protection money and break shit, break bones, and wreck places. Just your general, run-of-the-mill bruiser."

I nodded. "Sounds familiar." *And fun.*

"But when he talks about those days, that's when he's the happiest. Being boss isn't something that he went looking for. He's like you—street smart, tough, a consummate wise guy. An opportunity arose, and he took it. He wasn't groomed to be the next boss. The thing is, though, since he's been in charge, our organization has been better run and more well respected. So there's something to be said for starting at the bottom and clawing your way to the top." He shrugged and met my gaze. "This will probably sound stupid to a guy like you, but it makes me wish that I had a chance to do the same. He sent me off to school and made sure I didn't have to fight for everything the way he did. But sometimes I think maybe I would have been better prepared for this life if I'd been forced to do it the hard way."

As much as I hated to admit it, he was a smart kid.

"Look, if you want to get your ass beat and earn some

scars, I'm more than happy to take you out back and wail on you." I held up my hand to stop his protest. "Seriously, I will stomp a mudhole in your ass free of charge. Have you seen the movie *The Goonies*?"

A grin crept across his face. "You're a dick. You know that?"

"Seriously. When I'm done with you, you'll look like that guy with the face. What's his name? Sloth? You know the one. Got one eye toward heaven, one eye staring at a candy bar, teeth all out to here and an ear that can hear the ocean from Kansas."

He laughed, and I struggled to keep a straight face.

"Then you'll be a proper made man. Nobody'll fuck with you." I chuckled and rubbed my face. It felt good just to laugh and not think about all the shit bearing down on me.

Peter popped his head in the door. "The fuck is going on in here?"

"Nothing. Just schooling young Angus here on the importance of the truffle shuffle."

"I've got some news." Peter walked in. His jaw was covered in thick shadow, his clothes rumpled, and his hair in need of a comb. I supposed we were all tired and beat up, but we couldn't let off the gas. The Russians wouldn't.

Peter shot Angus a dark look.

"I can go." Angus began to rise from his seat.

I waved him back down. "Stay. You went with us last night to kick some Russian ass, so you're good with me as far as I'm concerned."

Peter gaped but didn't question it. "It's about the rat."

"Sit down and spill." I leaned forward, my elbows on the desk. Bloodlust began to rise in my veins as I thought about all the horrible things I would do when I found the traitor.

"Don't get too excited. I don't have a name. But I finally managed to get in contact with my Russian informant from Dmitri's operation. He verified what we heard about the woman Dmitri keeps captive."

"Is it my mother?" Sabrina, pale and small, stepped into the doorway.

I rose and led her over to my chair, positioning her in my lap. Her skin was cool to the touch, and I rubbed her arms to infuse some warmth.

"I can't say for sure, but she certainly fits what we know about your mother."

"We have to save her." Sabrina straightened her spine. "Dmitri has to pay for what he's done."

"I agree." The sureness in her voice reiterated what I already knew—things were coming to a head with Dmitri far more quickly that I'd expected. This newest complication of Sabrina's mother only increased our organizations' velocity toward each other.

Peter continued, "My informant verified that the rat has already reported our shipment will be at the river in three days. They're already preparing to take it by force, but they'll be bringing even more firepower than last time."

"Get with Sam. Make sure we have enough ordnance to blow them out of the water." I stroked Sabrina's hair, hoping that she could feel every bit of love I had for her through my touch.

"Already done. We're going to concentrate our men on the waterfront but leave enough on the air strip to defend it if shit goes south."

"Good. What else did you find out about the rat?"

"That's basically it. News about the river shipment traveled quickly from the rat to the Russians. The informant did mention that it's somebody close. But I've vetted everyone." Frustration leached into his voice. "Everyone. George, Tony, all the guys on the house security team, the guys on the gate. I've even put tails on a few of our men just to make sure. Fuck, I sweep the house for bugs every few days. I keep coming up empty."

If Peter couldn't find him, then he was practically stitched into the fabric of my syndicate. Invisible, like a fucking bedbug that couldn't wait to feast on my blood. "This guy is a ghost. But I know how to flush him out. We take the fight to Dmitri. I want you and David and Angus to pull every piece of information that we have on Dmitri's stronghold. Every way in, every way out, how many men on the ground level, how many on the penthouse level, what sort of firepower—everything."

Sabrina looked up at me, hope and fear dancing in her eyes. "That's dangerous."

"It needs to be done." I kissed her forehead. "If I can save your mother, I will. And there is no doubt that I will gut Dmitri. His reign is about to come to a bloody end."

Peter coughed into his hand. "Are we really going to do this?"

I ran my hand under Sabrina's shirt and pressed my palm against her waist. She'd lost so much. If I could kill Dmitri and save her mother, maybe I could give one little piece of her shattered childhood back to her. It would be worth it.

"Yes." Maybe I was just some street-fighting kid from the shit streets of Philly, but now I was the boss. And it was time that I embraced my role with open arms. No more fucking bellyaching, no more excuses. I existed for Sabrina and for the people who depended on me. And I wouldn't let them down. "Once we're done with the shipment, I want to hit them in the fucking mouth the very next night. While they're licking their wounds and scratching their balls, I want a team to torch the warehouse on the water and another team to go with me and cut off the head of the snake."

"About fucking time." David leaned against the door frame.

I shot a glance at him. "Where'd you come from? Is this the Avengers Assemble time or something?"

David crossed his beefy arms over his chest. "Yeah. If someone's talking about killing, my Bat signal goes off."

"Psycho. It's settled then. Protect our shipment, then destroy the Russians and take the spoils." I tipped Sabrina's chin up. "As long as my queen agrees, of course."

She glanced around the room, then met my eyes. "Kill them all."

Holy shit. My blood chilled, and my cock roared to life. How was that for a fucking answer?

"I'll drink to that." Peter went to the small bar next to the window and poured drinks for all of us.

Peter, David, and Angus stood around my desk and we all toasted the plan and to the queen of vengeance who sat sweetly in my lap.

# CHAPTER TWENTY-ONE

## SABRINA

THE NEXT FEW DAYS were full of preparation for the upcoming shipment along with quieter maneuverings concerning the eventual raid of Dimitri's safe house. Nate was in and out of the house at all hours, and no matter how hard I tried, I couldn't convince him to take me with him on his trips. He guaranteed me that the types of men he was meeting with weren't the sort that I would want to rub elbows with. I let him get away with it, because I had a much bigger ask on my mind.

"What are in the boxes that got delivered to the house earlier?" He walked up behind me and kissed my cheek before sitting down to breakfast.

"That's all the stuff I ordered for my room."

He draped his napkin across his lap. "We may as well send it all back since you'll be staying with me from now on."

I forked a piece of pancake. "Don't be so sure. Your decor could use a major update. Everything is so bachelor. The dark bedding, the mismatched rugs, the heavy drapes, the enormous closet that's half full of weapons. I could go on."

Nate smacked his hand on the table, faux surprise painting his features. "Well I never!"

I smiled with my mouth half full. "I'm just speaking truth to power over here."

He sipped his coffee. "Honestly, I couldn't care less if you decorated the walls with My Little Pony as long as you're in my bed every night." Scooting his chair back, he motioned me over. "Come here."

My cheeks warmed as I rose and crawled into his lap. He snagged a piece of bacon from his plate and pressed it against my tongue. I chewed and swallowed as he claimed a piece of bacon for himself.

Opal hurried in with two fresh glasses of orange juice. "I can help you with those boxes after I'm done preparing lunch. I'm curious to see what kind of household items are in fashion these days. This house has been occupied for decades, but the decor has remained the same for most of that time. It'll be nice to have some more modern things." She smiled at me and freshened up Nate's coffee.

"Sounds good. I'm looking forward to it." I shifted on Nate's lap as his erection pressed against my ass.

Opal hustled off to the kitchen through the swinging wooden door.

I smacked Nate on the arm. "Didn't you get enough this morning?" A slight ache between my thighs reminded me of how it felt to wake up with him inside me.

"Enough isn't a thing with you. I'll never get enough. You may as well get used to it. Besides, I already warned you that I'm a beast in the morning."

I ran my tongue along his lip and savored the saltiness from the bacon and the unmistakable taste of him. "What's on the menu for today?"

He sighed. "I'm meeting with Peter and David right after breakfast, then we're going to go over our game plan for tonight, then we need to make contact with our supplier and double check that the airport is secure. After that, we need to survey the spots along the river where the fake delivery is taking place so that we can get our men in position right when the sun goes down."

Nerves fluttered in my stomach, but I wouldn't turn back. If he truly wanted me to be his queen, then he would understand my request and, hopefully, grant it.

"What is it?" he asked, his gaze narrowing.

"What do you mean?"

"You're doing that thing where you hook your ankles together and bounce your knees against each other. It means that you want something. Usually badly. It's a tell you've had since I first met you."

I glanced down and found my ankles pressed against each other and my knees bouncing. Forcing them to stay still, I took a deep breath. "I want to go with you tonight—"

"Absolutely not. This isn't even—"

"Wait!" I slapped my hand over his mouth, but his frown still marred his eyes. "Let me explain." I pressed my palm tighter against his lips. "Will you let me explain?"

He gave me a curt nod, and I dropped my hand.

"I know you're going to say it's dangerous. I know you're going to say that I should stay here and let you handle it. But I want to stay with you. When we're separated, bad things happen. And maybe I can help. Staying here and sitting on my hands helps nobody. Maybe if I'd been with you that first night when you were attacked on the waterfront, I could've saved lives." I dropped my gaze and stared at my fingers as they nervously wrestled each other. "Maybe I could've saved Will."

"Sabrina." He ran his hand through my hair. "Will's death wasn't your fault. You did everything you could to save him. Even if you had been there, he was hit too hard. Nothing could have brought him back from that. And if you had been there, I would have been worried the entire time that something would happen to you. I wouldn't have been able to think straight, and I definitely wouldn't have been able to act when I needed to save lives and to fight off the Russians. Keeping you safe is a priority. You aren't a trained fighter. You'd be a sitting duck, one that Dmitri wouldn't hesitate to take."

I wanted to argue with him, to dispute what he'd said. But deep down I knew he was right. I'd only been training with David for a few days, and that was just for defense. Even so, the facts didn't change how I felt. I always wanted to be at Nate's side, whether that was here at the house or out in the thick of things.

"What if I just stay in the car? Or wear a vest?"

"You know that's not enough. We need to train you with guns and other weapons. I have no doubt that you will learn how to be an asset on the combat side of things." He gave a wry smile and shook his head. "Even though I tried my damnedest to keep you away from this life. We see how that worked out."

I brushed the tip of my nose against his. "It's not my fault you're a softy and always give me what I want."

"You and that sassy mouth." He ran his hand down to my ass and squeezed. "I like that you want to come. I really do. But you're not ready. And I need my head in the game at all times until the Russians are done and dusted."

He was right, and I hated that he was right. But I could still help out. I wriggled my ass against his erection. If I couldn't go with him to the battlefield, I would give him something that would guarantee he would do everything in his power to return home to me. Leaning close to his ear, I whispered, "Tell me how badly you want to fuck my ass."

He gripped me tighter and yanked me against his chest. "You're such a bad girl."

A knock on the dining room door caught our attention.

Peter strode in. "Sorry to interrupt, but it's time for the meeting."

Nate groaned. "Right now?"

I nibbled his ear. "Since you're going to be out of the house all day, this is a limited time offer."

Nate shot up from his seat and tossed me over his shoulder. I squeaked as he marched through the dining room.

"Whoa." Peter held his hands up. "The meeting—"

"Can wait," Nate finished for him. He carried me past Peter, and I gave a little wave as Nate powered me up the stairs, to our room, and tossed me onto the bed.

"Strip." His voice was low and edged with gravel as he hastily removed his clothes.

I took my time peeling off my t-shirt, shorts, and underwear.

"You are such a naughty little tease." Nate opened the bottom drawer on his nightstand and pulled out a small black box.

"What's that?" I pressed my thighs together as I took in his beautiful form.

"You aren't the only one with a talent for ordering things off the Internet." He opened the box and pulled out a small bottle of lube and a pink vibrator.

Curiosity tickled me in all the right places as I watched him set the items on the nightstand.

"Spread your legs."

I obeyed, wanting everything from him all at once.

He got on his knees and pressed his mouth to my pussy. His tongue eased along me, each stroke tantalizing and perfect. He reached for the vibrator and clicked it on. The low hum made promises, and the little device delivered as soon as he touched it to my clit.

My back arched, and I moaned low in my throat as the new sensation washed over me.

Nate glanced up, his eyes warm in the morning sunlight. "What? They don't have vibrators at boarding school?"

"No way. Your roommate would hear." I could barely get the words out, the vibration against my clit frying my brain.

"So you're only used to this?" He slid two fingers inside me.

I nodded over and over again. "Uh huh."

He pulsed his fingers in and out and drove me crazy with the vibrator. When my legs began to shake, he eased off and slid his fingers to my asshole, rubbing the sensitive skin and spreading my wetness.

"Over." He grabbed my hip and rolled me to my stomach, then pulled me to my knees. Reaching around, he pressed the vibrator to my clit again, and I buried my face in the sheets.

Before long, a wet sensation had me staring back at Nate. He was pouring lube on my ass and spreading it with his fingers. I was so close to coming, but then he pulled the vibrator away and made me wait. It was maddening. Over and over, I was almost there only to be denied. But his teasing seemed to have a purpose, because he eased his finger into my asshole, then added another as his delicious torture continued. When he added a third finger, I didn't know if I could take it. But his use of the vibrator told me I could. The vibrator told me I wanted more. I agreed with it, rocking my hips against the little device and working his fingers.

But then he pulled it away again, and his fingers

disappeared too. More lube and then the vibrator thankfully returned. Something much thicker than a finger pressed against my asshole, and I froze.

"Don't go tense on me. Just let yourself go." He circled the vibrator on my clit, convincing me that he was right.

I relaxed as he pushed his head against me. The tight ring of muscles rebelled at first, but he didn't give up. As long as he kept that vibrator right where it was, I'd let him do anything to me. With increased pressure, he slipped inside.

I moaned into the mattress and stilled at the slight sting from the intrusion.

He rubbed my ass. "Such a good girl with such a tight little asshole." Easing in farther, he repositioned his knees between mine and pulled back a little bit, then moved deeper than he'd ever been.

The sensation was strange but erotic. I couldn't deny that I wanted more, and he gave it to me. He pulled back again and slid tight inside me. But he pulled the vibrator away.

I protested by slamming my hands on the mattress, but he didn't return it.

"I can't keep looking at your ass taking my cock. If I do, I'll shoot faster than a teenager with a warm sock."

Turning my head so that my cheek rested against the mattress, I said, "Then stop looking, but don't you dare stop with the vibrator."

"Yes, ma'am." He pressed it against me, and I jolted.

I ground my pussy against that little humming spark

of sex as Nate pulsed his cock in my ass. It was so wrong but so good. His fingers trailed along my lower back, his grunts growing more desperate with each thrust. I was so full, his cock eliciting tickling and tight sensations all along the inside of me.

Then something magical happened. He clicked another button on the vibrator and it moved faster. I clutched the sheets so hard my knuckles hurt, and his throaty groan was the beginning of my end.

"I'm coming." Did the words pass my lips? Were they just in my mind? I didn't care. I was diving off the top of orgasm mountain, floating through the rainbow of bliss, and splashing down in the crystal clear waters of holy-shit-I'm-in-heaven.

"Fuuuuuuck." Nate shoved forward roughly, but I didn't care. My orgasm had sent me somewhere far away, somewhere I wasn't sure I wanted to come back from.

He pulled out, and warm spurts of come splashed my ass. I'd been moaning for so long that I lost my breath.

When every last bit of euphoria had turned into sated exhaustion, I shied away from the vibrator. "Too much." My voice was muffled in the sheets.

He clicked it off and tossed it on the bed then fell on his side next to me. My ass was still in the air, still covered in his seed, but I didn't care.

"You're gonna kill me one day. You and that sassy mouth. But if I die with my dick inside you, I'll die a happy man."

"That was so romantic." I tried to roll my eyes but they just shut. Too worn out.

He stroked his hand down my arm. "Yeah, I thought so too. I may sell that to a greeting card company. Maybe copyright it."

He never failed to make me smile, even when he was being ridiculous. Maybe especially when he was being ridiculous.

"I love you."

"You let me fuck your ass. If that's not true love, I don't know what is." He rose and went to the bathroom, returning to clean me up and lay next to me.

My mind began to come back, all the worries and cares settling on me like a weight. I can only imagine how heavily it all sat on Nate's shoulders. The air shifted in the room, as if my worries sucked the oxygen away.

He wrapped his arm around me. "I'm coming back, you know."

"I know."

"You're a worrier. I get that. But I need you to trust me." He dropped a tender kiss on my lips. "Can you do that?"

"Of course. I trust you with my life, my future, my everything."

"That's my girl." He rose and began dressing. "I'm going to leave David with you tonight. More for my peace of mind than anything else."

"He's not going to like that." I sighed as Nate covered his fine ass with his boxers. "Last time he was stuck with me, he paced the entire time and grumbled about drawing the short straw and having to be the babysitter."

Nate laughed. "That sounds like him."

I snuggled into the sheets. "Maybe this time I'll try to sneak up on him and take his knee out."

"That would teach him a lesson." Nate sat next to me on the bed and leaned over, smoothing his palm down my cheek. "Spend the day planning what you want to do with our room. My only rules are no pink and don't touch my guns. I'll have Peter get someone to design a new safe for them so you can have that closet space all to yourself."

"You sure know the way to a girl's heart."

He gave me one long, luxurious kiss, then stood and strode to the door. "Yeah, apparently, it's through her ass."

I threw a pillow at him, but he darted out the door before it made contact.

# CHAPTER TWENTY-TWO

## NATE

Peter fidgeted in the seat next to me as we watched the runway. "The flight's on time—should be here in 15 minutes."

"How about our guys on the river?" A never-ending current of tension vibrated through my body. I wouldn't be able to relax until I got back home to Sabrina.

"No news is good news. Our decoy boat should be chugging up the river right about now. If they're going to ambush us, we'll know as soon as it happens."

"They will." There was no way Dmitri would pass up this chance to disrupt my operations even more.

Peter shifted again, his sharp eyes scanning the darkness around the edges of the lit runway. "I don't like doing this without David."

"I need him taking care of Sabrina."

"I don't disagree. But it never hurts to have some extra firepower."

I smirked. "I'll be sure to tell him you've been belly-aching for him."

"Always gotta be a dick, don't you?"

"I got a rep to protect." Despite the light ribbing, we both kept our attention on the runway. We needed this score, and we needed it to go down without a hitch. An irritating tickle in the back of my mind warned me that shit was never easy. Never. But I was hoping that my luck would change.

After a few more moments of tense silence, a light appeared in the sky, blinking in a way that could only be our approaching aircraft.

Peter hit a quick-dial number on his phone. "What's the word on the water?" He tapped the speaker button.

"Quiet. The boat's almost to the dock," Angus's voice came back.

The hackles on the back of my neck rose. "No sign of the Russians?"

"No. The boat's pulling up now. We've got lookouts on the highway and up and down river. No one's made a peep." Angus paused. "Something feels off."

"I feel it, too." I glanced at Peter.

Movement beyond the runway caught my eye. "Look." I pointed as a line of men emerged from the gloom, submachine guns tucked at their sides.

"Fuck!" Peter stared. "I had three guys out there."

"Not anymore." I snatch the phone from Peter's lap. "Get your guys to the airstrip now."

"What's going on ove—"

"The Russians are here. Get your squad here as fast

as you can. The rat..." I trailed off and glanced at Peter. The rat had to be someone close enough to know the real plan. Whoever it was told the Russians, and now we were really fucked. But I had kept that information close, which only left Peter, David, and Sabrina—all of them loyal, or so I had thought.

I tossed the phone, pulled out my gun, and pointed it at Peter. To his credit, he didn't reach for his piece, even as gunfire began to erupt along the runway.

"Nate. It wasn't me." I had never seen Peter more serious, his grave eyes trying to convince me. "David and I are solid."

"There's no one else. It had to be one of you." Even as I said the words, I couldn't believe them. The Ravens had been with me from the start. They had always had my back, no matter what. The thought of them turning on me made me question the entire foundation of what we'd built together. On top of that, terror lanced through my heart. I'd left David alone with Sabrina. He was supposed to protect her, but what was his real agenda?

"I know." He shook his head. "It doesn't make sense. But you have to trust me. The same way I've trusted you. I'm not going to say you're like a brother to me just to save my hide. But it's true. You are."

"Fuck." It was the only thing I could manage as I weighed his words, holding his life in my hands.

Bullets thunked into the side of the SUV as the sounds of out-and-out warfare ratcheted up outside.

Peter held his hands up. "If you're going to do it, go

ahead. But I swear to you on my life and my brother's life that we would never betray you."

Everything in me believed him. Maybe because I was sentimental. Maybe because he'd been with me, always on my side, for the past five years. Maybe because I was fucking stupid. Yeah, the last one was probably the right one.

I lowered my gun.

He took a deep breath and dropped his hands to his lap. "Thank you. Can I get back to work now?" He didn't wait for an answer and picked up his handheld to bark instructions at our men as the plane landed to a hail of gunfire.

I palmed my Uzi and a Glock, then jumped from the SUV and took a defensive position behind the landing gear of the nearest plane. Dozens of men raced towards us, all of them set to "destroy" mode. *Fuck.*

We were outnumbered, outgunned, and outmaneuvered, but we would fight for what was ours. My thoughts strayed to Sabrina, and I prayed that she was safe as I rose and began spraying our attackers with bullets.

# CHAPTER TWENTY-THREE

## SABRINA

AVID'S PHONE RANG, AND he answered it immediately. "Yeah." His thick, dark eyebrows drew together as he listened. "I'm coming...I don't give a fuck what he told me to do. I'm coming." He stashed his phone in his pocket and hurried to the door.

I rose from the edge of the bed, my stomach lurching with turmoil and worry. "What is it?"

"The Russians knew. Somehow they found out that the real shipment was at the airport. It'll take our guys half an hour to get there from the river. By that time, it'll be over." He opened the door, then paused. "Take this." He handed me a pistol from his holster. "This is the safety. Just flick it off. If anyone comes through that door, pull the trigger."

The weight of the gun surprised me, but I gripped it and tried to seem brave, even though I was falling apart on the inside with worry for Nate. "Please hurry."

"I will." With that, he left and closed the door behind him. I flipped the lock.

My leaden legs carried me back to the bed where I sat and played out worst-case scenarios of what was happening at the airstrip. My eyes tried to tear up, but I wouldn't let them. I would be strong and wait for Nate to return. He had to come back. He promised me, and he had never let me down before. He wouldn't start now.

After David left, the house became eerily silent. Every little sound caught my attention, and I held onto the gun as if it were a lifeline. Footsteps in the hall had me aiming at the door.

A light knock, and then Opal's voice floated through, "Can I wait with you?"

"Yes." I tucked the gun behind me and unlocked the door for her.

She hurried in, her eyes wide. "David left in a rush. Is everything all right?"

I hugged her, hoping her motherly touch would soothe my nerves. "No, they had a shipment tonight. The Russians were waiting for them." Anguish twisted my voice. "They're in a fire fight for their lives." *And I'm here, being useless.*

Pulling away from my embrace, she squeezed my upper arms. "I'm sure they'll be fine. They probably took enough men to the airport to last for a little while, at least."

"Wh-what did you say?" Ice prickled through my veins.

She smiled. "Oh, I was just saying that I'm sure it will be all right."

"How did you know about the airport?" I thought back to all the times when Nate had discussed business in front of Opal. She was always on the periphery, bustling in with coffee at just the right time to hear tidbits of conversations. Cold realization dawned inside me. Opal had been the rat all along.

Her smile faded and she pulled a pistol from her skirt and pointed it at me. "It took you long enough to figure it out."

I stared at the barrel, unable to focus on anything else, though I slowly reached around for the gun tucked in the waist of my jeans.

"Not a chance." She aimed at my forehead. "Turn around." Her voice was cold, completely devoid of the motherly tones I had grown used to. The same soft tones that had lulled Nate, Peter, and David into a false sense of security.

I did as she said, turning my back to her. She ripped the gun from my jeans and shoved me forward with wiry strength.

I stumbled and dropped to my knees as gunshots ricocheted from downstairs. Turning, I stared up at her. "Why?"

She held the gun on me as gunshots sounded from below and boots pounded up the stairs. "This house has belonged to great families for a century. Families that have led the most respected organizations in the city. Sometimes the country." She sneered, the wrinkles in her face growing deeper. "Then Nate Franco comes along. No pedigree. Just some thug who thought that he could rule over the rest of us when he should've been shining our shoes. He doesn't deserve this house. He doesn't deserve my service. I've been skimming from the household account, saving up for this day. Nate and his whore and his trash friends will be gone, and this house's great tradition will be reinstated."

"You'd replace him with the Bratva?" I rose higher on my knees and tried to formulate a plan to knock her on her ass.

"The Bratva have a rich tradition, a long history, and a respect for the way business used to be done. I'm no fan of the Russians, but I'd much rather serve them than an American mutt who should never have risen to the top."

I leaned forward, ready to spring, when the door behind her burst open.

She turned. "Here's your little bitch, as promised. I expect you to keep your side of the agreement and allow me to stay on as the head of the—"

A gunshot boomed through the room, and Opal dropped to the floor, her dead eyes looking through me.

Dmitri tucked his gun into the holster at his chest. "Dumb bitch." Turning his gaze to me, he gave me a wide smile. "Little *kukla*, we meet again."

I lunged for the gun in Opal's hand. Dmitri was faster, kicking it away and tackling me to the ground. He settled on top of me as I screamed and tried to claw his face. Grabbing my wrists, he pinned them to the floor, crushing them with his weight. I tried to remember my training, to channel my inner David to get out of this situation. But every time I tried to buck Dmitri off, he chuckled and forced me back down. On the third attempt, he slammed my skull against the floor and sparks burst in my vision.

"I never took you for much of a fighter." He leered. "Though I guess I should have. Your mother put up quite a fuss when I first got her. She's different now. Broken, like you're going to be."

I spit in his face. "I'm going to kill you."

"No." He licked my face, his hot tongue making me gag. "You're not. You're going to be mine for as long as I want you. And when I'm done with you, I'll give you to my men to pass around. And when they're done with you, I'll kill you. Slowly." He put one hand on my neck and squeezed. "I'll do it with my hands just like this so I can see the life leave you. When your little doll eyes go dark, I'll be the last thing you see."

"Fuck you," I gritted out as he increased the pressure on my windpipe. "Nate—"

"Is dead or dying. My men at the airfield had very specific instructions. They'll bring me his head before the night is out. I'll set it on a special shelf in my room so he can watch as I fuck you."

"No. You're a liar." The words caught in my throat as he squeezed. Nate wasn't dead. I don't care how many men Dmitri had sent for him, he couldn't be dead. My heart repeated the denial over and over even as my mind began to process Nate's slim odds of survival. "No," I repeated as he stared at me with unfathomably dark eyes.

"Don't worry, little *kukla*. In a few hours, you won't even be thinking about him anymore. You'll be too concerned about what I'm doing to you." He whistled, and three large men entered the room. "Take my prize out to the car."

I struggled as the largest man grabbed me by the hair and yanked me up. He threw me over his shoulder as another man slid zip ties onto my wrists and ankles and stuffed a handkerchief into my mouth. I gagged and tried to spit it out as I was carried down the steps. The harsh smell of gasoline met my nose, and I saw George's body lying in a pool of blood by the foot of the stairs. The bodies of two Russians at the front door told me that George had died trying to defend this house, to defend *me*. I tried to kick the man who carried me, but he gripped my thigh hard enough to make me scream.

As they carried me outside, smoke was already pouring from the back side of the house, orange flames lighting up the night sky. I wriggled and elbowed my kidnapper in the back, though I knew I wouldn't escape.

The Russian thug sat me down next to an open car trunk and backhanded me so hard my vision went black. By the time I was able to open my eyes, there was nothing to see except the midnight interior of the closed trunk.

# CHAPTER TWENTY-FOUR

NATE

G UNSHOTS PELTED THE EXTERIOR of the hangar. Peter and I knelt behind pallets full of airplane parts and machinery. I'd lost more men than I cared to think about, not that I had time to think when the reaper was breathing down my neck.

I reloaded my Glock. with my last clip. My Uzi was long gone. Peter was down to two handguns, no reloads. Outgunned and outnumbered, all we could do was hunker down and make our last stand. Several sets of footsteps echoed through the cavernous space as our assailants, cocky with victory, made their way toward us. My men from the waterfront wouldn't make it in time. We'd been mowed down man by man, the airfield turning into a slaughterhouse. Dmitri's men took no prisoners.

Peter's grave face told me it was over. But I already knew. I only wished that I'd been able to get a message to Sabrina, to warn her that my protection was about to disappear. I took solace from the fact that she had David with her. When I didn't return tonight, David would know to grab the cash from my safe, take Sabrina, and get out of town. I had to put faith in him, and push away any thoughts that he could possibly be the rat. Peter was by my side, fully aware we were about to die together. His steadfastness told me that his brother would stand by me just the same.

"Hey, Nate!" A voice I didn't recognize with a thick Russian accent catcalled me from across the hangar. "I know you're in here. Hiding like a little bitch."

I leaned over and peered through the blades of a rusted turbine. A tall Russian in a shitty suit strode out in front of a line of two dozen of his soldiers. His cocky swagger needed to be taken down more than just a few notches. I eased my Glock between two of the turbine blades.

He kept coming, a stupid grin on his face. "I've been thinking about putting you down for a while now."

"That's funny." I squeezed the trigger, delivering a slug between his eyes. "Because I don't think about you at all."

As the dickhead fell backwards, a raging surge of gunshots formed a deafening wall. Peter yanked me down as bits of metal sprayed around us. My forehead and ears stung from exploding shrapnel as the Russians let loose what seemed to be a never-ending barrage of bullets.

"I think you pissed them off," Peter yelled over the din.

I grinned. "Any asshole that tries to start a villain

monologue before he kills the star of the show deserves a bullet in his face."

Peter patted his chest over his heart. "You finally admit that *I'm* the star of the show. It's about goddamn time."

I laughed even though I knew that we were one bullet away from the grave. If I had to die, at least I was doing it with a friend at my side. The gunshots died down as the footsteps grew closer.

I met his eye. "Sorry I pulled my gun on you."

He shrugged. "You didn't pull the trigger. I guess that's what counts."

It was a smartass absolution, but an absolution all the same.

"Ready to go guns blazing?" I lifted my pistol.

"As long as I take some of them with me, I'm cool with it." Peter maneuvered into a crouch next to me, both of us ready to use our last gasp of adrenaline.

"On three." I gave Peter a final nod. My thoughts tried to stray to Sabrina one final time, but I only allowed myself the brief mental image of her cornflower blue eyes as she looked up at me, a mischievous smile on her lips. "One." She told me she loved me. "Two." I told her she was the only one. "Three."

We burst out from behind the pallets and fired wildly while rushing to fresh cover behind a Cessna. I'd almost made it when I chanced a look behind me. Peter had fallen, one of his pistols clattering away. I rushed back and grabbed under his arm, yanking him toward the Cessna.

"No!" He tried to pull his arm free while also firing the last of his bullets. "Leave me."

"Fuck you." With a final pull, we collapsed behind the Cessna's tire as the Russians yelled and cursed in their mother tongue.

Fire cut across the side of my neck, and I could feel hot blood running down inside my collar. Peter clutched at a wound in his stomach, blood blooming along his light blue shirt.

I tossed my Glock and pressed my hand to the wound. "I'm empty."

Peter's gun fell from his hand. "That was kind of anti-climactic."

"Funny. Your mom never says that."

He chuckled but clutched his torso.

Heavy sets of boots approached in the now quiet hangar. It was the sound of the end. No more fighting, no more running.

My thoughts strayed back to Sabrina, her sassy tongue and tender heart, as the Russians came into view.

*I love you, Sabrina. Can you hear me? I love you.*

# CHAPTER TWENTY-FIVE

### SABRINA

W HEN THE TRUNK OPENED, I was blinded by the lights. The glare died down as rough hands yanked me from my tiny prison and hustled me through a parking garage to an elevator. Blinking hard, I stared around at the men who held me, but none of them were familiar. My hands and feet had gone numb from their bindings, and my tongue felt buried in sand from the handkerchief in my mouth.

They held the elevator doors open for about a minute until Dmitri appeared. He strode in, a huge grin on his face as he took me in his arms. I tried to lean away from him, but I was trapped.

"Were you this inhospitable to Nate?" He spoke in my ear. "I don't think so." His hands ran down my back and squeezed my ass as the elevator shot upward.

I wanted to knee him in the crotch, but my legs were pinned together by the zip tie at my ankles. My mind screamed, *"Get off me!"* But my dry throat wasn't able to push a sound past the handkerchief. Not that it would've mattered.

The elevator stopped. Dmitri released me when the doors opened, and his men dragged me into a magnificent penthouse with stunning views of the city. Two armed men stood guard at the elevator, and a handful of Dmitri's goons were scattered around the main living area and the open kitchen. My heart sank. There was no way I'd be able to get past all of them.

"Take her to my room." Dmitri strode toward the kitchen while I was dragged down a dim hallway and into a large bedroom.

At the foot of the bed with black sheets, two small cages sat. Inside one, contorted into a painful fetal position, a woman with blonde hair and light blue eyes stared at me. She was naked, her eyes feral, and no recognition sparked in them. But somehow I knew, maybe through some connection that I could never understand, that she was my mother. Seeing her like this cut a new hole in my heart, one that I feared could never be repaired.

His men shoved me to my knees next to the empty cage. One reached under the bed and pulled out a length of iron chain with a shackle at the end.

The other cut my zip ties and grabbed a handful of my hair. "*Snyat' odezhdu.*"

*Strip her.* I cringed back and put my hands in front of me to defend myself. The man with his hand in my hair wrestled his arm through my elbows and held me still as the other one stripped off my jeans. I pressed my knees together, refusing to let this happen to me. Tears burned in my eyes as the man ripped my legs apart and peeled first my jeans and then my panties off.

His eyes focused between my thighs, and I kicked at him, nailing him in the jaw with the side of my foot. He roared and grabbed a handful of my shirt, yanking it forward. The seams burned along my skin as they pulled apart, the fabric no match for his brute strength. He did the same to my bra, stripping it off me with calculated violence until I sat naked, tears streaming down my cheeks.

He licked his lips and reached for the shackle. I tried to kick again, but he grabbed my calf and squeezed until it burned. Then he affixed the cuff to my ankle. When he was done, he sat back and stared at all the parts of me he didn't deserve to see.

The man holding my hair released me. *"Poyekhali."*

*Let's go.*

The one who'd stripped me shook his head and pointed at me, arguing in Russian. The words were garbled, but the meaning was all too clear. He wanted to hurt me in the worst way possible. But the other Russian warned him that Dmitri would kill him when he found out. The threat worked, and the brute backed off before reluctantly following his comrade from the room.

When the bedroom door shut, I collapsed and hugged my knees to my chest. My entire body shook as my fingers roved to the shackle and my ankle. *Get your shit together, and get out of here.* My inner voice sounded a lot like Nate's. Maybe he was coming to save me. Maybe he was storming up the stairs to the penthouse right that second. But that wasn't a risk I could take. I needed to get out of here, and I needed to do it fast.

I sat up and peered at my mother through the bars of her cage. "I'm Sabrina." Crawling closer, I tried to reach the simple bolt on her door. "I'm your daughter." If I could slide it open, she'd be free.

She didn't look at me, only tucked her head tighter against her knees.

"Mom." The word felt alien on my tongue. The shackle dug into my ankle as I reached for her cage. My fingers slipped off the bolt. I pulled farther, ignoring the pain in my ankle, and slid the bolt free. The gate swung open.

"Mom, you can come out." I scooted back toward the bed and yanked on the chain. It was latched to something underneath the sturdy wood frame. Turning back to my mother, I found her in the same position she was in when the door was shut. "Mom!"

She finally looked at me, her light blue eyes glassy and vacant.

"The door is open. I need your help." I shook the chain. "If I can get free of this chain, you and I can leave here together. Just come out."

Her gaze traveled over the open gate, but she made no move to exit the cage.

"She won't move." Dmitri leaned in the doorway, a satisfied smile on his face. "Will you, my dear?"

My mother seemed to cave in, shrinking into the smallest possible version of herself.

"Nikita and I go way back, don't we?" Dmitri shed his jacket and walked into the room.

I scooted back against the bed and pulled my knees up to hide as much of myself as possible.

He tossed his jacket on the bed and began unbuttoning his shirt. "I knew her when she still belonged to your father. A beautiful woman with an even more beautiful child." A wistful smile crossed his face. "God, how I wanted her. I would watch her day and night, creep into her room when your father was away, dream about her. But then your father showed me his true nature. He used me." The smile faded and the cruelty remained. "Over and over. I often wondered if she knew about him. I asked her several times once I got her in my possession. She denied it. But I wasn't sure if I believed her." He shrugged and his hands went to his belt.

A shudder wracked me, and I glanced to the door, looking for any avenue of escape.

Dmitri knelt and pointed at my mother's cage. "You see that? Blind obedience. She won't leave that cage until I tell her to." He reached out to touch me, but I slapped his hand away. "You're fiery now, but it will fade just like Nikita's did. Soon, you'll be in this cage." He patted the empty one. "And you won't come out until I tell you to. And if I tell you to strangle your mother, you will. And if I tell you to suck every cock that walks through that door, you will."

"Never."

Dmitri smirked. "Your mother said the same thing." He snapped his fingers and stood.

My mother uncoiled from her cage and crawled to him. Her body was marked with a highway of scars—cuts, bruises, burns. Some of them fresh, some of them old, all of them painful. A thinner, longer chain ran from her ankle to a bolt in the floor at the back of the cage.

"*Sosat'.*" Dmitri delivered the sick command in a stern voice.

My mother knelt before him and unzipped his pants.

I looked away as she pulled out his cock, but Dmitri grabbed my hair and forced me to watch as she took it in her mouth. My gorge rose, and I dry heaved, but Dmitri held me fast.

"You see?" Dmitri slapped my mother's face as she sucked him. "This will be you in no time. I broke her spirit. Now I'm going to break yours."

Spit pooled in my mouth as the urge to throw up tried to overcome me. "Nate will come for me."

Dmitri laughed. "Nate and his associates are dead. All of them. My men are on their way here with Nate's head." He pointed to a shelf on the wall between two windows. "I've already got a place picked out for it."

The floor seemed to disappear, or perhaps I sank through it. My heart constricted, as if an icy fist crushed it between cutting fingers. Nate couldn't be dead. I would have known, wouldn't I? I would have felt it. A million denials twisted inside me. But the finality in Dmitri's tone, the sadistic satisfaction in his eyes...

I shook my head. "I don't believe you."

"You don't have to. It'll all become clear soon

enough." He yanked my mother from his cock and threw her to the floor. "Now it's your turn."

"I'll bite it off." I snapped my teeth.

"I don't think so." He pulled a knife from his pocket and flicked it open. Pointing it at me, he stepped closer, his halfway flaccid cock waggling in the cool air.

"Mom." I choked on the word as she lay where he'd thrown her.

"She won't save you." Dmitri shook his head at me as if I were an unruly child. "Don't you understand?" He grabbed her hair again and dragged her until she sat in front of me.

She didn't say a word as he ran the blade down her breast, drawing a line of blood right on top of a series of similar scars. Her eyes remained glossy. She wasn't there. Tossing her aside again, he reached for my hair. I kicked out my foot, catching him right below the knee.

He yelled and fell to the side as I scampered up onto the bed and yanked at the chain.

The noise drew one of the earlier henchmen into the room, but Dmitri stood and waved him away. "Get the fuck out." He went to the door and slammed it, then flipped the lock.

I tugged at the chain, the metal biting into my ankle as I fought like a wild animal with its leg in a trap.

Dmitri returned, knife in hand. "You're going to regret that."

"Fuck you!" I whipped the chain toward his knife hand, but it was several inches too short.

He took the opening and launched himself at me, his

thick frame pinning me to the bed. I fought until he pressed the blade against my throat, warm blood trickling across my skin.

"Let's start our first lesson. You need to learn who owns you." He shoved his knee between mine.

"All of this belongs to Nate!" I yelled in his face. "You can't take anything from me, because I've given it all to him. You can do whatever fucked up things you like, but I will never be yours."

He blinked, his dark eyes growing narrower. "I'd like to test that theory." His other knee joined the first, and his cock head pressed against my inner thigh.

Bile rose in my throat as I tried to send my mind somewhere far away from the monster on top of me. Nate's eyes, my favorite green flecked with hazel, and his smiling face appeared. How could seeing him hurt so much?

"Spread wider, *kukla*." Dmitri's hot breath at my ear brought me back to the here and now. He pushed closer, his cock nearly at my entrance.

If he'd been telling the truth—if Nate truly was dead —maybe I should simply buck up against Dmitri, let the knife slide inside me and cut off my life. End the torment before it began. It would only take one swift movement.

Before I could move, a painful crack across my nose pulled a scream from me. Then Dmitri's weight shifted, his knife dropping to the bed as he grabbed at his neck. I shoved him away, then saw my mother behind him, her chain wrapped around his throat as she pulled with all her strength. "Don't you touch my daughter, you *kusok der'ma*," she hissed.

Dmitri tried to stand up, and my pushing was helping his momentum. Instead of letting him go, I latched onto him like a monkey, wrapping my legs around his torso and using my weight to pull his body down, the chain tightening as my mother pressed her knee against his back.

He shot one hand out toward the mattress, reaching for the knife. I grabbed it first, slicing his fingers as I pulled it from his grasp. I clutched it close, then shoved it up. My arm jerked as the blade glanced off his ribs, then sank between them.

Surprise lit his dark eyes as I twisted the knife. He gurgled as hot blood poured out of the hole in his heart, coating my chest as the blood vessels in his eyes popped.

Blood leaked from his throat where the chain dug in. When I was certain he was dead, I let go and shoved him to the side. He lay face down on the bed as I scrambled from beneath him. My mother perched on his back, still pulling the chain with all her might, her thin body shaking from the effort.

"Mom." I put a hand on her shoulder. "He's dead."

She shook her head and kept pulling. "He's not. It's a trick."

I squeezed her frail arm. "It's over."

She blinked hard, her wild eyes adjusting, as if she were finally seeing me. "He's dead?"

"I promise." I gestured to myself, covered in his blood. "I stabbed him in the heart." I glanced down at his body. "And you are on the verge of taking his head clean off."

Her grip loosened on the chain, her hands red and raw from pulling so hard. "I couldn't let him." Her eyes watered. "Couldn't let him hurt you, too."

I pressed my palm to her face. "I'm so sorry. I didn't know—"

"You couldn't have." She grabbed a handful of the duvet and wiped some of the blood off me. "No one knew where I was or what happened to me."

I tugged the sheet from beneath Dmitri's body and wrapped it around her shrunken frame. "I'm here now. We're getting out of here. I promise."

"But the chains..." She glanced at my ankle, then her own, her eyes reminding me of the ones I saw in the mirror every day. There was so much I wanted to know, to tell her, but there was no time. If we didn't find a way out soon, we'd be dead before our jailbreak truly began. Killing the warden was only half the battle.

"There has to be a way to get free." Dropping to all fours, I felt beneath the bed for where my chain terminated into a metal loop.

"His guards won't come back in. Not for a long while." She shuddered. "They know not to bother Dmitri while he's having his fun."

I felt around the loop and the metal plate that had been set flush into the wood floor. I wouldn't be able to budge it. Sitting up, I inspected the cuff at my ankle. It was similar to a handcuff, but not as seamless. The home-made mechanism had a couple of screws holding it together.

Climbing back onto the bed, I wedged my feet under Dmitri's body and kicked him over onto his back. His head lolled to the side, flesh and bone visible, his spine showing through. The blade still protruded from his chest. I yanked it out as my mother stared at his face, as if wanting to be sure that he was truly dead.

I pressed the tip of the knife into the small screw that held the back of the shackle together. It slipped out, and I cursed quietly, then tried again. Once I got the hang of it, I was able to twist it until the screw came loose and the bolt on the other end dropped to the bed. Tugging at the metal, I was able to open the cuff enough to slide my foot out.

"Here." I handed the knife to my mother. "Work the screw out." I gathered my clothes from the corner and threw them on as she twisted the blade.

Once I was dressed, I sat next to her and took the knife, working the screw out faster than she could with her shaking hands. When the shackle was gone, she rubbed her ankle, as if it were the first moment in a long time since she'd been free of it. The thought cut me, but I couldn't dwell on guilt. We had to get out of the penthouse.

I rose from the bed and rummaged through the nearby dresser, hoping for some sort of weapon. "Do you know where he keeps his guns?" I whispered as my mom continued to rub her ankle, a faraway look once again clouding her eyes.

"Not here." She pointed at the side wall. "In the bedroom next door." Another tremor shook her, and tears flowed freely down her cheeks.

*Shit.* We wouldn't make it two steps out the door without some sort of weapon. Our little knife wouldn't do a damn thing against the goons with guns right outside.

I darted to the windows overlooking the city. They didn't have an opening mechanism, just sheets of glass. Not that it mattered, we were thirty stories up, and there was no way down.

I returned to the bed and pulled my mother to my chest. Her tears drew some of my own. It was as if she were letting out all the emotion she'd hid from Dmitri for so long, her body no longer able to hold it back.

"I'm so happy I got to see you." She pulled back and stroked my cheek. "My beautiful girl. So glad I got to see my Sabrina again."

"Don't give up." I gave her a weak smile. "We are getting out of here."

She shook her head, her sad eyes cutting through my false bravado. "I wish that were true."

# CHAPTER TWENTY-SIX

## NATE

I GLARED AT THE closest Russian as Peter grunted in pain. Blood coated my fingers as I tried to stanch Peter's wound.

The big Russian fucker aimed his pistol at me, a smirk on his face. "*Dosvidaniya ublyudok.*"

"Fuck you too, cunt."

I expected a bullet to the face. It never came. The hangar lights went out, the entire place plunged into darkness. I threw myself on top of Peter as the Russian fired.

Then the roar of the rotary gun met my ears as bullets riddled the planes, the equipment, and the squad of Russians who stood in a group nearby. Pained groans and cries rose amidst the ongoing carnage from the bruiser with the modern Gatling gun. It had to be the Butcher. No one else would have bothered to come to our aid.

A smattering of return fire erupted nearby, but David quickly destroyed the shooters with another round of slugs from the rotary gun. When the hangar quieted again, only the groans of the injured remained.

"Boss?" David's voice bounced off the metal sides of the hangar.

"Back here! Peter's hurt bad."

"I'm coming." David ended the groaning men with a handful of shots as he picked his way to us. When he rounded the Cessna, his gaze fixed on his brother, and a particularly vicious rage fell over his face like a black cloud.

Leaning down, he easily lifted his brother—not a small man—into his arms. "Your neck." He hitched his chin at me.

"It's fine." I didn't know if it was or not, but I wasn't in as bad of shape as Peter. "Let's get him to the hospital. Then I'll worry about me."

David set off toward the airstrip, moving quickly as he stepped over the dead. I followed and helped him load Peter into the back of a black SUV.

I pulled myself into the passenger seat as David screeched tires out of there. Digging my phone from my pocket, I dialed Angus.

He picked up right away. "We're almost there." His voice was strained tight.

"Too late." I pressed my palm to my neck and glanced back at Peter, who lay pale and silent in the back seat. "It's over. But I'll need my guys to clean up, get our dead and see if we have any wounded, then take the shipment to our warehouse."

David tore down the road, his knuckles white on the steering wheel.

"I'll see to it." Angus wasn't one of my guys, but I'd quickly grown to trust him and depend on him—perhaps more than I should have.

I ended the call and immediately dialed Sabrina. It went straight to voicemail. A prickling of worry flashed across my mind. I dialed again. Voicemail.

"Did Sabrina have her phone when you left?" I asked David.

"Yeah, she was in your room."

I was about to dial her again when my phone lit up with an incoming call. "Yeah?"

"Boss, it's Morris, from the house." The guard's voice was wheezy.

"What is it?" I gripped the phone hard. "Is Sabrina okay?"

"They burned it down." He coughed, a gurgling sound that didn't bode well. "Took her. The Russians took her. They just left." Another violent cough. "It was Opal. She let them in."

"Opal." I slammed my hand on the dash. "What the fuck?"

He coughed and tried to speak again, but it was garbled.

"I'm sending an ambulance. Hang on, Morris." I ended the call and dialed 911, reporting a shooting and fire at the house.

I dialed one more number.

"Yeah?" Con's sleepy voice hit me on the second ring.

"How fast can you get here?"

"What's wrong?" The sleep cleared from his voice in a heartbeat.

"The Russians took Sabrina."

"Fuck." A rustling sound and Charlie's murmured voice in the background. "I'll call in a favor at the small airport out here. Jump a plane, be there in two hours, tops."

"I don't have that long." Desperation leaked into my voice. "Dmitri took her. He could be hurting her right no—"

"I'm leaving the house. I've got to make some calls. Hang on till I get there." The line went silent, and I wanted to throw it against the windshield.

David pulled into the emergency room of Taylor Hospital, a rundown joint south of Philly. At least they'd have lots of experience with gunshots. We jumped from the car, and David gingerly pulled Peter into his arms and carried him inside.

A nurse rushed out from behind the front desk. "Sir, you can't just—"

"He's dying." David's cold voice shut her right up. "Save him. If you don't, you're next."

The nurse blanched and reached for the phone.

"If you aren't calling a doctor, you're dead." David strode forward, his brother limp in his arms.

She swallowed hard, her dark eyes wide. "I-I'm calling our emergency surgeon to the OR up on three. Take the elevator"—she pointed to it—"to the third floor. There will be a nurse waiting to start triage."

"David, I'm sorry, but I have to—"

"Go get her." He headed toward the elevator, his broad back blocking my view of Peter. "Keys are in the ignition. Once he's out of the woods, I'll come help."

I didn't have time for any reassuring words or to worry about Peter. My thoughts turned to Sabrina, to what sort of hell she was going through. Dashing from the ER, I jumped into the SUV and raced out of the parking lot as an ambulance rolled up, its lights flashing.

A few more phone calls, and I was on my way to Sam's to pick up some heavy-duty firepower. I would save Sabrina or die trying.

# CHAPTER TWENTY-SEVEN

SABRINA

M Y MOTHER EYED THE door as I used the knife to hack a hole in the drywall between Dmitri's bedroom and gun room next door. "We don't have long."

I redoubled my efforts to quietly destroy the wall, my hands coated in white dust as I created a vertical slit with the knife. "Do you, um"—I wiped the back of my hand across my forehead—"do you scream sometimes?"

She hugged her arms across her middle, the white t-shirt we'd grabbed from the closet several sizes too large for her. "Yes." Her wide, haunted eyes made me ache for her.

"Can you do that? I'm going to try to punch through here, and the sound would cover it." I stood and lightly knocked on the drywall, double checking the stud locations so I could avoid them.

"I can scream." She walked to the bed and sat, then closed her eyes. Her body shook, as if she were reliving one of the many traumas Dmitri had visited on her. A blood-curdling cry ripped from her lungs, one that would reverberate in my nightmares for the rest of my life.

I punched the wall, pain bolting up my arm with the effort. Another scream, and I hit it again, denting the drywall and pushing it inward along the path I'd scored with my knife.

A low chuckle came from the hallway, Dmitri's henchman getting off on the pain. I fisted both hands and punched, my knuckles burning.

"Stop." I shook my head and backed away. "It won't work." I'd barely made any progress, and a few of my fingers had gone numb.

"He's usually done by now." She covered her face. "They'll come soon. They'll find out, and they'll kill us."

I went to her and pulled her into my arms. I wanted to tell her she was wrong. But the reality was that we'd been shut in this room for hours. The guys in the hall would soon realize something was wrong, and when they did, we wouldn't be able to stop them. Not with a dull knife and a chain against guns.

"What are we going to do?" The hopelessness in my mother's voice spurred me onward. I had to keep trying.

"We're going to fight." Returning to the wall, I prepared to strike again, but an explosion shook the building.

The power flickered, then shut off completely as shouts and gunfire erupted from the hallway. Men beat on the door and yelled for Dmitri.

I grabbed my mother and pulled her into the bathroom, slamming the door and locking it.

"What's going on?"

"Nate." I herded her into the sunken tub and joined her as the gunfire grew to a deafening level. "He came for me." I wrapped my arms around her, both of us curled up as bullets flew overhead, easily piercing the walls. "For *us*."

Yells tore through the air as the gunfire became more sporadic.

"No!" An agonizing wail. "You're dead."

A deep laugh from the hallway chilled my heart. "No, that's you." A single gunshot, then the *thunk* of a body falling to the floor.

I knew that voice. My nightmare. It was the man who killed my father right in front of me—Conrad Mercer.

"Jaysus at the blood." An older man's voice with a distinct Irish accent. "You boys didn't even need our help, did ya? Angus called in the cavalry for no good reason." Was it Angus's father, the one I'd met at Nate's house?

A yell, another shot, another thunk.

"He almost got the drop on me." The older man whistled. "Thank ye, Con."

"My pleasure."

"Where the fuck is she?" Nate's voice was edged with panic.

"Nate!" I yelled and started to rise from the tub.

"Wait." My mother clutched me close. "Make sure it's safe first."

A bang told me someone had kicked the bedroom door in.

"Sabrina!" Nate turned the bathroom door handle. "You in there?"

"Yes." I untangled myself from my mother's arms as Nate burst through the door, the wood splintering from his assault.

He rushed to me, his face covered with cuts and blood running from a deeper slash along his throat. "Are you okay?"

"I'm fin—"

He stopped me with a kiss that seared straight down to my soul. Wrapping his arms around me, he lifted me from the ground and squeezed me tight, as if he were afraid I'd disappear.

When he pulled away, I gasped in a breath as he ran his hands all over me. "Are you hurt anywhere?"

"No. It's oka—"

"Did he..." His voice trailed away as his eyes darkened.

I knew what he was asking. "No."

He finally took a breath, then looked past me at my mother. "You all right?"

She climbed from the tub. "I don't know." Her eyes darted around, then landed on the shadow across the doorway.

I followed her gaze, and my heart stopped. My nightmare stood there, his dark hair mussed, a scruffy beard on his face, and the same striking eyes—light blue, but hiding a darkness. I clutched Nate.

"I told you. Con's a friend." Nate smoothed a hand down my back. "He's a good guy."

Even Con arched a brow at Nate's "good guy" pronouncement.

"Did you lasses make this mess?" Back in the bedroom, Colum, the Irish boss, toed Dmitri's body.

"Yes." My mother found her voice. "I'd do it again if I could."

Colum grunted his approval. "I don't blame you one bit. Nasty piece of work, this one."

"He suffered, but not nearly enough." The steel in my mother's voice surprised me. "I wish I could have taken my time."

"You and me both. I promised that fucker a painful death." Nate shrugged. "But as long as he's not breathing, I guess I can deal."

I avoided looking at Dmitri's dead eyes and turned my attention back to Nate. "You're hurt." Pressing my fingers to his throat, I tried to inspect the wound.

"Just a bullet graze. Bleeds like a motherfucker, though." He pulled my hand away and kissed my palm, then pressed his palms to my cheeks. "I'm sorry."

"It's not your fault."

"It is. I should have figured it was Opal." His jaw tightened as he said her name.

"You couldn't have known. David vetted her, right?"

"Yeah. She'd been in the life for so long that we assumed she knew the penalty for disloyalty better than anyone." He pressed his forehead to mine. "I'm sorry."

"You're here. That's all that matters." I kissed him, soft and sweet. He answered, his tongue sweeping against mine as he pulled me tight against him.

Con cleared his throat.

Nate pulled away reluctantly and eyed the hitman. "Cock block."

As the kiss haze cleared, I pulled Mom to my side, keeping her close.

"Nice to see you again, Sabrina." Con kept his voice even as he turned his attention to me.

I couldn't return the sentiment, so I stayed silent.

Con seemed to respect that, giving me a small nod before looking at Nate. "We done here?" He used the sight on his pistol to scratch his cheek.

"We're even." Nate nodded. "And you're dead again."

"Good. I'd like to stay that way. Dead, gone, dusted." He grumbled and shoved his pistol into the back of his pants. "I only killed maybe a dozen or so. Pretty shitty haul for me."

Nate smirked. "I got at least fifteen. Maybe you're losing your touch."

"Shut the fuck up. I saw your pansy ass taking pot shots from behind me."

"Why do you think I called you, man? I needed a human shield."

The corner of Con's lips twitched. "I knew I shouldn't have answered when I saw 'Nate the dipshit' on my caller ID."

"Bullshit." Nate swiped at the blood on his neck. "You were dying for some action. I bet you acted all butthurt to Charlie about having to come out here, but you had that same old hard-on for me like you always do."

"Nate," the warning in Con's voice would have stopped any sane man in his tracks. Not my Nate.

"Do you put my picture on the back of her head while you're doing it doggy—"

Con's fist shot out faster than seemed possible. Nate's head reared back, but the hit wasn't much more than a tap. He rubbed his jaw. "Okay, I was mistaken. You still got it."

Con gave a perfunctory nod.

Colum stepped toward Con. "I don't suppose you'd want to come back to work for me and the—"

Con's low growl shut him right up. "I'm dead. You never saw me. If I hear different, I'll be back for you."

The Irish boss's eyes widened and he dropped his gaze. "Never mind then."

Nate walked me through the bedroom and into the hall, my mom following with us. A contingent of Irish stood outside, their guns still at the ready in case any of the Russian corpses on the floor decided to show signs of life.

Everything that had happened over the past few hours rippled beneath the surface of my mind, some of the terrors breaching while others mulled around in the depths. "Dmitri set the house on fire."

Nate squeezed my waist. "It's a total loss. And there's more. Peter got hit in the airport firefight."

"Is he all right?"

Con opened a door to a stairway next to the elevator. Nate hustled me in first, followed by my mother.

"He's in surgery. I'm not sure how it's going to go."

We took the stairs in silence, and when we finally emerged from the building, the cool night air was a balm on my nerves.

Colum directed his men into the waiting vehicles and told them to lay low for the day. Con flipped Nate off, then strode away down the street, turning into an alley and disappearing into the dark night without another word.

"The deal is done, Nate." Colum held out his hand, and Nate shook it. "You won over Angus, and you've won over me, too. Let's hammer out the details in a few days' time." He climbed into a waiting car as sirens started to wail nearby.

"Come on." Nate opened the passenger door of his SUV, which he'd parked on the curb, and helped me inside, then assisted my mother into the backseat. Climbing into the driver's side, he said, "I need to check on Peter. I can drop you two off at—"

"Not a chance." I rested my hand on his. "I'm sticking to you from here on out. Wherever you go, I go."

He pulled the back of my hand to his lips and kissed it. "What did I do to deserve you?"

I spent the ride to the hospital fussing over his cuts and the ugly gash on his neck, though he didn't seem the least bit bothered by any of it and took every opportunity to drop kisses on my hands, my arms—anywhere he could place his lips. My mother sat quietly and stared out the window, as if her eyes were readjusting to life outside of Dmitri's cage.

When we arrived, I checked my mother in at the ER

for a full checkup. She balked at first, then gave in when a kind nurse helped me lead her to her room.

"I'll be back." I smoothed my hand along her blonde hair. "I'm just going to check on Peter."

"I'm okay." She squeezed my hand. "As long as you're safe, I'll be fine."

I took Nate's hand, and we walked to the elevator.

A couple of orderlies gave Nate some curious stares, probably because he looked like he needed a room. But he'd been adamant about refusing treatment until he knew how Peter was doing.

I hit the button for the third floor. "Have you had any messages from David?"

He shook his head. "I don't know what to expect."

"We'll get through it."

He reached out and hit the stop button on the elevator. "I need to tell you something first."

Cornering me against the wall, his intense gaze held me to the spot. "You're everything to me. When I heard that Dmitri had taken you..." He gritted his teeth.

I pressed my palms to his chest. "It's okay."

"No, it's not." Shaking his head, he continued, "You're my queen. I should have protected you. Without you, all this is nothing. Before you came back, I was just going through the motions. I was the boss, but in my mind, I was still the foot soldier who was only playing at being in charge."

"But you've been so strong."

"I've been strong because of you. When you walked

back into my life—" He smirked. "Strutted, I suppose is the right word for your sassy little walk."

I smiled and rubbed my nose against his.

"When you came back, I realized that what I'd built didn't mean shit if I didn't have you to share it with. Instead of playing at being boss, I *became* the boss. I stopped worrying about whether I was good enough, strong enough, because you believed in me."

"I always have. From the day I first saw you." I stroked his cheek. Nate was my touchstone, the one person in my life I would always depend on, because he always came through for me. Maybe that was the foundation of my love for him, but I'd built so much more on top of it.

"I'm going to work every day to earn that faith."

I ran my fingers behind his ears and into his hair. "Every night, too, I hope."

"Fuck, I love you." He grabbed my ass and yanked me to him, his kiss rough and perfect. I lost myself in him—the messy, scarred, perfect man whose love I cherished above all else.

# EPILOGUE

## NATE

W AS I STANDING IN the right place? I felt like it was the right place, but Sabrina's mother was giving me a sort of confused stare from the front pew, Colum sitting at her side.

"Con." I stage-whispered to my best man.

"What?" He wore sunglasses, and he should have looked like a total douche in them, but instead he was cool as shit.

"Am I standing in the wrong spot or something? Nikita is giving me the eye." I turned to glance at him.

Con's lips twisted into a smirk. "Where you're standing is fine, but you've got lipstick smeared all over your chin."

"Oh, shit." I reached up and rubbed my chin and my lips.

"You're not supposed to fuck the bride before the wedding. Bad luck or some shit," Con intoned as the priest gave me a hard glare.

"No, I'm not supposed to see the wedding dress. That's the bad luck. I didn't. She was naked."

Peter leaned forward to peer past Con. "You fucked her in the church?"

I finished wiping my face clean. "God didn't mind. It was like he was getting some free Skinemax all up in his house."

The priest's face went from displeased to full-on constipated.

Charlie shushed us, her delicate features highlighted by white hydrangeas in her hair.

Con lowered his sunglasses and took her in from head to toe. "I'll deal with you after the ceremony."

Charlie, color rising in her cheeks to match the pink of her dress, said quietly, "You'll have to catch me first."

Con laughed low in his throat. "Consider it done."

David shifted his large frame, his tux probably straining to stay together at the seams. "It's ten minutes past time. What the hell are we waiting—"

The organist began to play, and the full-to-the-brim cathedral quieted. The stained-glass windows filtered the morning sun, and the hand-painted ceilings soared away from the rising congregation.

I watched as the vestibule doors opened, and then everything stopped. My ears rang, as if I were shell-shocked, as Sabrina—her dress some sort of lacey affair with long sleeves and a low neckline—practically floated down the aisle. Even through the veil, her face lit up as she saw me, each of her measured steps sending my heart into a faster gallop.

She was more beautiful than I could have even imagined, and it was hard to believe that she'd come here to marry *me*. For once, words failed me—even the profane ones—and all I could do was stand and watch my destiny approach.

I took her hand as she walked up the steps, and we stood face to face as the priest began speaking about the qualities of true love. His words fell on deaf ears. I already knew what true love was. She stood right in front of me, hope in her eyes and faith in me in her heart.

———

"What is taking so long?" I lay on the bed, my cock at full staff as I stared at the bathroom door.

As soon as the ceremony was over, I'd grabbed Sabrina, had our first dance at the reception hall, then whisked her away to our penthouse suite for the first night of our honeymoon. She'd been in the bathroom for at least ten minutes, and I was on the verge of crushing the door when it finally opened.

My eyes widened as she swept out wearing only her veil, her heels, and her wedding ring.

"Holy shit."

She strutted in front of the bed, the sheer fabric tickling the hard buds of her nipples as the rest of the veil flowed out behind her. I rose and went to her, lifting the veil so I could kiss her cherry lips. She moaned as I palmed her tits and walked her back until she dropped on the bed.

Scooting her to the middle, I laid her out with her veil spread beneath her.

"I want to take a picture of this."

"Nate!" She tried to sit up, but I pushed her back down.

"Okay, fine. A mental picture."

She smiled and spread her legs wide. "Go ahead."

*Fuuuuck.* "Forget the picture, I want a taste." I bent my head to her pink pussy and gave her a long lick.

She lifted her hips, pressing her sweetness to my mouth. I licked her clit, rubbing my tongue all along her spot as she looked down at me, her gaze locked with mine. She moved to my rhythm, using my tongue to heighten her own pleasure. My cock throbbed, demanding I get inside my prize, but I wouldn't give in, not until I had her worked into a frenzy.

After a few more minutes of my attention, her legs began to shake, her cries growing more desperate. I had her. Crawling up her soft body, I settled between her thighs and pushed inside her slowly, savoring each noise she made, each scratch of her fingernails as I claimed what was mine.

I wanted her to feel loved, to feel how much I needed her in each measured stroke. Her breathing grew heavier, her eyes heavy lidded as I worshipped her, kissing her lips, nibbling her neck, and working my way to her tits. I sucked a nipple into my mouth sliding my tongue across the taut skin as she arched for me. Wrapping my arm beneath her, I lifted her from the bed and took as much of her tit into my mouth as I could, then sucked her nipple until she writhed and bounced on my cock.

So much for my slow pace. I sped with her, my cock hardening even more as I pulled her on top of me. Her veil tickled my thighs as she rode me, chasing her pleasure and grinding on me as I smacked her ass. She moaned, loving the punishment as much as the reward. My palms hummed with the heat of my impacts as I spanked her some more, giving her that little edge of pain that she needed.

Watching her tits bounce and feeling her slick pussy work me was almost too much, but I stilled my hips, letting her do the work. She was a vision in white, a wedding wet dream that I would never forget. Each grinding surge of her on top of me had my balls pulling tighter, and I was ready to explode.

She dug her nails into my chest, her mouth open wide as her hips froze. God, she was so fucking hot when she came. I pushed up inside her as her pussy walls convulsed and her moans rolled through the room. I slammed her down on me, holding her in place as my cock kicked and shot my release inside her. Each burst of come pulled a grunt from me, and I kept my gaze on her the whole time, taking in each shudder and whimper as she rode the wave of her orgasm.

When she was spent, she collapsed on my chest. I eased my hands beneath her veil and rubbed her sweat-slick back.

"I think I'm dead." Her breath came out in a whoosh.

I laughed and kissed her forehead. "That was just the first act. We have a lot more to go."

She smiled against me, then dug her teeth into my pec.

"Mmm." I reached down and palmed her ass. "That's my girl."

She rocked against me, my half-mast cock coming back to life. "I am, you know."

"What?"

"Your girl." She rested her elbows on my chest and stared down at me. "I always will be."

"I know. I'm never letting you go." I squeezed her ass. "I'm hoping that when you're done with your law degree, I can retire and you can support me."

She snickered, her eyes sparkling. "So you want to be a stay-at-home dad?"

My heart leapt. "You want kids?" We'd only ever discussed it in passing, and I didn't want to pressure her into a family when she was so young. But, as always, she surprised me.

She nodded and rubbed her nose against mine in that special way of hers. "Not until after school, but yeah. I think it'd be great to have a little Nate running around with my good looks and your smart mouth."

I didn't think my life could get any sweeter, but with Sabrina, anything was possible. "I think you mean *your* smart mouth."

She kissed me, her tongue tangling with mine. "You know you love it."

I bit her bottom lip, savoring every last bit of her. "You got me."

Her lips turned up in an unforgettable smirk. "Believe it."

## ACKNOWLEDGMENTS

As always, thanks to my biggest fan Mr. Aaron for putting up with me as I sat, stared off into space, and possibly drooled a little while thinking up Nate wise-cracks. Thanks to my girls for running screaming into my writing room because one of them farted on the other, or because they wanted juice, or because they wanted to know where the balloon went, or because the cat wouldn't play with them, or because one of them didn't like triangles—actually, no thanks to my girls at all, the damn heathens.

I can't begin to say how much I appreciate the readers who loved Dark Protector enough to send me demands for Nate's story. I kept back-burnering him, but he got his way eventually. A shout-out, as always, to my readers group, Celia Aaron's Acquisitions. You guys are my safe place where I can post about all sorts of ridiculousness, though I must say I don't appreciate the tentacle porn turn we've taken recently. You know who you are. *cough*

Thanks to Vivian for reading this book after fearlessly escaping the herd (school?) of man-eating sharks in Hawaii. You did well.

Thanks to Mel for threatening that if I ruined the ending, she'd kill me.

A big thank you to Stacey at Spellbound for the final (super rushed, because I'm a jerk sometimes) edit. And a high five to Give Me Books for getting the word out for me.

Perfect Pear, as always, did a fabulous job on this cover. I promise I will learn to trust you. But seriously, how many times do you roll your eyes when I say, "I don't know if I like that," and then you say "oh my god, I said it was just a rough mockup! Give it a minute, jeeeeeeeezzzz"?

Thanks to my cover model, Amadeo Leandro, for being so, so tasty. Brazilian models, amiright? Daaaaaaaamn.

And of course, to you, dear reader. Thank you for following along with my alphabet soup journey of danger, shenanigans, and sexy times. Please stick around for a while, because I have a very different treat in store for you this October. (Hint: It's a fantasy romance. A hot one.)

Xoxo,

Celia

## Contemporary Romance

### Kicked

Trent Carrington.

Trent Mr. Perfect-Has-Everyone-Fooled Carrington.

He's the star quarterback, university scholar, and happens to be the sexiest man I've ever seen. He shines at any angle, and especially under the Saturday night stadium lights where I watch him from the sidelines. But I know the real him, the one who broke my heart and pretended I didn't exist for the past two years.

I'm the third-string kicker, the only woman on the team and nothing better than a mascot. Until I'm not. Until I get my chance to earn a full scholarship and join the team as first-string. The only way I'll make the cut is to accept help from the one man I swore never to trust again. The problem is, with each stolen glance and lingering touch, I begin to realize that trusting Trent isn't the problem. It's that I can't trust myself when I'm around him.

### Tempting Eden

A modern re-telling of Jane Eyre that will leave you breathless...

## Jack England

Eden Rochester is a force. A whirlwind of intensity and thinly-veiled passion. Over the past few years, I've worked hard to avoid my passions, to lock them up so they can't harm me—or anyone else—again. But Eden Rochester ignites every emotion I have. Every glance from her sharp eyes and each teasing word from her indulgent lips adds more fuel to the fire. Resisting her? Impossible. From the moment I held her in my arms, I had to have her. But tempting her into opening up could cost me my job and much, much more.

## Eden Rochester

When Jack England crosses my path and knocks me off my high horse, something begins to shift. Imperceptible at first, the change grows each time he looks into my eyes or brushes against my skin. He's my assistant, but everything about him calls to me, tempts me. And once I give in, he shows me who he really is—dominant, passionate, and with a dark past. After long days of work and several hot nights, I realize the two of us are bound together. But my secrets won't stay buried, and they cut like a knife.

## Bad Bitch

## Bad Bitch Series, Book 1

They call me the Bad Bitch. A lesser woman might get her panties in a twist over it, but me? I'm the one who does the twisting. Whether it's in the courtroom or in the bedroom, I've never let anyone - much less a man - get the upper hand.

Except for that jerk attorney Lincoln Granade. He's dark, mysterious, smoking hot and sexy as hell. He's nothing but a bad, bad boy playing the part of an up and coming premiere attorney. I'm not worried about losing in a head to head battle with this guy. But he gets me all hot and bothered in a way no man has ever done before. I don't like a person being under my skin this much. It makes me want to let go of all control, makes me want to give in. This dangerous man makes me want to submit to him completely, again, and again, and again...

## Hardass

## Bad Bitch Series, Book 2

I cave in to no one. My hardass exterior is what makes me one of the hottest defense lawyers around. It's why I'm the perfect guy to defend the notorious Bayou Butcher serial killer - and why I'll come out on top.

Except this new associate I've hired is unnaturally skilled at putting chinks in my well-constructed armor. Her brazen talk and fiery attitude make me want to take control of her and silence her - in ways that will keep both of us busy till dawn. She drives me absolutely 100% crazy, but I need her for this case. I need her in my bed. I need her to let loose the man within me who fights with rage and loves with scorching desire...

## Total Dick

## Bad Bitch Series, Book 3

I'm your classic skirt chaser. A womanizer. A total d*ck. My reputation is dirtier than a New Orleans street after a Mardi

Gras parade. I take unwinnable cases and win them. Where people see defeat, I see a big fat paycheck. And when most men see rejection, it's because the sexiest woman at the bar has already promised to go home with me.

But Scarlett Carmichael is the one person I can't seem to conquer. This too-cool former debutante has it all—class, attitude, and a body that begs to be worshiped. I've never worked with a person like her before—hell, I've never played nice with anyone before in my life, and I'm not about to start with her. This woman wasn't meant to be played nicely with. It's going to be dirty. It's going to be hot. She's about to spend a lot of time with the biggest d*ck in town. And she's going to love every minute of it...

### Filthy and Rich: A Billionaire Menage Romance Box Set

*Sensually dirty and filthy rich, these five smoking hot billionaire ménage stories will leave you breathless. Includes stories by New York Times bestselling author Opal Carew, Sheryl Nantus, Celia Aaron, Charlotte Stein, and Calista Fox.*

### Legally Screwed

When a lawyer goes into a mundane appointment for estate planning, she has no idea she's about to meet two super hot best friends who do everything—everything—together. And that what they want more than anything is to have her in their bed, over and over again...

## Dark Romance

## SINCLAIR

### The Acquisition Series, Prologue

Sinclair Vinemont, an impeccable parish prosecutor, conducts his duties the same way he conducts his life--every move calculated, every outcome assured. When he sees something he wants, he takes it. When he finds a hint of weakness, he capitalizes. But what happens when he sees Stella Rousseau for the very first time?

## COUNSELLOR

### The Acquisition Series, Book 1

In the heart of Louisiana, the most powerful people in the South live behind elegant gates, mossy trees, and pleasant masks. Once every ten years, the pretense falls away and a tournament is held to determine who will rule them. The Acquisition is a crucible for the Southern nobility, a love letter written to a time when barbarism was enshrined as law.

Now, Sinclair Vinemont is in the running to claim the prize. There is only one way to win, and he has the key to do it— Stella Rousseau, his Acquisition. To save her father, Stella has agreed to become Sinclair's slave for one year. Though she is at the mercy of the cold, treacherous Vinemont, Stella will not go willingly into darkness.

As Sinclair and Stella battle against each other and the clock, only one thing is certain: The Acquisition always ends in blood.

## MAGNATE

### The Acquisition Series, Book 2

Lucius Vinemont has spirited me away to a world of sugar cane and sun. There is nothing he cannot give me on his lavish Cuban plantation. Each gift seduces me, each touch seals my fate. There is no more talk of depraved competitions or his older brother – the one who'd stolen me, claimed me, and made me feel things I never should have. Even as Lucius works to make me forget Sinclair, my thoughts stray back to him, to the dark blue eyes that haunt my sweetest dreams and bitterest nightmares. Just like every dream, this one must end. Christmas will soon be here, and with it, the second trial of the Acquisition.

## SOVEREIGN

### The Acquisition Series, Book 3

The Acquisition has ruled my life, ruled my every waking moment since Sinclair Vinemont first showed up at my house offering an infernal bargain to save my father's life. Now I know the stakes. The charade is at an end, and Sinclair has far more to lose than I ever did. But this knowledge hasn't strengthened me. Instead, each revelation breaks me down until nothing is left but my fight and my rage. As I struggle to survive, only one question remains. How far will I go to save those I love and burn the Acquisition to the ground?

## ACQUISITION: THE COMPLETE SERIES

Darkness lurks in the heart of the Louisiana elite, and only one will be able to rule them as Sovereign. Sinclair Vinemont will compete for the title, and has acquired Stella Rousseau for that very purpose. Breaking her is part of the game. Loving her is the most dangerous play of all.

*includes Sinclair, Counsellor, Magnate and Sovereign

## Blackwood

I dig. It's what I do. I'll literally use a shovel to answer a question. Some answers, though, have been buried too deep for too long. But I'll find those, too. And I know where to dig—the Blackwood Estate on the edge of the Mississippi Delta. Garrett Blackwood is the only thing standing between me and the truth. A broken man—one with desires that dance in the darkest part of my soul—he's either my savior or my enemy. I'll dig until I find all his secrets. Then I'll run so he never finds mine. The only problem? He likes it when I run.

## Dark Protector

From the moment I saw her through the window of her flower shop, something other than darkness took root inside me. Charlie shone like a beacon in a world that had long since lost any light. But she was never meant for me, a man that killed without remorse and collected bounties drenched in blood.

I thought staying away would keep her safe, would shield her from me. I was wrong. Danger followed in my wake like death at a slaughter house. I protected her from the threats that circled like black buzzards, kept her safe with kill after kill.

But everything comes with a price, especially second chances for a man like me.

Killing for her was easy. It was living for her that turned out to be the hard part.

### The Bad Guy

My name is Sebastian Lindstrom, and I'm the villain of this story.

I've decided to lay myself bare. To tell the truth for once in my hollow life, no matter how dark it gets. And I can assure you, it will get so dark that you'll find yourself feeling around the blackened corners of my mind, seeking a door handle that isn't there.

Don't mistake this for a confession. I neither seek forgiveness nor would I accept it. My sins are my own. They keep me company. Instead, this is the true tale of how I found her, how I stole her, and how I lost her.

She was a damsel, one who already had her white knight. But every fairy tale has a villain, someone waiting in the wings to rip it all down. A scoundrel who will set the world on fire if that means he gets what he wants. That's me.

I'm the bad guy.

———

### Short Sexy Reads

## The Reaper's Mate

This job. Boring is too colorful a word for it. I've been escorting humans to the afterlife for millennia. I'm over it. But when you're the son of the two greatest reapers of all time, reaping is in your blood. My latest appointment is with one Annabelle Lyric, a twenty-eight year old New Orleans party planner. Snoozefest. But there is one bonus to this assignment: it's Halloween night. In New Orleans. And she's attending a posh party whilst unaware of her impending demise. I've been tasked with taking Annabelle's soul right after the masked ball.

The good news? I'll fit right in with all the costumed partygoers. The bad news? That hits me when I realize Annabelle is much more than my next victim, she's my fated mate.

## Christmas Candy

A Christmas novella where everyone gets their just desserts.

Olive had a major crush on Hank in high school. She was the too-smart, slightly chubby girl who gawked as Hank ran track and made all the cheerleaders swoon. After high school, the two went their separate ways. Olive opened a yoga studio and swore off sweets while Hank traveled the world. No problem, right? At least there wasn't a problem until Hank moved back to town and opened a candy shop across the street from Olive's studio. Now, Olive will do everything she can to shut her old crush down. But Hank has other plans, and all of them end with an Olive sundae.

# ABOUT THE AUTHOR

Celia Aaron is a recovering attorney who loves romance and erotic fiction. Dark to light, angsty to funny, real to fantasy—if it's hot and strikes her fancy, she writes it. Thanks for reading.

Sign up for my newsletter at celiaaaron.com to get information on new releases. (I would never spam you or sell your info, just send you book news and goodies sometimes). ;)

## Newsletter Sign Up

*Stalk me:*

www.celiaaaron.com

Printed in Great Britain
by Amazon